▼

CHEATERS

a n d   O t h e r   S t o r i e s

▲

DEAN ALBARELLI

▼

CHEATERS

and Other Stories

▲

St. Martin's Press ⹂ New York

Grateful acknowledgment is made to the editors of the following magazines and anthologies, in which these stories originally appeared in slightly different form:

The Southern Review and *20 Under 30: Best Stories by America's New Young Writers:* "Honeymoon"

Poetry East: "O Sole Mio"

The Virginia Quarterly Review: "Infatuated"

The Quarterly and *Cape Discovery: The Provincetown Fine Arts Work Center Anthology:* "Grace"

The Hudson Review: "Cheaters," "Flames," and "Passengers"

Storm (U.K.), *Witness,* and *Voices of the Xiled:* "Winterlude"

Boulevard: "The Orthodox Brother"

Design by Pei Koay

Library of Congress Cataloging-in-Publication Data

Albarelli, Dean.
   Cheaters and other stories / by Dean Albarelli.
     p. cm.
   ISBN 0–312–14294–3
   1. Manners and customs—Fiction.   I. Title.
PS3551.L245C44   1996
813'.54—dc20   96–1218
                                              CIP

First Edition: August 1996

10 9 8 7 6 5 4 3 2 1

for Sara

For generous support that aided the completion of these stories, I'm very grateful to James Michener and the Copernicus Society of America; The Writers Room, Inc. (New York City); the Vermont Council on the Arts; and the Fine Arts Work Center in Provincetown.

And for their many varieties of support, my unbounded thanks to the Albarelli and London families.

I'm also enormously grateful to the following individuals for their invaluable advice and faith: Margaret O'Brien (to whom "Honeymoon" is fondly dedicated), the late Peter Taylor, Nina Ryan, Dorothy Antczak, Frederick Morgan, Paula Deitz, Ron Koury, Charles Ruas, Hutha Sayre, George Witte, and, of course, Sara London.

D. A.

▼

CONTENTS

▲

▼

CHEATERS

a n d   O t h e r   S t o r i e s

▲

▼

WINTERLUDE

▲

Hampson could already taste the mothballed misery of another Midwestern Monday, could feel his angry funk in free fall: just "laid off" at the paper; a note in the morning mail saying his rent would soon increase; and an hour ago, for some reason, lightbulbs blowing out in the kitchen and bathroom of his tiny apartment. By the time he found a parking space at the shopping center, off beside the enormous snowbanks, his car had begun drawing attention with its tubercular sputter, a blue-black cloud pluming from the exhaust pipe. There were days, and this was one of them, when he could almost believe things had been better before Alicen left. Not that she'd "left" precisely—in fact he'd told her to go, wouldn't have it any other way—but "left" was how he tended to think of it now.

He pulled the parking brake and felt in his shirt pocket for the very last floater, washing it down with a handful of snow from the roof of his car. For several weeks now he'd been relying each day on the little melt-in-your-mind masseuse, though he didn't like thinking it was a habit. Still, he liked even less the few times he'd been flat out of pills and presidents these past weeks; better by far the groggy release of chemistry than the stupid spates of spleen and self-pity he stumbled into without it.

He'd just turned up Aisle 4 in search of lightbulbs when he glimpsed it, but only momentarily, so he had to wonder if he'd seen correctly. The girl—she was college age, wearing a grey wool overcoat—stood close to the display shelves in the kitchenware section. She seemed to have slipped something, something shiny, a fancy winged corkscrew maybe, into one of the big pockets at the side of her coat. Seeing Hampson, she began twisting one of the coat's black buttons in her free hand. He pretended not to have noticed, occupying himself with the lightbulbs he'd located. The girl began humming to herself, touching at several items on the shelves before moving off to another part of the store.

When he got to the Express Lane she was standing in line two lanes away. He could see her purchases at the end of the black conveyor belt: a box of Tampons, a tin of Planters cashews, and a bottle of liquid wash detergent. He tried to discern evidence of anything in her pocket, but the coat was big and bulky and the pocket looked normal.

The cashier swept up Hampson's items and smiled, a bottled blond with rather unattractive dark roots showing close to her scalp. She poked her painted nails at the register, and his lightbulbs totaled $3.37; Hampson dug into his jeans and found he had three ones, a quarter, and several pennies. Reluctantly, he wrote a check, his forearm casually hiding a full page of unbalanced transactions. He knew there was at least forty dollars left in the account, but that was all until his severance pay was processed. And then what? He hadn't been quite so poor since college. That was one thing you could say for marriage anyway—Alicen's passbook had almost always had four-digit numbers in the balance column.

He handed the woman his check.

"Do you have some ID?" she asked.

He produced a laminated state press pass—coat-and-tie photo—and a long-outdated ID from the university he'd attended in the East.

"Do you have a Sale Days Courtesy Card?"

"No. I've got a driver's license. A local library card . . ." Alicen had never left the apartment without a couple of credit cards in her wallet, but Hampson was too disorganized to ever be responsible for such a thing.

Blond-on-Black took his flimsy, dog-eared driver's license, a thick square of unlaminated paper perforated down the middle, and inspected it. "This is a driver's license?"

"Yes, it's from Vermont. They don't use photographs. It's valid, though. I mean, my check's not going to bounce."

"I'm sorry, if you don't have a Courtesy Card, you at least need a local driver's license." She shrugged sympathetically. "There are a lot of transients in this town."

Transients, he thought, do I already look so unemployed? Funny word to issue from the peroxided head now staring at him. "Jesus," he said, "how do I get a 'Courtesy Card'?" The man behind him was shifting his weight and sighing.

The cashier reached beneath the counter and pulled out a letter-sized form with questions in fine print on front and back. "You just fill this out and bring it to the manager's office, over on the plat—"

"Oh, fuck, forget it," he said. He stuffed the checkbook into his coat pocket. "You're not gonna take this check?"

"I'm sorry, I can't."

He crumpled the check and glanced at the lightbulbs. "You're a very accommodating woman, you know? And by the way, you should give your hair the treatment again real soon." He walked off thinking *stupid what are you saying Jesus contain yourself.*

When he stepped outside, the college girl was about twenty yards away, shoulders hunched, walking quickly to her car. He hoped she *had* ripped something off. Just what the place deserved. And then, still full of an angry rush of adrenaline, he had an idea.

The girl was heading for a little red Saab parked beside one of the enormous r-shaped light posts. The floater hadn't quite kicked in yet; his knees felt briefly the way they had in high school, the first time he'd set his skis into the track of the fifty-meter jump. He picked up his pace. "Uh, excuse me, miss."

She turned quickly, wide-eyed with surprise, half slipping on the snow-dusted ice.

"Sorry, didn't mean to startle you," Hampson said. He paused. He was being too polite.

"Yes? What is it?" the girl said.

"David Forbison, store security. Uh, I think you might have left the store with something unpaid for?"

She furrowed her brow and shook her head, slowly stepping backwards. "No, everything's right here in the sack. I have the receipt."

She was too nervous; he was convinced now he'd seen her take something. "Well, I believe I'm right, ma'am, and we ought to check it out." He glanced around to make sure no one overheard them. "Would you please come back into the store with me?" He guessed this would quickly establish his credibility.

"No, I won't. I haven't done anything." She seemed short of breath. A rather fetching young fräulein, genuine yellow hair, rosy round cheeks.

"Well, would you at least reveal the contents of your pockets for me?"

"The contents of my pockets are none of your fucking business. It's getting cold out here—please leave me alone."

"Ma'am, I think you must realize I'm empowered to arrest you. I'm trying to keep this from being any more awkward for you than it needs to be. Now, if you could just reveal the contents of your pockets for me, we could have this all over with."

"What do you think I—you can't just . . ."

But her eyes were beginning to well up now. A man carrying a large shopping bag and a new yellow broom glanced at them as he walked by. The girl waited until he'd passed to speak. "Look, don't arrest me. Please. I did take the corkscrew. But this store *owes* me money. I bought a colander here last month that got all rusty the first week I had it. I mean, this place owed me that much at least."

"You could have returned it. We have a very reasonable refund policy."

"They'd never have taken it back," she said, brushing her cheek with a mittened hand.

"Anyway," he said, "that's not the point now."

"Do you have to arrest me?" Her voice cracked. "Can't you just take it back in with you?"

"That's not really possible. Look. I'll tell you what." He glanced back toward the store. "You look pretty cold, could we talk in your car for a minute?"

She looked newly concerned now, but after a moment said, "I guess," without taking her eyes off him. She got in and unlocked the passenger door, leaving her own door slightly ajar. The car had an expensive cassette deck, and there were half a dozen tapes spread out across the dashboard. The girl settled her hands in her lap, her glance not quite meeting his.

"What's your name?" he asked pleasantly.

"Betsy," she said.

"Betsy what?"

"Betsy Dance."

"Is that really your name?"

"Yes! Honestly."

"It's a nice name." He'd scrunched around in the seat so that he was facing her profile. He noticed now that her nose must have once been broken, a minor angular flaw amidst the gentle curves of her face. "You seem like a nice girl, Betsy. Probably go to the university, right?"

"Uh-huh," she said. "I do."

"Probably never done this kind of thing before." Maybe she had, maybe she hadn't. People loved it when you discerned fine qualities in their faces. "Am I right?"

She turned slightly. "No, you're right. I never . . . I've never . . ." She shook her head.

"Okay," he said. He paused. He was glad he'd let the short scruff of beard grow recently; he still felt somewhat disguised beneath it, his awareness of the whiskers somehow making it easier to adopt this paternal moron tone, when he was probably only seven or eight years older than she. "I'm not real eager to get you into trouble, Betsy. But I've got a job to do. I mean"—he snuffed hard, a little nuance of character for the role—"I'm hired to do a specific kind of work here, and, you know, it's not always pleasant, but I do it." He paused again, uncertain now whether he could really go all the way with this. "So. I've got this . . . 'obligation' to my employer. And then I've got the problem of commissions."

"Commissions?"

"Right. See, the security staff gets a flat salary here, but we also work on commission. Which means if I apprehend a shoplifter and then let him go—or let her go—I'm letting money flow right out of my own pockets. See?"

"Yeah, I see." She pulled at the tassled end of her wool scarf. "How much do you get for busting someone? I mean, apprehending."

"Well, it varies. It goes up each time. Me, I've got a pretty good record. I've stopped nine shoplifters just since the first of the year, so my bonuses are increasing, see?" The floater had settled in. He was having to work hard now to keep from indulging the ignoramus accent that kept trying to creep into this ludicrous delivery.

"Well," she ventured, "maybe I could help you out a little and you could overlook it? I mean, with all due respect. Not a bribe or anything, but just . . . you know?"

"Well, that's a possibility, Betsy." He caught himself staring at a hole in the leg of her jeans, where the soft blond hairs of her knee showed through.

"If I give you ten bucks, can we forget it, please?"

He maintained an even expression and settled his gaze on her until she let out a nervous and slightly impatient sigh. "Betsy, you don't already have a criminal record, do you?"

"No, of course not!" She blushed deeply.

"Because the boys inside there ain't the type to slap your wrist and send you home." He sighed and peered back toward the store windows as if checking for someone. Betsy Dance glanced back that way too, her eyes widening with anxiety.

"I mean, maybe I'm wrong," he said, "but I figured it'd be worth a little more than ten dollars to you not to catch a criminal record." He lifted an old Dylan tape from the dashboard and examined it, then slid it into the cassette deck. "Not to have a cruiser come take you downtown, where you'll get your pretty little fingers all covered with ink."

The tape wasn't playing; her pretty little fingers stuck a key into the ignition, and suddenly Dylan was crooning, *Winterlude, winterlude, my little apple . . .*

"You hear what I'm saying?" Hampson asked. "You really want your name in the Day in Court column, where all your professors can read it over their morning coffee? I mean, Betsy, think about it: *ten bucks?*"

"Well, how much do you want?" Her left hand edged toward the door handle.

Good question—how much *did* he want? The Saab, her Italian shoes, her general demeanor spelled sugar daddy, which meant this little prank might just be good for, what, a hundred? Solid chunk of the next rent check. "I just want it to be worth my while, Betsy, to do you a favor when I'm putting my job on the line. I mean, I could get my ass canned for letting you go."

"All right, all right, look. I'll give you . . . seventy-five dollars. If that's not enough you can go ahead and bust me."

"That sounds about right." He nodded.

She drew her upper lip over her teeth and removed her wallet from her shoulder bag. "I've got a ten . . . and a couple ones here," she said, her fingers shaking slightly as she sorted through the black leather wallet. "Can I write you a check for the rest?"

"A check," he said, considering. "Sure, just give me the ten and make out a check for sixty-five."

Her hand continued to shake as she quickly completed the check. She asked him his name and didn't seem to notice that he was now Chris Hampson and not David Forbison. She tore the check out and handed it to him. He glanced it over, folded it in half with the crisp new ten, and slid them into his coat pocket.

"Oh, I almost forgot," she said, reaching into her own coat pocket. Hampson heard a solid *clink* and saw a flash of metal. He braced against the door thinking *Jesus, she's got a weapon,* but it was only the shiny silver corkscrew, which she held out to him.

He stared at it, then pushed it back to her, his fingers registering the cold pink skin on the back of her hand. "You keep it, Betsy. We'll call it compensation for the rusty colander." He unlatched the door and a fragile pencil length of snow fell from the edge of the roof onto his shoulder. "Be good now," and he was out of the car and walking across the parking lot. His knees were shaking, and a perverse triumphant laugh strained to burst from his lungs.

Three weeks later, his savings dwindled, living on Kraft macaroni and cheese, Hampson had picked up part-time hours at a bookstore on Dubuque Street. He still dropped floaters at home most days, and had noticed that sometimes now, if he went for a day or more without, a certain anxiousness descended on him and an activity as simple as aiming toothpaste onto his toothbrush would cause his hand to shake. He'd also had the runs on and off for a week, though maybe it was just the lousy diet.

He'd been half tempted to phone his mother and ask for a small loan—two or three hundred bucks—but it was easier to avoid communicating with her. She had received the news of his impending divorce as if he'd announced his membership in a satanic cult. And with his father and older brother recently sentenced for a billing scam in their fuel-oil delivery business—yet another of the new year's glad tidings—he doubted she had extra cash on hand.

Besides, he'd just met a young med-school student specializing in pharmacology, a white-robed rube who hadn't yet figured out the street value of floaters. Doing business with doe-eyed Dr. Discount might just allow him to maintain his frequent flyer status. If he could continue economizing—cheap pills, a few dollars a day for food, gradually selling off his books and records—the job at the bookstore might just see him through.

Wednesday evening he was working the register near the front window when he happened to notice Betsy Dance, in her oversized coat, stroll into the bar across the street. It wasn't quite closing time yet, but he began ushering the few remaining customers out of the store. In ten minutes he'd locked up and was pushing into the smoky dimness of the Prairie Dog, its customers an odd mixture of local working-class folk and the cheerful, shallow, well-fed and ill-informed undergrads he'd come to detest. Betsy Dance was sitting at the bar alone. She had a Coke in front of her and was writing on a sheet of paper. Hampson settled unnoticed on the stool beside her and spoke quietly: "Your check bounced."

Still writing, she turned slowly, a look of mild curiosity on her face until their eyes met and she recognized him. She started suddenly, knocking her drink over on the polished surface of the bar. A young bartender rushed over with a cloth. "Never get hired that way," he told her with a wink.

Hampson squeezed a quick smile at him, but sat waiting until the guy had finished wiping the wood dry and moved off.

Betsy Dance glanced behind her and swallowed, then turned back to Hampson. "I'm sorry," she said quietly. "I didn't think it would do that."

"I think you did," Hampson said. "I think you tried to screw me, Betsy. Think you tried to corkscrew me." Immediately, and almost involuntarily, he had adopted the persona of his store detective.

"Look," she said, "not here, please?" She began jotting a number on the sheet of paper and Hampson started to say, "Oh no, Betsy, you're not gonna—" but she ignored him and called to the bartender. "Excuse me? I've got to run—could you please give this to Zack for me? And tell him I *can* manage Thur—"—she glanced at Hampson—"Thursdays, it's no problem."

She grabbed her grey coat from the stool beside her, glanced briefly at Hampson with a disdainful scowl, and headed for the door, Hampson close behind.

A group of frat boys came jostling through the door as Betsy Dance stepped outside, four of them carelessly and unwittingly blocking Hampson's path. When he got to the sidewalk she was already thirty yards away, sprinting toward Iowa Avenue, coat clutched against her side, left arm pumping madly.

"Jesus!" he said, and he took off after her, wondering, as his stomach began rumbling with hunger, just what he planned to do if he caught her.

She stopped in the middle of the street to let a car pass, glancing behind her once, and then tore in front of a bus, making a beeline for a cluster of university buildings. Hampson dodged an elderly couple and heard the man swear at him as Betsy Dance sprinted up the walk that led to the Scientific Research Center.

He was out of breath and feeling wild by the time he reached the heavy glass doors of the building. Two or three students sat smoking in the lobby, warming themselves on the narrow bank of radiators that lined the bare brick wall. The place had an early-evening emptiness about it: dim lighting, the distant whirring of a janitor's heavy waxing machine. He walked straight ahead into the huge lecture theatre, but it was empty. Unless she was behind the lab table. He jogged down the carpeted steps: not there. Back out to the lobby, where there were restrooms down the hall and to the right. He felt a little dizzy now, his short sidewalk sprint a good deal more exercise than he'd had in the month or so since he'd begun eating so frugally. He knocked on the door marked WOMEN, got no response, and stepped in. Nothing. Pushed the stall doors open, one two three, to be sure she wasn't trying any movie tricks. On the way out he caught a glimpse of his red and sweaty face in the mirrors. What the hell was he doing? He was angry now, though he knew it made little sense. When his bank statement had arrived three days ago and he'd learned her check had not been covered—meaning the check he'd sent his landlord was about to bounce—he'd been furious, shouting obscenities and kicking a hole in the kitchen wall.

Now he walked quickly down the wide corridor to the big corner classroom on the left. And past it to a staircase. A trace of wet footprints there. And likewise on the second-floor landing. Department of Biology. A maze of corridors and offices. Come out, come out, wherever you are. There. A noise. Down there in the gloom, the sounds of someone sniffling. Louder now. A light switch on the wall. No, keep it dark.

Distinctly now, he heard the rapid panting breath of a girl in tears. And, as he walked nearer, pathetic as all hell, the moaned word "Ple-ease." Followed by "Sto-o-op." Which he did. Overwhelmed by a sudden discomfort of self-disgust.

"Betsy, what do you think I am, anyway?" he pleaded, surprising himself with the sudden surrender of his goon persona.

She was huddled into a corner at the end of the corridor. "I don't know," she said whimpering. "Can't you just stop? Please. I can give you the money. I mean it."

"Betsy, I don't even want the money. Look, I'm just gonna come down there and talk to you."

"No, please, leave me alo-oh-oan," she said. The pathetic vibrato of wet fear in her voice somehow summoned for him his older sister, the night his father had stunned all of them and taken his belt to her in the kitchen.

"I will, I'll leave you alone, but I'm going to talk to you first."

She stopped whimpering, but she was still cowering against the wall, sniffling and breathing in jerky heaves.

"Betsy, look, you're making too much of this. I'm not even a security guard really. I was just pulling your leg that day." She was edging into the corner as he drew near. "I thought you looked like a nice girl and I wanted to meet you," he said, almost believing now that it was so. "It was the only way I could think of."

"Yeah, right," she whined skeptically.

"I mean it," he said, "I just got a little . . . carried away."

He was only a few feet away from her now, feeling awkwardly threatening as he peered down on her in the dim corridor. "Can I sit? Do you mind if I sit?"

She moved her head slightly to one side and back, indicating No, but now he wasn't sure to which question. He sat.

Her coat was on the floor beside her; she hugged her arms to her chest, shivering.

"Why don't you put your coat on. Here," he said, and he draped it over the front of her and around her shoulders. "Come on, take it easy," he said. "I'm not what you think, okay?"

"Well, I'm not what *you* think."

"How do you know what I think?"

His question hung there and she shrugged slightly, causing

the coat to slip down off her shoulders. He moved closer to replace it, and she huddled into its warmth. He glanced at her hand on the floor, a jade-and-silver ring on one of her slender pink fingers; after a moment he took her hand and held it. She tensed briefly, but didn't withdraw it, and he began rubbing her fingers warm.

"Give me the other," he said after a minute, and he reached beneath her coat for her right hand.

"No. Stop."

"Why?"

"Because. I don't know you."

"Come on, Betsy, don't get so Emily Post on me all of a sudden."

"I'd just like to go home," she said. "Can I go now?"

He gestured to the empty corridor.

She clutched her coat and started to get up, but as she leaned forward to raise herself, her face almost deliberately near his it seemed, he met her mouth with his lips, causing her to rear back and bump her head against the wall. He started to apologize, but she was kissing him back now, an aggressive and toothy mouth-merging which for a moment he half construed as a bizarre sort of attack: her mouth mashing his lips, her slightly imperfect front teeth clicking and grinding the enamel of his own incisors. She finally unleashed a warm dart of a tongue, simultaneously reaching behind her head and rubbing her bruised blond scalp.

He was kneading her breast through her sweater—through two sweaters, really: a black turtleneck and, beneath it, a thin cashmere crewneck with a price tag or designer's card still affixed—he was doing this when she whispered suddenly, "I have a key."

"What?"

"I have a key. To this office." She gestured her chin at the door behind him.

It had been more than five months since he'd slept with a

woman—that is, since Alicen's farewell fuck. He hadn't much thought about sex since then, but suddenly his need was so fervently urgent he was ready to lie naked on cold linoleum, on a goddamn metal desktop if she was fussy, this Betsy. But this was an office with tenure: an old and well-preserved Persian rug, several large and handsomely framed Currier and Ives prints, and, against the windows, a black leather sofa. There was even a quartz space heater.

Betsy Dance stood watching him silently, speaking only to answer that the office belonged to someone she'd worked for. She pulled the two sweaters off all at once, revealing her marvelously pert little pointed breasts, smooth pink nipples that hardened before his eyes in the cold. Over the next thirty minutes she was oddly silent, save for her high-pitched song of orgasm, a throaty three-note theme that quickly brought Hampson to a squirming shudder of his own. At one point, he thought, she had begun to say the name Stewart, or at least "Stew," though maybe it was just "It's too . . ." Too what? Good? Big? Not likely. No, it was probably "Stew." Which was okay, he guessed, since the whole time he held her heaving pink and white body, there was one red word that rang out in his own head: Alicen.

All in all, a most unusual February afternoon.

But lying alone in his own miserable bed that night, his fingers absently kneading the dried residue of sex from his pubic hairs, it was not the girl's reticence or purloined cashmere, nor even her little conical breasts or distinctive come music that Hampson found himself dwelling on. The thought that held him now was why, since she had that key, had she not let herself into the office before he found her?

Afterwards, as he was driving her home, he'd asked her about herself. She was from Northfield, Minnesota, she allowed, a bio major, parents divorced, one older brother. Northfield, Hampson said, isn't that where Jesse James nearly bought it? She nodded, silent and vaguely moody now, and a moment later he thought he saw her dab a single tear from the edge of her nose. He considered making a joke about her belated concern for the James gang, but thought better of it.

When he let her off, neither of them said anything about calling or seeing the other again. And though he often thought fondly, in the days that followed, of their odd tryst on the black sofa, he was just as glad now that he'd made no last-minute plans or promises.

Instead, Betsy Dance called him. About a week later. At the bookstore. She was very sorry to bother him, but she thought he might be willing to help her. Could he? She sounded nervous.

"Well, yeah, if I can," Hampson said. "What's the problem?"

"I'm at the police station. They won't release me unless I post bail."

He let go a short stunned laugh. "What'd you do?"

"I'd rather talk about it later, but can you help me?"

Hampson turned away from Perrin, the store owner, who was chatting nearby with a customer. Whispering now, he asked, "Were you shoplifting?"

"Sort of."

He blew an exasperated bit of static into the mouthpiece. "That other time wasn't the first, was it?"

"No," she said quietly. "It wasn't. That's why they're being tough now."

He was silent.

"But, Chris?"

"Yeah?"

"In the office that night? That was a first."

"Bullshit," he said, and Perrin turned around with his brow furrowed.

"It's not . . . bullshit," she said. "And I do need your help."

"Isn't there anyone else you can call? What about your family? I mean, your old man gave you a Saab to come to school with, he's not about to stiff you bail money."

"The car's my neighbor's, and she's out of town." Her voice was trembling. "My father lives in California—I've been trying to reach him all day. Please, Chris, don't make me spend the night here. I need two hundred and fifty dollars. I've got a waitressing job at the Prairie Dog—I'll be able to pay you back. I can give you a hundred as soon as I get home."

"What about your mother?"

"She's a—away. Somewhere. I don't know."

"Betsy, I'd like to help you, but I don't even *have* that much—in the bank or anywhere else."

"Please, Chris. Don't say no."

"Betsy, look, just keep trying your father. Anyway, you must have friends here . . ."

"I don't *know* anybody at this goddamn school."

"Betsy, I want to help you," he said, "but I honestly can't. Really, I'm sorry. Look, I have to get back to work here." He hung the phone up gently.

When his shift ended, he got Perrin to advance him his next check and walked over to the police station. A young officer led her out to the booking desk, and she said a simple, "Thank you, Chris," looking calm and self-possessed and even rather prim. But when they got outside she hid her face in his parka and began sobbing. He stopped and stood patting her back, but she said, "No, let's get out of here," and he led her to his car.

Twenty minutes later they were in the kitchen of her apartment. Betsy had stopped crying and sat with both hands wrapped around a mug of tea. Neither of them had spoken for some time.

"Betsy, why do you need to do that shit, anyway?"

"Don't," she said. "I'll go get the money right now. Just don't do this to me." She got up and headed for the bedroom.

He wanted to say the money could wait, but in fact it couldn't. Even if she gave him a hundred now, he was still down by fifteen Hamiltons. And getting thinner by the day on a new stringency diet of Ramen soup (five packages for 99¢).

While she rummaged through drawers in the bedroom, he tilted back in his chair and quietly pulled open the fridge: a bowl of tuna fish salad with diced pickles that would do very nicely. Plus a little square of lasagna with some honest-to-God meat in it. He eased the refrigerator closed and sat waiting for her.

She brought out a stack of tens, fives, and ones—her waitressing money, apparently—and counted out a hundred and fifteen dollars. "There—I owe you a hundred and thirty-five now."

Hampson nodded and slid the money to the edge of the table. "I thank you," he said.

She sat down and glanced at him, picking at a button on her blouse. "I really do appreciate it."

"No problem. About the balance, though . . ."

"Well, I could write you a check if you want." Behind the damp trace of tears an ironic imp gleamed, tugging slightly at one corner of her mouth.

Hampson watched her for a moment and then removed her hand from its nervous picking. "You're a funny girl."

"Funny ha-ha?"

"Funny peculiar, too."

"Well, well."

"You wouldn't happen to have any lasagna just lying around?"

Her Mickey Mouse alarm clock said 8:15. They'd been dozing for over an hour. He traced his thumb along the goose bumps of her upper arm, felt himself getting hard again as her wrist grazed his still-sensitive penis. There was a child's bright watercolor on the wall, a large matted piece with a green girl and a blue man sitting beneath a large and limbless brown tree. There were also several family photographs—pictures of her father and brother anyway.

"How come there are no pictures of your mother here?"

She shrugged.

"Why?"

"I don't know. We don't really get along."

"Why is that?"

"My mother . . . is just . . . a bitch," she said.

"Wow, never knew anyone with a bitchy mother before."

She allowed a small smile. "Now you do."

Over the next few weeks a routine of sorts ensued, including, on weekends, makeshift meals and gin binges in Betsy's apartment (weekdays she seemed to get by on popcorn); regular bouts of daytime sex (a strictly nocturnal activity with Alicen); and occasionally helping Betsy with a writing assignment ("Degradation and Revenge in *The Scarlet Letter*"). She never visited his own apartment, and only rarely urged him to spend the night at hers.

He was still doing floaters most days, but convinced himself his need was less urgent now. Betsy didn't know about the pills; the few times she'd asked if he was high, he claimed he'd been drinking. He figured she was troubled enough without another dubious habit. Still, his sailing solo had less to do with altruism than anxiety over maintaining his modest stash.

Most weeknights Betsy worked at the Prairie Dog. Alone in his own apartment, Hampson would lie in bed reading a book borrowed from work, or take to the medicine cabinet and levitate. Their relationship seemed somehow tentative, but there were nights when he lay in bed feeling a sad and almost sentimental longing to visit her, even in the collegiate chaos of the bar, though he knew that doing so would only be a disappointment.

*   *   *

Early one evening in the first week of March, he was working the register at the front of the bookstore when Alicen walked in with one of her old comrades from law school. His heart drummed up and his face went hot. He hadn't seen or spoken with her in at least three months. She was living in Des Moines now, working for some slime-bag law firm that handled farm foreclosures. She claimed she was planning to take her knowledge to the other side eventually, but it sounded like rationalization to him.

"Chris!" she said in apparent surprise. Her dark straight hair was cut short now, with a subtle, unbraided rat's tail in back—no doubt a daring bohemian touch among the pinstripers at the firm. "You're still here."

"Well, yeah."

"I just mean, I thought when you got, when you left the paper you were . . . I don't know," she dropped her voice discreetly, "I thought you didn't like it out here."

"I don't."

"I know. I mean, I figured you'd left town by now."

He shrugged. "I need some cash first."

"Oh. I wish I could help you," she said.

He rolled his eyes.

Sonia, the comrade, touched Alicen on the arm and said, "I'll let you two talk, I've got to look for something."

Alicen nodded and stepped closer to the register. "Don't be nasty with me, okay?"

"I'm not being nasty."

"Is it really just cash that's holding you back?"

Hampson studied her face. Did she know about Betsy? He doubted it. Doubted she'd care. "What do you mean?"

"I just mean, I don't know, up-and-coming young journalist, *Register* nominates you for a Pulitzer, so now you're a bookstore clerk?"

"The *Register* also fired me."

"So? I heard they bent over backwards to keep you on. You

could have told them you were going through a divorce. What are they supposed to do when you hardly turn anything in for over a month?"

"Where'd you hear that?"

"I saw Roger what's-his-name at a party in Des Moines. He also said you'd been overdoing it with Percodan or something."

"Roger. The guy's a Christian Scientist, he thinks taking Tylenol's like sucking Satan."

"He wasn't talking about Tylenol," she said, her eyes suddenly zeroing in on his, gauging, he guessed, his pupils.

"Get lost," he told her, his eyes squinting disdain.

"All I'm saying is, other papers don't know they let you go. Send your clips around. Show them the series on the farm crisis. I know it's been a bad time, but come on. It's not as though you don't have options."

"What are you getting at—you're ashamed to have a former husband who works in a bookstore?"

"Give me a break. I just hope you're not letting a couple of . . . adventitious setbacks ruin you."

"Is that what they call it in the legal world—an 'adventitious setback'? That must be what the scarlet A stands for. I always wondered about that."

"Don't be a jerk, cut it out."

"Fuck you."

"Jesus, Chris, you're such a prick. I'm trying to help you. Anyway, I thought what's-his-name at the *Tribune* said they might have something up there."

Hampson shrugged.

"Did you go up there and talk to him?"

He shook his head and glanced toward the door. Betsy had just come in and stood about ten feet away, scanning the magazine rack, uncertain whether she should approach him just now. "Hi," he said, summoning a lackluster smile, and she jumped her eyebrows, lifting a single mittened hand.

Alicen turned and took Betsy in. She caught Sonia's eye at the back of the store and motioned to her. Sighing, she turned to Hampson again and leaned closer. "Get it in gear, Christopher," she said quietly. "Life's not just going to wait for you, you know." She buttoned her expensive coat and glanced again at Betsy. "Life's not, but she is, I gather." Betsy, he noticed, was keeping a covert eye on Alicen.

He didn't answer, just met her eyes evenly until she shrugged and said, "I give up. Good-bye, Christopher."

"See ya," he said flatly.

It was in fact a far more civil encounter than he might have expected—particularly on his part. But then, why parade his hurt any more than he already had? He'd swallowed enough pride just consenting to that awful and silent final fuck the night she'd left. Two minutes of a strange tumescence packed as much with rage as with lust, and then, before either of them had even approached a climax, he had suddenly gone soft, his limp penis shrinking from Alicen as if in distaste. The more he'd tried to stay hard, the more clearly he saw the scene he'd happened upon a week earlier: Alicen, black hair wild on their living-room floor, receiving the bare-assed thrusts of David Forbison, her fellow editor at the *Law Review.*

Betsy wandered over to the counter now. "Was that your wife?" she asked quietly. He was a little surprised she'd stood guard there by the magazine rack; for all the nights she'd nestled close in recent weeks, he still detected a certain indifference in her affection that he expected to preclude anything like jealousy.

Which was fine with Hampson. In three years he'd thrashed his way through enough of the conjugal jungle to do him in for a lifetime. Why suffer another safari when you could always visit the zoo? Nonetheless, he knew that cash and lassitude were no longer first on the list of things keeping him here. There was also this Betsy. Betsy Banditti. Betsy of the Five-Finger Discount. That night when he'd asked her about her mother, when he'd found her so reticent, had seemed to establish a set of ground rules to which he was more than willing to adapt. Rule Number One being: *Don't ask*. There were benefits to such reticence. Privacy is dignity, after all, and Hampson—betrayed by his wife, fired by his editor, his father and brother serving five years each—Hampson simply didn't want to be asked.

But walking home with Betsy after his shift had ended, she did just that. "She stuck you, didn't she?" Betsy said.

"What?"

"Her. Your wife. She hurt you, right?"

"When?" he said, annoyed now.

"I don't know. Sometime. It's obvious."

"I guess."

"You don't have to tell me about it." She paused. "Just tell me this: Do you feel sometimes like you'd like to get even with her?"

He slowed and watched her face for a moment. In the cold like this, the two points of skin where her nose had once been broken showed up whiter than the rest of her snowy complexion. "I don't even think about her." He shrugged. "Why?"

"I don't know. I just wondered."

"Okay, Betsy, you show me yours and I'll show you mine."

"What do you mean?"

"Hey, let's be candid, okay? Somebody stuck you, too, right? I mean, you're asking me don't I sometimes want to get even. There's somebody *you* want to get even with, isn't there?"

"Maybe," she said.

"So . . . ?"

"You said you'd show me yours first," she said.

"Forget it, Betsy, I don't even want to play."

"But I'd really like to know," she said. "I care about you, Chris, I'd like to know what happened." He glanced at her. Maybe there was more affection there than he'd realized. "Really," she said.

He blew a purse of air and shook his head, scuffing at a chunk of snow. "I told you I used to work for the newspaper."

"Uh-huh. You told me you were a store security guard, too."

"I covered eastern Iowa for the *Register*. You can look it up if you want. Anyway, I was supposed to cover a very angry farm rally in Decorah one afternoon. But about eight miles from town I came on this accident. Big tractor trailer loaded down with new Buicks, lost half its load in the middle of Route 80."

Betsy shook her head slightly. "I'm not sure you understand what I was asking about."

He turned and fixed her with an icy glare. "I'm getting to it, Betsy, just hold your fuckin' ponies."

"Sorry." She touched his arm in apology.

"The *real* accident was the three-car pileup behind all the Buicks. Which I arrived at about a minute after the whole thing happened. Not a cop or ambulance in sight yet. I get out and in the first car I stop at there's this old lady with a wig half hanging off her head. The car radio's going, she's mumbling to herself, and when I open the door I see her forearm's barely attached at the elbow. Let me know if I'm boring you, Betsy, because I'd just as soon drop it."

"No, tell me."

He dipped his chin into the collar of his coat. "The husband was already gone. And her arm might as well have been. Her elbow was like a little geyser of blood squirting into her lap. I tied a tourniquet on her, which meant she'd probably lose the arm, but at least she wouldn't bleed to death. But when she realized about him, she started tearing her hair out. I mean literally, her real hair. With her one good arm. So I hold her down and wait till the emergency crew arrives.

"And shit, the last thing I wanted to do then was drive to a fucking farm rally in Decorah, write up my little six-hundred-word piece on it. So I turned around. Thinking about this woman and her husband, and I remember, I thought, God, I hope Alicen's home. I felt this real . . . a real intense devotion, like I'd never felt before. Made all the little fights we'd been having look like nothing, you know? Who cares about that shit, people can die. It was a real wake-up call." He paused. "Yeah. Like wake up, asshole. Because she was home all right. She was home, and she wasn't alone. So. Is that the part you were waiting for? There you go. 'The Good Samaritan,' for modern-day viewers."

"That's awful," Betsy said. She slipped her arm around him.

They stopped at the edge of a driveway as a car backed out, then continued in silence for a minute.

"Tell me about Stewart," he said finally.

Her head jerked, fully alert.

"It is about Stewart, isn't it?"

Betsy stopped. "How do you know that?"

"You said it once . . . in your sleep."

"Oh . . ." She toyed with the zipper of her parka. "You're not going to like this, but you know that office we were in that time?"

"That's Stewart's?"

"Not exactly, it belongs to the professor he worked with. Stewart was getting a Ph.D. Or still is, I guess. We'd go up to Northfield now and then, to spend the weekend at my mother's house." Her voice became deliberate as she kept it from veering into emotion. "She and I were going through a, uh, well, we had more or less of a truce since I'd left for school. Before then we used to fight a lot. Real screaming scenes. And worse. That's why my nose is so ugly."

"She broke your nose? I mean, it's not ugly at all, but she broke it?"

"She clobbered me with a bag of carrots when I was twelve, and it never got set right. I think 'cause she was afraid I'd tell the doctor. Before that I was actually kind of pretty."

"Betsy, you're very pretty, it's barely even noticeable. Was that typical, though?"

"Well, it was the only time she broke my nose. But things were getting a little better the last few years. Plus she seemed to like Stewart. Which was new. In high school she'd always hated my boyfriends. She either made fun of them or wouldn't talk to them." She shrugged. "And . . ." She drew the word out slowly, as though she would stop. "Stewart was giving a paper in Chicago one weekend, so my roommate and I— I had a roommate then—we decided to go to Northfield together. I needed some things, and I thought," she jerked her shoulders, "I thought I'd surprise my mother. And when we got there, Stewart's car was in the driveway, so I figured the seminar had been canceled, that he came right up there to see me. Except he hadn't even known we were going. Anyway . . . anyway, *you* can imagine the rest of it."

Hampson waited. "What?"

"What do you think?"

"You mean he and your mother . . . ?"

"The two of them. In the shower together," she said, her voice cracking slightly.

"Jesus." He saw her eyes glaze over. "How old is your mother?"

"Forty-three. But she looks about thirty."

Hampson shook his head.

"The point is," she said, swallowing unshed tears, "we ought to get even. Don't you think?"

"Get even," he said hollowly. That was the point? The point, he would have thought, was that given such similar experiences, maybe there was some odd logic in the crazy crossing of their paths.

"Well, why not?" Betsy said.

He turned and studied her face. Her complexion was wonderfully ruddy now, the evening chill and the quick burst of emotion combining to heighten her elfin Nordic features.

"I know she hurt you, Chris, and I could help you get her back. I mean, not get her back, of course, but get back at her. Or at the guy if you want. But if I do, you'll help me too, won't you?"

He licked the inside of his mouth, thinking. So she wanted to get even. Was that such a base instinct? *Nemo me impune lacessit.* Nobody fucks *me* over and gets away with it. Nobody fucks my mother and gets away with it, either. So why should David Forbison screw Alicen with impunity?

Vengeance; it was simple logic, really, the oldest logic on earth: Eat from that tree and I'll fix *your* wagon—and your little serpent, too.

"What is it you want to do exactly?" he said.

About a week later Betsy was getting dressed for the second shift at the Prairie Dog while Hampson sat gloomy, drinking gin and tonic on the easy chair in her bedroom. "I put a full tank of gas in your car," she said, pulling a pair of wool tights on over her underwear.

He nodded, feeling his pocket for the two unfamiliar housekeys she'd given him.

Betsy tugged the waistband of the thick black tights high on her belly, halfway to her bra. "That way you won't have to stop up there." She snatched a denim skirt from the closet and stepped into it. "It'll be better if nobody sees you afterwards. Don't you think?"

"Mmm."

"Don't be so glum, Christopher. It's not a murder, for Christ's sake. Plastic surgeons do it all the time." She walked to the dresser and as she passed him mimed a slow blow to his nose—"Pow!"—but he didn't respond. "And remember," she said, "don't get hung up over the cash and jewelry and stuff. If you get it, great, but that's just, you know, the cover."

"I've got it, Betsy, okay? I've got it."

"Sor-*ree*," she said.

He sipped at his drink and added gin from the bottle on the floor beside him, glancing at her Mickey Mouse alarm. A month ago he'd considered the clock pathetically tacky, but now he found it rather touching. What a fucking sap. Always thinking a woman might be the missing piece of the puzzle forming his half-assed picture of happiness. Only to find each time that his jigsawed vision of joy was missing much more than he'd guessed. "You're sure we're gonna be business as usual after this?" he asked.

Betsy turned from the closet. "Of course! Why not?"

"I don't know, I mean, suppose you resent me for it? Christ, Betsy, she's your fucking mother."

"That's just biology," she said. "Is that what's bothering you?" She came and stroked his cheek.

He shook his head once, then shrugged, poking a finger at the wedge of lime in his drink and holding it beneath the surface. "Tell me some more bad shit about her," he said.

It was snowing outside of Northfield. A jeep had gone off the road near the interstate exit, but it didn't look like much; a state trooper was already on the scene laying chains. Not that Hampson would stop anyway. No dodges, he was going through with this thing. He'd nearly said no the day before, but Betsy was bent on it now. Besides, cash in the kitchen freezer, jewelry in the bedroom—if all went as planned, he could bag the bookstore job and score enough floaters to lie back and levitate until spring. Then maybe get his amputated ambition out of hock. Make a down payment on some incentive.

In any case, he was ready now to kick some ass. Deviate some septum. Whatever. That perfect patrician nose upon which, according to Betsy, her mother had always prided herself. Bango. Say bye-bye. Just let me at that nose and we can call it a night. Then again, better hope she resists a little or it might look pretty suspicious: *Thief Ignores Valuables; Hammers Homeowner's Nose.* Even some hick Northfield cop might trace the motive there. Not that any old Sherlock could ever fathom the mind of Betsy Dance.

He switched his high beams on and took another swig from the thermos of gin and tonic. By now it had cut through the blissy passivity of his pills, nudging him into the anger this evening would hinge on. So: remember to feel for it— cartilage caving in on the knuckles. That's how it was with Charlebois on the playground all those years ago: felt it *and* heard it. A right satisfying sensation, too. This, though? How satisfying could this be? Still, if it made Betsy happy. A strange girl, but also a girl he was beginning to love, he realized. Be a pity to spare the rod and spoil the relationship.

Which brought him back to the more troubling aspect of this little errand. Not the criminal violence of it, but the fact that the whole thing confirmed Stewart—Stewart whatever-his-name, Stewart the Ph.D.—the whole thing confirmed old Stew as the guy Betsy couldn't get over, the ugly tattoo on her heart. But then, this might be what it took to banish the bas-tard. And what's a little humble pie to a man who's found his wife humping her brains out on the living-room floor?

Dakota Street wasn't hard to find. A pleasant neighborhood of upper-middle-income homes, turn-of-the-century places with spacious yards and wide driveways. The type of people who took notice, no doubt, of a rusty and unfamiliar out-of-state car parked on the street. For which reason Hampson continued on for several blocks, down the hill to a condo unit with a half-filled parking lot. He was shivering now—the cold in part, but little anxiety quakes as well. He cut the engine and got out, stood beside the car pissing a gin-and-tonic valen-tine into the snow. Oh, the things we do for love. Then stuffed the ski mask into his coat pocket and hoofed it back up the hill.

Dakota Street. Except for the solitary scrape of a distant driveway being shoveled, the neighborhood was quiet. A good chance she'd yell, scream, whatever. Neighbors . . . ? Just get the goddamn door closed.

Two seventeen was the number he wanted, but as he neared 207 he slowed, realized the sporadic shoveling was just ahead. So let's just take it across the street here, collar turned up against the cold. Let these nice tall pine trees obscure us, that's the ticket. Should have been over here anyway. Don't let that G-and-T buzz make us careless now. So: addresses ascending by twos means 209, 11, 13, 15 . . . shit. Betsy, what am I walking into here? You said she motherfucking lived alone! What's this guy doing out in her drive—whoops, no, strike that, all systems go here. Little M/F confusion there, Houston. Back to full throttle. Slight of figure, long of hair, yellow of boots—definitely an F. As in Fractured.

Her back was to him as she shoveled, Hampson making his way from tree to tree until she was only thirty yards away. His heart was doing a mad percussion number now, but his breath had lodged somewhere between mouth and lungs, unmoving.

Across the street Jenna Dance stopped and unzipped her parka, leaning on the shovel. A good sign: only one light on in the handsome brick house. Maybe best to follow right in behind her when she finishes.

She pulled her white knit hat off now and ran her hand through her hair—hair as blond as Betsy's. He could only see her in profile, but she didn't look especially malevolent; be easier if the bitch had fangs. Never mind that, though, keep the venom flowing. It's going to happen.

He dropped to his knees as she approached the last section of unshoveled driveway near the street. Almost alarming how much she looked like Betsy. Prettier, though. A more perfect face. At least for the moment.

A car rolled around the corner, and Hampson lay down on the sidewalk, hidden by the snow piled high on either side. When he stood again she'd finished the driveway and was walking into the garage. He pulled the keys from his pocket. Soon as she starts closing that garage door. Get in there and wait for her. Get her while she's winded.

But she came back out carrying a small sack. Salt? Clomping through the snow to the largest maple tree in her front yard. Not salt. Birdseed. Filling a goddamn feeder. Wonderful, I'm here to mug St. Francis of the frozen fucking north. Only, forget it, lady, I'm not the least bit touched. So you're a bird lover, big deal. Hitler and his generals used to weep over Shakespeare, it didn't make them human. Just get in the house so we can dance this number.

But she wouldn't. She zipped her coat back up and sat on the top porch step, her breath drifting off in vapors. By now he had to piss again, finally indulging himself in a quiet steamy leak into the snow, kneeling this time for minimum noise.

For five, ten, it had to be fifteen minutes, she sat there looking meditative, depressed maybe, chin cradled in her mittened hands. Eventually she leaned down and scooped a handful of snow from the top of the shrubbery, holding it to her face and nibbling from it.

Don't do this, he thought, just cool it with the sensitive shit. Feeding the birds, nibbling snow, you're still a bitch.

But either the gin was wearing off or he'd pissed the last of his venom into the snow, because goddamn it, he had some second thoughts now. And yet how simple, to land one nose-breaking blow, rifle her jewelry box, her secret cash stash. He thought of Betsy, in bed the night before, hovering over him for hours on her knees. Melting into her sheets, her mouth, he'd said to himself, yes, I'll do it for this girl; a crazy criminal thing, but she's been wronged and I'll do it.

And yet. And yet. Better to break Alicen's goddamn nose. That was the face he'd gladly do damage to. What happened here, though, in that house across the street, it wasn't his life.

He stepped out from behind the tree, and she started suddenly—her hands dropped stiffly to her lap. He watched her and spat into the street, locked eyes with her as she rose and walked hurriedly into the garage. In a second the automatic door kicked into action, slowly creaking closed. Bitch.

He stepped into the street and picked up a slender, palm-length piece of curbing cement that had been scraped loose by a snowplow. It had the vague shape of a trumpet, though it arched and sailed through her big front window rendering the precise chiming notes of a percussionist's triangle.

He got back to Iowa City just before midnight, and when he saw the police cruiser outside Betsy's apartment he panicked briefly, thinking, in a quick burst of paranoia, that someone had seen his plates in Northfield. Then he noticed a small crowd gathered in the driveway, students mainly, each holding a big plastic cup of beer, and he relaxed. Another neighborhood party out of control. Goddamn weekend began Thursday nights now in these college towns. When did they study? Books? Ideas? Social justice? Their idea was just to be social. Book a flight to Florida for spring break. Most of the little pricks were voting Republican now, which was fitting, since their main aim in life was having a grand old Party.

An officer blocked the door to the back stairs of the house, refusing to let Hampson in, though he claimed he lived there, refusing even to hint at what had happened. Betsy would be at work for another hour, but he was worried now; hers was the only apartment accessible by the back stairs.

No one in the crowd seemed to know what had happened except that an ambulance had recently come and left. He was about to try a second assault on the stairway when he noticed Reed—"Lieutenant Loose Lips" to knowing reporters—swaggering Reed, who succumbed to glottal gab at the merest hint of newsprint.

"Reed!"

He was getting into a cruiser parked across the street, but turned and smiled. "Hampster. Looking pretty scruffy these days."

"What's going on?"

Reed shook his head. "Sorry, Crisco, still in the middle of

something here. Catch me tomorrow—I'll give you some quotables."

"Strictly off the record, man. What is it? Off the record, Reed, just two guys talking."

Reed glanced around. "Love quarrel, looks like." He smiled and waggled his tongue in a perverse manner. "Vicious stuff, Girl who lives upstairs, waitress, runs into an old beau on the job. They start flirting, she brings him home, they do the nasty and they're lying in bed. Thirsty now, right? Girl gets up to open a bottle of wine. Comes back and stabs him in the vitals with a corkscrew."

"Jesus! Betsy? She stabbed him in the—heart?"

"You know that chick? Not the heart, man, the *vitals*: bitch skewered his poor dick. But hey—who knows?—maybe he was a lousy lay. Come too fast, could be your last. Ha!" He released a taut man's belly laugh and mock punched Hampson's shoulder. "I *know* you'd love to quote me on that one." He opened his car door and got in, slammed the door and rolled the window down.

Hampson was reeling now, dizzy, wanted only to go sit on the curb.

"So. Let it be a lesson to you, Crisco."

"What?" he mumbled vaguely.

" 'What?' " Reed imitated. "Fucking-A, man, you're just no good without a notebook, are you." Then, peering closer, "Jesus, you don't look good, guy."

Hampson nodded, his mouth hanging open dumb, mumbled some inarticulate sound as he crossed the street.

Reed tore off with his cherry top flashing, snow spraying from behind his tires.

The crowd, mainly college boys in shirtsleeves, had begun to disperse, heading back across the street to the party still in session there.

"Hey, guys, check this," someone called, and everyone drifted back to the driveway. Sitting on the curb, Hampson turned to see two cops escorting Betsy out the door and down the icy driveway to the waiting cruiser. She wore her parka and mittens, but he could see her hands were cuffed in front of her. Her mouth was bruised and swollen on one side. He started to stand and she saw him, her eyes came alive suddenly. "Chris!" she called, and the beer-guzzling college boys turned to look at him. But before she could say anything more, an older officer set his hand on her head and ducked her into the back seat.

He stumbled into his own apartment ready to crash, the gin and the drive finally taking their toll, though his chest still surged with a sick anxiety. He went to the medicine cabinet and popped a floater, kicked off his boots and got under the covers fully dressed, but soon the phone began ringing. For a solid minute he listened to it. Ten minutes later the same thing. Her one call. A short time later it rang again. When it stopped he got up and removed the receiver, went back to bed, then got up again and unplugged the jack, stood wrapping the cord around the disembodied phone. He found a cardboard box and set the phone in it. Dropped papers from his desk into the box as well. Then walked to the closet and swept his clothes from the rack. Lifted his suitcase to the bed, opened it and emptied each of his drawers into its gaping mouth. The big bottom drawer, a disaster of chipped veneer, he carried to the next room, filling it with his few kitchen-wares and a stack of books.

He got back into bed then and slept for four hours, rose at six o'clock and stripped the covers. In the medicine cabinet there was a small vial with a half dozen more floaters in it. Brushing his teeth he eyed the brown container, then twisted the plastic lid off and poured the remaining pills into his hand. Dropped them into the toilet. Pissed and flushed.

By ten o'clock he was forty miles outside of Chicago. He

passed the exit for Aurora and about a quarter mile later came upon an attractive redheaded girl in tight jeans and a green down parka, holding a hand-lettered sign that read EVANSTON. His foot came off the pedal and his hand felt slowly for the turn signal as he studied her. Their eyes met. A tall soft-looking girl, with a pierced nose apparently. Sort of a gangly hip innocent. He held the directional stick without moving it. His foot dropped back to the pedal and pressed. The girl, an amber world of possibilities, receded in his rearview mirror.

"Hoof it," he whispered.

▼

HONEYMOON

▲

My grandfather remembers walking down Sackville Street with Michael Collins in 1916, so you might say we've a history of nationalists in the family. I used often try to picture him there with the Big Fellow when I chanced to be on O'Connell Street. It wasn't easy, what with buses painted with bright hailstorms of Smarties, storefronts flashing neon, and the ersatz hell of McDonald's. Around the General Post Office I could get a fair glimpse of what they might have looked like. Collins, tall, boyishly masculine, the eyes of people upon him. My grandfather would not have matched him in height, but I'm sure he bore himself with equal poise. I don't recall just how they happened to be together, but it was so.

This day, walking past the GPO, I did not picture them, but recalled walking there with my grandfather years before, at age seven or eight. He had stopped to show me the bullet holes and pieces of lead in the building's pillared columns, remnants of Easter Week. I had rubbed my finger into the holes gingerly, with respect; touching history it felt like. I now wondered if such scenes would etch themselves as fondly upon the memory of my own son. I was to be married in a week, and questions of a family had begun occurring to me.

Just beyond the GPO, I passed a young punk rocker whose hair was dyed green and orange, of all colors. He had all the gear: tight black pants, bulky tennis shoes, safety pins, the haircut with the cultivated cowlick. He stopped outside a record store where the window displayed a hideous poster advertising a new album by the Sex Pistols. I couldn't help wondering what must his parents think when he steps into his tidy little home in Clontarf or wherever.

Further south, crossing the quay to the bridge, I slowed to watch a workman cleaning Daniel O'Connell's statue. The Liberator. The demagogue who balked in the fields of Brian Boru, is more like it. Unable to call a British bluff. Grandfather called him the Deliberator for that. "Wasn't he the t'in edge of the wedge among our heroes, though," was what he would often say.

Around the base of O'Connell's statue sit four angels with long thick hair that would, were they not mere stone, most certainly be blond. I studied the angel on the right as the morning crowd pressed by. At one time I had believed her to be not just an angel but my guardian angel, that dear protectress who, as Grandfather said, was always close by. She was beautiful, and had a bullet hole in her left breast, a wound sustained in Easter Week.

Soon I reached the green gate of Trinity. I had only twice been within the hallowed grounds since taking my degree two years earlier. My mother has lived in Dublin all her life, and never once set foot in Trinity. My father nearly threw me out of the house when I decided to study English and history there, even though it was by then nearly seventy percent Catholic. I entered the front gate, where Oliver Goldsmith, self-consciously ugly, hides his face in a book. Edmund Burke looks across at what was once the Irish Parliament and, being a logical man, registers no surprise that it should now be the Bank of Ireland.

I followed two culchies with thick Kerry accents—dressed straight off the dusty bargain racks of McBirney's—down into the Buttery and ordered a pint. Something about culchie clothes in the city always depresses me, especially in the pretentious atmosphere of Trinity, and I started thinking about this culchie's mother packing him off to Dublin, poor lad, so far from home with so little taste.

But I was feeling less sorry for the culchies than for myself this morning. I was to meet an American student who was selling his passport. It disturbed me to have been tapped for so menial a task, all the more so as I'd recently spent six weeks in Syria, learning to "pick oranges" as the standard joke went. Doubtless the lads at the office had fed Ferguson some ripe tripe: "O'Toole's a schoolteacher; he's nothing to do in the summer. Let *him* pick up the passport."

From the description, I recognized the American's denim jacket with a silver-studded peace symbol on the back. He was sitting at the bar and kept looking at his watch; after a short while he got up and left. I followed him across the cobblestones, watching his back and remembering Ferguson once telling me that the symbol was really "the footprint of a chicken."

It occurred to me that perhaps Ferguson was testing my commitment or toying with me to see if I'd balk by sending me on what was practically a messenger-boy job. Because while in Syria, of all times, I had begun to reconsider my involvement. Of course, Ferguson couldn't know that I was entertaining such thoughts. I hadn't mentioned them to anyone. Even so, ridiculous as it sounds, I had more than once heard the man discuss his belief in extrasensory perception, which he claimed to have often experienced. And even if he was just taking the mickey out of someone, or using the line to intimidate a man, there have been times when I've thought those bedroom eyes of his have read men's thoughts even as the thoughts occurred.

The American was glancing behind him, and I looked

down as we passed the ugly new Arts Block and a Calder piece called *Cactus*. More likely Ferguson had sent me simply because I knew Trinity.

I walked across College Park, where the grass was stained with faint lines of white lime, which had marked the 800-meter track earlier in the summer. I forgot about Ferguson, but all those doubts that had begun in Syria sprang up again, persistent as the blades of grass my peace-loving friend was trampling ahead of me. Especially doubts about the occasional "visits to my uncle" in Belfast. Someone else could do those jobs. They had to be done, but someone else could do them. There were dozens of headers who wouldn't mind the few extra quid they could pick up in my place.

The entire dilemma was ludicrous, really. My commitment had always been such that I gave myself completely to anything they asked of me. (I'd even written part of a speech for Ferguson to deliver at the Easter Week rally a year before.) And having learned much in the way of destruction for constructive change, as it were, I was sent off to Syria to train with the elite. Who turned out to be a lot of smelly Arabs with Soviet guns and money, men who never bathed, and leered over my fiancée. And there I began to sense that I wanted no part of this life. It was not the same organization my grandfather had known. It was tainted and tawdry; backed by opportunists, loaded with the hooligan element and naive neo-Marxists, and a few deluded romantics like myself.

Somehow it has always been that way with me; just when I become quite serious about something, or committed to it, or proficient at it, I lose interest in the thing. Here at Trinity it was distance running. I had good luck in my first season of cross-country. In most matches I could expect to place in the top ten, and by third year I was usually the team's first or second finisher. But during track season my interest began to falter. I thought maybe it was just the atmosphere of the track, running eight loops around an 800-meter oval, over and over.

I was sure the feeling would pass by the time cross-country began in the fall. But it didn't. And in the spring I was captain of the track team, running worse than ever, and no longer caring a great deal about it, walking to the starting line without a drop of adrenaline flowing in me. And then running circles.

The American was standing, hands pressed deep in his pockets, in a deserted dressing room of the Pavilion. He was nervous. I told him we realized, of course, that to get back home he would eventually have to report the loss of his passport. But he was not to do so until the following May. Since this was August, it gave us a long time to make use of the document. Ferguson had told me we would want to be getting a man into and out of the States. I told the American that if there was an emergency in which he would have to leave for home, he was to contact us first. But it would be best if there were no emergencies. "Mind now, you tell anyone, and it's big trouble for you, understand?" He nodded his head so that his little wire glasses slid on his nose and said yes he did. His hand was shaking when he gave me the little blue book. I looked inside; there was his picture, coat and tie, with a sloppy signature across the edge of the photograph: Kevin Blanchard. I gave him the fifteen £20 notes, which he seemed to pocket happily enough, glancing at and half thumbing the wad, but not bothering to count it.

I had wondered earlier about giving him the full sum. With marriage and an expensive flat only a week away, it seemed reasonable to consider changing the price. He was nervous enough that he would probably have taken much less, but I abandoned the thought, said a solemn "Cheers," and left. It was as well not to have stolen money hanging over me. Given my upbringing, I could almost envision repentant nights on my knees if I were to pull it off, but if I failed, I'd have no knees at all. I only realized how much the idea troubled me by my sudden relief; I nearly added "Thanks" as I turned into the corridor messed with pellets of mud and bloody tissues from the rugby players. Of course, it was best to be curt and keep him frightened, but my not thanking him was also evidence of the general rudeness I had conditioned myself to in Syria. The Syrians were forever commenting on my "pleases" and "thank yous."

"Why do you always be so bolite? Never mind to say 'thank you.' You are so Breetish."

The irony, apparently, escaped them.

Going out the back gate of Trinity, I met Professor Baxter, who had been one of my lecturers in Irish literature. A man whose very life revolved around *Finnegans Wake,* he was a Brit, and was said to be a closeted gay. The closet, however, was a walk-in, allowing Baxter ample latitude. His affected speech rather betrayed him. "Ah, Master O'Toole, and where *did* you acquire such an exquisite tan?"

"Hello, sir. I've been in the Mideast."

"Ah, yes, the fertile crescent. For Joyce, you recall, the region was emblematic of life itself."

"Yes, sir, Plumtree's Plotted Meats and all that—I mean Potted."

He smiled his curious smile of a Saxon. I used to wonder if he found me attractive. I had forgotten the days when I had been the first to arrive at his tutorial, sitting alone with him in his office, anxious for the others to arrive, yet sharpening my confidence on that smile and his attentions. I always imagined that I was frustrating him. Life itself, indeed! After his lectures on *Ulysses*—"Once again, I urge you to note the redemptive claims of the theme of fertility"—we would laugh at how he must know "bugger-all about fertility."

I returned with the passport to the office on Tara Street. Ferguson was there, and asked me to stay a moment. We went into his office. On the wall behind his desk there was a silk-screened poster of men in sunglasses and "blackberries" that had been used for a rally in April. He sat down, removed his silver watch, and began winding it. "Would you like to visit your uncle again?"

"For what?" I asked, hoping he did not think I meant money.

"The stuff you and the girl brought back from Syria. The blessed 'try-nye-tee' of her immaculate conception," he said, winking at me.

Mary, my fiancée, had come to meet me in Syria toward the end of my two-month stay. She was only nineteen, and it was the first time she had ever been out of County Dublin. It was, perhaps, rather frivolous, but we had never been apart in the three years we'd known each other. After several long-distance phone calls during which she'd get weepy and try to persuade me to come home early, I had finally encouraged her to leave the bakery for a few weeks and join me. I said it would be a sort of early honeymoon for us, but Mary's religious streak runs deep, and she took a room in a hotel next door to my own.

She was raised almost entirely by her father; her mother died in childbirth. Terence, the older brother, told me their mother had been warned not to have any more children after his own birth, and when she became pregnant with Mary, her death had been almost inevitable. Since then, Mary's father, Mr. Wolfe, had turned zealously to religion. He kept her life at home pious and sheltered. He was more than suspicious of me for a time, though I soon enough saw how to play him. Just happening to run into Mary and her father at nine o'clock Mass on a regular basis helped him overcome his suspicions.

When I think of the years I first started seeing Mary, I always remember the two of us watching television with her father in their tiny living room. It's six o'clock, we're waiting for the news, and the Angelus bells come on with a picture of the Virgin Mother. Mary and her father cross themselves, and he looks peripherally at me to see if I'm doing the same. It's

not something I'm accustomed to doing, so I make an ambiguous motion with my right hand to push my hair off my
forehead, and then scratch at my stomach. By now he's shifted his eyes away, so I can forget the lint on my left shoulder.

I continued to attend nine o'clock Mass on Westland Row,
crossed myself to the tune of Angelus bells, and, more natu-
rally, voiced my republican politics until Mr. Wolfe no longer
regarded me with suspicion at his front door.

He was not altogether pleased about Mary's plans for Syria,
to say the least. In fact, at first he told her she could not go, but
when he realized that wasn't going to mean much (she'd
already found a reduced-fare ticket and paid for it), he decided
she might as well go with his blessing. His blessing, of course,
was accompanied by Mary's understanding that this was not yet
an official honeymoon. ("Please God, child, I needn't tell you
that.") He knew pretty much what I was doing there, but he was
an old republican himself once the lines were drawn. It was
really because of him, I suppose, that my involvement always
had such a romantic appeal to Mary. Less appealing to me was
that after two weeks in Syria, she had to take part in that dubious romance.

Before we returned home, I was asked by one of our people
to smuggle, with Mary's assistance, a package of trinitro-
toluene and cyclonite back to Dublin. There was very little for
me to do, actually. The Syrians who worked with us provided
Mary with a false front, which was hollow and strapped
around her back, to appear as if she were pregnant. I expected her to be terrified with that package nestled against her
belly, but she was not. She was most disturbed by the possibility that someone might recognize her in that apparently
expectant condition at Heathrow Airport.

If Mary was relatively calm, however, the entire return trip
was ruined for me. I stared out at the plane's vibrating wing,
and each of the few times I tried to fall asleep, my nightmare
came to me. It was a dream stemming from something that

had occurred a year before, and it was always the same. I had been in Belfast, staying at a safe house where I was arranging to bring two men down to the south. One of them had been in the basement of the house making up a package like the one Mary carried, when it went off. I had been on the upper level and was unhurt. When I went downstairs, I saw the girl who lived in the house lying on the floor beside the bath. She was wearing only a pair of jeans, no blouse. I could see her breasts quite plainly, all white and stretched slightly flat. A movement at her hip distracted me, and I saw her skin opened like a seam there, while parts of her insides oozed onto the linoleum tiles. It sickened me, but I just stood staring at her breasts. There were shouts in the street outside, and I knew I should have run, but I stayed and stared at her face and breasts for a full minute. In my dream this girl would somehow become Queen Elizabeth, and, although I know fuck-all of anatomy, I was always able, in the dream, to identify her liver as it spilled out of the seam. Sometimes I saw her kidney and appendix, too, but more often it was just the liver.

I gave up on trying to sleep on the plane, only wanting to get to Dublin, where we could rid ourselves of the package. When I finally delivered it to Ferguson the next day, I ran from his office all the way to the bakery, where Mary kissed me in front of her father and sent me off with a bag of warm doughnuts. I thought then that I had heard the last of that package, but now Ferguson sat before me, still smiling over his pun.

I picked at a hangnail on my thumb, avoiding his eyes. "When?" I asked.

"Saturday night."

I smiled at him. "I'm getting married Saturday. I'll be having my own fireworks."

"You're a bleedin' ballocks," Ferguson said, pushing back in his chair. But he congratulated me. He sighed, and said he would find someone else to do the job. "Just be sure you're not honeymooning in Belfast Saturday night."

On Friday night I took the bus to Mary's house. When I got there, I could tell she had been crying. We watched the telly for a bit with her father, but since he obviously wasn't going to bed, and we couldn't talk with any privacy in the kitchen, I suggested we go out for a walk.

"What is it?" I said as we crossed the front garden.

"Daddy," she said.

"Well, don't make me beg you, Mary."

"You know he thinks you're just great, Shane," she began.

"Shite, you mean he doesn't want us getting married now?" I scuffed at the gravel the old saint had so carefully laid out on his driveway a few weeks before.

"That's not it, Shane."

"Well, what?"

"He thinks maybe I'm not enough to you."

"A fine time to decide that."

"No, he just worries for me. He worries for both of us. But he said he wants me to be sure that I'll be a companion, and not just an outlet for you—a sanctuary." I could tell these were her father's words. "From the violence and all." She seemed to say it as a question.

"And is that how you think it is?" I asked her.

"No, I don't. Should I?" she asked.

"Of course not. What else did he say?"

"Mainly just that."

"Tell me everything, Mary," I said. We always told each other everything then, although I had not told her about the dead girl and the dream.

"Well, you know what his politics are, Shane. He's said before that he doesn't see an end in sight. But he doesn't think anyone really wants one. Anyone. He says half the provisional wing doesn't want a settlement, they just want to fight."

"Well there's fuck-all glamour and romance to fighting, Mary, if that's what you and your father think."

"I know," she said, "but that's just what he's getting at."

"What do you mean, 'that's just what he's getting at'? Speak fucking English."

"He thinks maybe I'll just be a warm bed for you when you have to get away from all of that." Once again I could hear her father's phrasing. "Shane, he said I'm not much of an intellectual companion for you. He doesn't think I'll hold your interest very long."

"And you believe him, do you?"

"No."

I couldn't help yelling at her. "Then why are you crying, Mary?"

"I don't want to believe him. I mean, I know I'm not as smart as you are, that I haven't read enough, I never went to college. But I think I'm a good companion for you . . . Or is he right?"

"All right," I said, "I'll tell you, Mary. In a way your father's right. Being with you *is* a relief from all of that. And you do make it easier for me. But without you I would still do that— and without that I would still love you. I would," I said, but I felt less sure of myself now. I could see that in many ways Mary had become a habit for me. Perhaps if her father had said these things long before, I would have sensed my own doubts. Several times I had regretted not being better acquainted with girls who had been to college with me. And even though intellectual women often annoy me, Mary's simpleness sometimes annoyed me more. "Believe me, Mary," I said.

She stopped and squeezed my arm, brushing her cheek dry on my sleeve. "I wouldn't believe the Hail Mary out of your mouth," she said, a vague smile dimpling her left cheek. She had a whole arsenal of these old Dublin phrases, some of which I hadn't even heard from my grandfather.

We circled the block back to her house. Mary was bright

and smiling when we got there, and kissed me for a long while outside the door. Inside, her father was watching a talk show. "I've a whole telly full of channels to choose from," he said when we came in, "and this is the only thing on that's not utterly disgustin'."

"Oh, Daddy, you watch the disgustin' stuff most of the time anyway," Mary said.

"Sure, I haven't much choice, have I? With the old blinkers goin', I'm not able to read as I once did. I did read that article on television sex and violence in the paper this morning. Did you see the article, Shane?"

"No, not yet," I told him.

"Well," he said, "it's disturbing, the effects it's having on the young people. And it's only getting worse, mind you."

"Well," I said, "I suppose the steamy stuff on the dirty shows negates the effect of all that violence."

From the kitchen doorway, Mary shook her head at me.

Her father frowned. "Sure, it's not a thing to be laughed at, Shane."

"No," I said. I spoke politely to him for the rest of the evening, but I felt on the way home that he had betrayed me, saying what he had to Mary on the night before our wedding. And yet I also felt that he was right about me. Or was it only *his* misgivings that made me doubt myself now? As the bus sneezed along, I tried to think instead about the wedding itself, remembering that my good black shoes still needed shining.

The conductor, a man my own age, had pressed his face up close to a window and said to the driver, "Look at that, they're kicking the shit out of your man."

I turned and looked, but the street was not well lit, and I could only see myself and some other passengers reflected in the window. But when we pulled away from a light at the North Circular Road, I could see a man sprinting rigidly, without expression, from the direction of one of the seedier pubs.

"Pull over here, Johnny," the conductor said. He stood on the steps and swung out the door. "Do you want a lift?" he called. The man slowed cautiously. His hair was wild, his white shirt untucked. He mumbled something I couldn't understand. "That's okay," the conductor said, "come on."

He got on and sat in the front on one of the seats facing the aisle. The skin around his left eye was blue and puffing out like a golf ball, and his shirtfront was stained with blood; he seemed not to notice that the stuff kept dripping from his lips onto the shirt, his shoes, onto the floor of the bus in little splattering drops. His pants were ripped at the knee, which was also bleeding slightly, but otherwise he seemed all right. I turned to peer back in the direction from which he had come, but there was too much glare.

When he got off, I began composing a list of things I needed to pack for the next day. The bus passed near the office on Tara Street, and I remembered Ferguson's warning. "Just be sure you're not honeymooning in Belfast Saturday night."

We did not honeymoon in Belfast, but on Inishmaan, the middle of the three Aran Islands. Having driven to Galway after the wedding on Saturday, we flew in a nine-seater to the island, a beautiful, if barren, maze of stone walls. As there were only four cars on the island, we walked a half mile to the bed and breakfast, accompanied by Joe Flaherty, who had charge of the airstrip.

He was quick to tell us that the purest Irish anywhere is spoken on Inishmaan, and we were embarrassed to say that, yes, we did have some Irish, as he put it, but not enough to hold a real conversation.

It reminded me of the embarrassment I suffered at St. Peter's, where Sister Teresa, who came from the Gaeltacht, pandied our hands when we failed an Irish lesson. "I've yet to meet the child too ignorant to learn a second language," she

said, "especially the official language of our nation. It's a dis-
grace for an Irishman to speak only a foreigner's tongue."
Whack!

One spring day she had called us all to the window and
pointed to a man in a black suit, standing on the corner
below. "Now you see, children, *that* is a Protestant."

We all stared at the mundane figure, studying him for
traces of treachery. Finally, Aidan O'Malley said, "But, Sister,
he looks just like anyone else."

She nodded sagely and said in a whispery voice, "That's the
frightening thing about it."

Joe Flaherty left us, turning off the narrow dirt road into
his thatched home. Chickens hopped about his front garden,
and a hen was nesting in a circle of large, oval-shaped stones.
About fifty yards beyond Joe Flaherty's we stopped at a larger
two-story house to which he had directed us. Mrs. Mulkerrin,
a woman in her forties with a slight mustache and a substantial rear end, came to the open door. *"Dia duit,"* she said.

We answered, *"Dia's Muire duit,"* and she continued on in
Irish until I asked, "Have you a room vacant?" Mrs. Mulkerrin
switched to good, heavily accented English.

The house smelled of fresh bread and braised liver, which
was cooking on an ancient stove in the front room. Mrs.
Mulkerrin brought us to a simple upstairs bedroom, and said
she would have her daughter make up the bed. Just above the
wooden headboard, on the wall opposite the door, there was
an old and faded print of the Virgin Mother. Near the window, hanging crookedly over a porcelain washbasin, was a
framed picture of the Sacred Heart, apparently torn from a
magazine. I had been outside of Ireland often enough to realize the Sacred Heart was more or less our national organ. I set
our duffels on the floor and leaned over to straighten the picture of the man who wears His heart on His chest. "There,
now don't say I never did anything for You," and Mary gave
me a backhand in the belly.

After a dinner of meat, potatoes, and soda bread, we strolled the dirt roads of the island, the only apparent visitors, and certainly the only people holding hands. I could hear Mary's stomach rumbling, and told her she should have eaten a decent meal for once. She'd recently begun dieting, and it was all because of an American girl at the bakery who was constantly talking calories and health foods. She had given Mary a pamphlet with an index of food groups and calories that Mary began carrying everywhere. She wasn't even remotely overweight, but consulted her calorie chart every time she ate now. At dinner she had said to me, "Now, of course there are no calories in water, but do you not suppose there are calories in plain tea? I should probably be counting tea for at least a few calories."

We were sitting at the table in the room used mainly for guests' meals, and I was flipping through the Mulkerrins' guest book. "Mary, you look fine, don't be a bleeding fool," I said, suddenly irritated, for just then I came across the name Kevin Blanchard. I couldn't place it at first, but then I saw the home address and realized—the American student who had sold me the passport. He had been in the very house only three weeks before us. It made me uneasy, as if my privacy itself had been compromised and threatened. Of course, in a place the size of Ireland, there are things one should never expect to escape, but it was oddly unsettling nonetheless. I could hear Professor Baxter's voice, with his damnably affected theatrics, from the recesses of some Trinity lecture hall. "History is a nightmare from which I am trying to awake," he was saying.

Mary stood now on a crumbling little stone wall and threw some hay to a few sheep we were passing. She said she wished we had more than a few days to stay on the island, tossing her hair back like some film actress. It certainly wasn't costing us much, but I reminded her that her father would need her at the bakery, and that school would be starting for me very soon. I taught at an all-girls school, which hadn't much pleased Mary when I was first hired. But I would have to start planning my lessons soon; have to keep the girls intrigued.

"I'm still going to be jealous of all those little girls getting spoony over you," Mary said. I kissed her forehead, and we went into the island's only pub.

The night had become cool, and the men with their pipes gladly made a place for us near the small coal fire when we came in. I suspected they knew we were honeymooning. Joe Flaherty was sitting at the bar, and he'd guessed as much earlier when we'd spoken with him. The conversations in Irish were oddly comforting, although we could understand little of them. We ordered a pint and a shandy, and talked quietly, occasionally just listening to the music of their several conversations, frustrated at not understanding the laughter when a joke was made. After we'd been there a while, one of the younger men winked at me. He was slicing chips of pipe tobacco from a small plug with his jackknife. "Ah, 't'won't be such good weather as thish tomorrow, but a good day to shleep late," he said.

I wasn't sure if Mary copped onto him, but it was she who finally tugged my sleeve and said, "We'd better get started back to the house."

The night had grown completely dark in the half hour we spent in the pub. We had forgotten that there are no lampposts on the island. The narrow road was entirely black. We walked to the Mulkerrins' house holding each other closely, unable to see ahead of us except when we passed a home that still had lights on.

Mrs. Mulkerrin's daughter had made up the bed with a fancy quilt of green, black, and orange circle designs. I slid under the covers in my underwear and toyed with the bulky alarm clock, watching Mary while she modestly undressed. She had begun to remove her bra, but caught me staring and smiled in embarrassment. I didn't look away, and she made an if-you're-going-to-stare-I-won't-take-it-off expression; then slipped it off anyway and jumped into the bed. But a loud clanging beneath us had her jumping back onto the floor even faster, shivering in her underwear with her arms across her chest. Laughing, I got down on my knees and could see that Mrs. Mulkerrin's daughter had tied a large brass cowbell to the bottom of our mattress. I crawled under the bed, onto the cold floorboards, to untie it. In the darkness there, working the thin string out of the bedsprings, I was reminded of a night in Belfast, lying beneath a car lacing a fuse. My nightmare occurred to me under the bed just then, but I would no longer have to dread it with Mary beside me. Even to wake up wide-eyed in the middle of the night would not be such a horror now; not when I would find Mary's warm body nestled against me, not when she would hold me, and whisper her calming words.

Lying on her side in the bed, Mary pulled a barrette from her hair and kneaded my shoulder blades. "I can feel where you were an angel," she said. I had told her the story my grandfather told me when I was small, that our shoulder blades were once our wings when we were angels in heaven. Mary said I was a scrawny thing, and wrapped her arms tight around me, pulling me on top of her.

That night I saw, for the first time, Mary's small freckled breasts. They so fixed my attention that, until she shrieked, I didn't notice that she was grimacing in silent pain. She pushed me off from her and cupped her hand between her legs. I felt far away from her as she choked with light sobs and told me in a frightened whisper, "Shane, we're after doing something wrong; I'm bleeding."

Rain was streaking the window, and I heard drumrolls of thunder as a northward-moving storm pounded the island.

▼

PASSENGERS

▲

The first time I saw my father-in-law with his girlfriend was in a little diner at Malletts Bay, the two of them holding hands at a corner table overlooking the marina. He didn't see us come in, and I managed to push Margaret back out the door.

"What? What's wrong?" she said.

"Nell's father—at the far table in there."

She closed her eyes for a moment. "Did he see you?"

"I don't think so." As far as I could tell, he'd been too focused on his own companion to notice.

We got back to her car, and Margaret sat looking at me with her hands on the wheel. "Second thoughts?"

I shook my head. "You?"

"Not yet," she said. She started the car up and pulled onto the road.

I glanced back at the restaurant.

"We'll just go to my place," she said adjusting the rearview mirror. "I've got some pesto and stuff in the fridge."

Margaret had an apartment in town, but she and a girl-friend—another physical therapist—were renting a cottage at

Porter's Point for the summer. We'd only known each other a month or so. I'd stepped out of the pilothouse in the rain one night and slipped on the short ladder to the deck. The next day I met Margaret in the orthopedic outpatient clinic. Someone had given me something for the pain and I was pretty woozy, lying with my chin on the edge of the examining table, blurrily examining the only thing I could see, which happened to be Margaret's long legs in white stockings. "You've got a run," I heard myself say.

She laughed. "Why?"

"I don't know," I said, "you just do."

She'd been probing at the area around my spine, her fingers pushing now and then at the muscle just above my hip. "You want me to stop?"

I shrugged. "No. Why?"

"Why did you say I have to run?"

"Your stocking," I said. "Has . . . a . . . run."

Her laugh was quirky and girlish, a little shriek which she quickly reined in, setting her warm palm flat on my shoulder.

When she finished, she wrote several notes on a form sheet, clipping it to an unimaginative and embarrassingly childlike "pain drawing" I'd been asked to make. My rendering of a spine looked like a zipper; the flashes of pain I'd penned in resembled porcupine quills emerging from the simple figure's left hip.

"You'll have to go easy on your back for a while," she said. "Good thing you do your job standing, because chair sitting's definitely out."

It must have been the codeine and Valium speaking, because in six years of marriage I'd never strayed, never even indulged in heavy flirtation. "If I live," I said, "maybe I can lie you bunch sometime—I mean buy you lunch." I was too drugged to be embarrassed. I just laughed.

"You'll live," she said, "but I've already been lied to a bunch."

Later, though, as I was heading toward the lobby, she

walked up beside me and spoke quietly. "Ask me sometime when you're not all drugged up and I might accept."

A week later I stopped back. Between the prescription tranqs and the pain, I hadn't registered the fact that we weren't exactly contemporaries, though I dimly remembered the few stray greys sprinkled through her chestnut hair. She did a sort of double take herself as she greeted me in the waiting area, and I instantly regretted the fact that just that morning I'd shaved two days of stubble from my face. (Clean-shaven, I was still carded by bartenders.) We went ahead with lunch, and soon enough the fourteen-year gap didn't seem to make a lot of difference.

"You think Janice'll be there?" I asked. We were almost at the cottage.

"I didn't think of that. She could be, it's her day off. Sure you want to face her?"

Janice was the housemate. She was a little younger than Margaret, and had been perfectly nice to me the first week I was around, until Margaret told her I was married. After that it was icicles.

We turned off the dirt road at Porter's Point, and it looked as though Janice's car was gone. The cottage was situated on a small ledge, with the lake right there below us and cedar trees obscuring the place from the road. I walked to the fence at the cliff's edge, and could see that about eight miles to the south, toward town, the number two boat was starting off for New York.

Inside, Margaret opened a couple of beers. I eased into a wicker chair and adjusted the sticky cling of the back brace she'd fitted me with. It was stuffy inside, and Margaret began sliding windows open; glancing up, I noticed the pale, tender skin of her neatly shaved underarm, which somehow made her seem oddly delicate. I had the unremarkable thought:

she's someone's daughter. She was a tall, outdoorsy-looking woman, with a sprinkling of freckles across her forehead that came and went with days spent in the sun. She'd just turned thirty-seven, which she was a little sensitive about, though it was easy to see she'd attract the flirtations of tongue-tied patients for many years to come.

"Hungry?" she said.

"Not really." I stood up and tugged at the brace once more, but it still felt unnatural. On the wall near the sofa there was a poster-size chart of North American flowers, with capsule histories and various symbolic associations: marigolds and grief, daisies and innocence. I'd never paid much attention to flowers, but Margaret had an ambitious garden in town. Nell tended our own modest garden, and though it was pretty, it seemed to me, aside from the vegetable yield, to be basically futile and boring. "Haven't really had much of an appetite lately," I said.

"My fault?" She settled on the couch.

"Yes, but I think it's a compliment."

"Ah, Michael, you're so suave." She tapped her sandal against my leg. "How's your back?"

"This brace is a pain in the ass."

"It's supposed to go around your waist."

"Har-dee-har," I said, and I stretched out on the sofa with my head on her leg. We hadn't slept together, though things had gotten rather moist a few nights before. Her age intimidated me a bit, and when it didn't, she'd often throw up polite little roadblocks. I wasn't expecting a lot more than lunch just now, because I had to be back in town for the number two boat when it returned. It was just a T-class vessel, twenty cars maximum, which I'd been operating since March. I had to watch my step because they'd never had a skipper under thirty before, and there was a big to-do about letting a twenty-three-year-old into the wheelhouse, even the son of a four-bar man. Still, by late summer the thrill had begun to wear off, and sometimes I was tempted just to break off course and zig-zag through the islands, take the whole boatload of strangers on an unexpected tour of the lake.

Only a couple of months earlier, I'd happily envisioned myself up in the wheelhouse the rest of my working life, but I knew now that that was an unlikely scenario. Still, it was much better than deckhand work, which I'd done almost every summer since I was sixteen.

My back was throbbing, and I rolled onto my side, face to face with Margaret's thigh clad in loose linen shorts. Feeling for the shorts' cuffed hem, I rubbed at the tightly muscled skin just above her knee, noticing the line of blondish hairs where her shaving ended.

"You shouldn't lie on your side," she said, and I nodded, dipping my head and running my tongue along her wrist. I remember wondering, exactly what is it I'm after here? Not, I was sure, a mother figure, certain obvious facts notwithstanding. So what, then? Sex? Love? Friendship? Diversion?

I was a little confused, I suppose, maybe in need of a good couch session, though the one in progress seemed as likely a therapy as any. I slid my hand a bit further along Margaret's bronze thigh.

After a moment she pulled my hand away and held my fingers to her mouth. "Who was Nell's father with earlier?"

"A woman," I said, still a little surprised.

"Not Nell's mother?"

"No."

"Does that bother you?"

I shrugged, shook my head. "No."

She sipped at her beer, gazing at me over the glass. "Right."

Nell picked me up at the dock after the last crossing that night. She'd left Ethan napping at her parents' house, and brought a shirt and jeans for me, thinking I might want to go out for dinner, but I was too tired. Or at least I said I was. The more time I spent with Margaret, and the more I thought about her, the more I became annoyed around Nell and wanted to avoid being alone with her.

"Anything wrong?" she asked.

"No. Back's giving me a little trouble." It was only a partial lie.

"Your driving exam's Friday," she said. "Should we cancel it?"

"No, why? You think I'm gonna blow it again?"

"Of course not. I'm just thinking of your back. You drive fine."

That was a generous exaggeration. I watched her a moment, admiring the way she casually held the steering wheel in the fingers of her left hand, her elbow resting on the door. The fact was, I didn't like cars, and I didn't drive very well, either. It should have been simple after piloting the ferry, and among the crew it was considered a laugh riot that I had a license for one and not the other, but I still didn't like getting out on the road with other drivers. Occasionally I would, but I only had a learner's permit, so it was illegal to drive alone. Lately I'd been doing that more often, mainly to visit Margaret, but Nell kept reminding me our rates would go sky high if the insurance company ever found out, which was a considerately subtle way of saying "accident."

She leaned over to tune the radio to a song I didn't recognize, and watching her sing along with furrowed eyebrows, her lips silently enunciating, I caught a glimpse of Becca, my younger sister. They'd always looked a little alike—ringlety hair, the same sort of straight Roman nose and high cheekbones—which I think was the first thing that made me think I'd like Nell. She was working a summer concession near the lakefront at the time, and between crossings I'd buy frozen yogurt from her. By the fall we were seeing each other steadily, then on and off in the winter, when one of my friends started asking her out. I knew that a few times they'd gone dancing or to movies. It wasn't till then, though, that I realized I'd begun to feel possessive about her. And it occurred to me that maybe we shouldn't be so on-and-off casual about things after all. At the time—we were both seventeen—I thought that maybe if I turned the heat up a little, if we began sleeping together, I could clear the deck of any interlopers.

I had the house to myself one weekend about this time, because my parents had driven Becca and a couple of friends to a swim meet in New York. When I woke up Sunday morning, hours after Nell had snuck home, I could hear my older brother and his wife, who lived outside of town, talking quietly in the kitchen. I went downstairs and noticed a small pile of jewelry on the dining-room table: my parents' watches and wedding bands, my mother's half-dozen silver Navajo bracelets, and a brass-and-copper bangle I'd given to Becca on her thirteenth birthday.

A thud of panic hit me, and though I instantly knew the gist of what had happened, I also made myself not know. The next ten or twenty seconds were a sea of possibilities, and during that odd stretch of time before anyone spoke, I resisted the logic of what I saw on the table. When I walked into the kitchen, my sister-in-law looked at me strangely, her eyes raw from crying. The car, somewhere in upstate New York, had been sideswiped on an icy stretch of road near Route 87, rolling down an embankment and falling through shallow ice at the edge of Lake George. One of Becca's friends survived, though she lost her leg, a girl I still see downtown sometimes.

Nell spent most of the next few months staying at my house. And though we slept in the same bed, we seemed for a short time to have forgotten about sex. Sex hadn't forgotten us, though, because eight weeks later we learned she was pregnant with Ethan.

* * *

He was asleep on the sofa when we got to her parents' house. Jack and Louise were sitting in the kitchen eating ice cream, arguing quietly about Jack's vacation week.

"We'll talk about it later," he said, looking weary. He crumpled his napkin and smiled apologetically at us, a thin handsome man in his early fifties.

"If you'd told me, though, I'd have remembered," Louise said. "I'd have taken the week off myself. Nell, did you know Dad was taking next week off?"

Before Nell could answer, the pager clipped to Jack's belt went off, and everyone stopped talking while he wrote on a napkin the number being repeated through heavy static. "Excuse me," he said, and went to use the phone in his study, squeezing my shoulder as he walked past. He came back out a few minutes later with a jacket on. "I've got to make a house call," he said, "shouldn't be too long."

I glanced at him, wondering. He stood lighting his pipe and gazed directly back at me for a moment. "Are we still on for Sunday, Michael?" He'd asked earlier in the week if I could borrow my brother's truck to help him move some furniture, not that I'd be of any use lifting.

Louise dabbed at a spot of ice cream on her pant leg. "I don't think we want that stuff here, Jack. You can give it to the Salvation Army."

"What do you mean," he said, "it's nice furniture. Nell and Michael might be able to use some of it."

"I'd like to know where you're planning to *store* all of it," Louise said.

"I don't know, in the carriage house for now. It's nice stuff."

Louise looked at us and made a dubious expression. Their relationship, in the six years I'd known them, was generally one of respectful discord. I tended to think of Jack as the more reasonable and sympathetic of the two—Louise was unrelentingly contrary in his presence—but now I wondered if she didn't have her reasons.

"Well, whatever," Jack said, and he kissed Nell on the forehead before leaving.

I went to the living room to get Ethan, who was sprawled across the sofa with his mouth open. Without thinking, I bent over to lift him, but before I could get my arms beneath him my back locked and I let out an involuntary groan that woke him with a start. He covered his face, then said slowly, "Dad?"

"Uh-huh."

"Oh." He closed his eyes again.

"Nice to see you, too." I sat down on the sofa, combing my fingers through the silky strands of his blond bangs, all plastered to his forehead with sweat.

"Did you see Champ today?" he asked, his eyes still closed. The latest fixture in his fantasy life was the Lake Champlain Monster, a creature reportedly sighted several times in recent months and thought by many to be the poor relation of Scotland's aquatic celebrity.

"Yeah, I did, but only from a distance. A lot of people had cameras on the boat, and you know how shy he is."

"What was he doing?"

"Oh, just sort of swimming around. Poking his head out now and then."

"Mmm," he said sleepily. "Why don't you take a picture of him?"

"Oh, he doesn't like that, Ethan. He's really a very private sort of guy."

"But I don't think he'd mind if *you* took it."

"Well, I don't always know when I'm going to see him. And I can't leave the helm to go take a picture. I'm busy with other things."

"Mmm," he said. "Mom said maybe it's a girl."

"What!"

"Champ might not be a boy."

"Oh."

"I'm pretty sure he is," he said. "Unless there's more than one. Maybe there's a whole family." And he was out again.

I drove on the way home, already nervous about Friday's exam. At the first traffic light Nell shifted in her seat and looked at me. "I don't know what it is, but you seem a little strange tonight. Lately in fact. Something you're not telling me?"

"No, I'm just trying to concentrate on the road." There was, in fact, more traffic than I felt comfortable with.

"Everything go okay on the boat?"

"Uh-huh."

"How's that new kid working out?"

"Nelson? Don't ask. Dave calls him 'Admiral.' "

"Did he get rid of the Walkman?"

"Reluctantly." I switched the high beams on. "Kid's a trip. Oh yeah, I meant to tell you, a seagull flew smack into one of the wheelhouse windows this morning. Shattered it. I could hardly see out the port side, had to have Nelson come up and tap the glass out."

She squinted. "Did the seagull . . . ?"

"Yes, but I'm sure it never knew what happened. Scared the crap out of me, though. I took the boat off course without even realizing. Anyway, after Nelson finishes up he says, 'Well, I'm going down to the cellar to give Dave a hand.' "

"The *cellar*?" she laughed. "Was he serious?"

"Yes. So I told him: you can go below, or you can go down to the engine room, but there's no fucking cellar on this boat." I glanced at Ethan on the back seat. "Is he out?"

"Yes, but please watch it. He got frustrated over something this morning and started muttering 'sun in the bitch' to himself."

I laughed. "Sorry."

We drove in silence for a minute. "By the way," she said quietly, and she glanced back at Ethan again.

"Yeah?"

A car approached, and the driver flashed his high beams on and off. Nell said calmly, "You're blinding him, Michael, take your brights off."

I dimmed the lights and held tight to the wheel until the other car had passed. "What?"

"This is kind of a strange thing to ask, but have you ever wondered if my father might be seeing someone? I mean, another woman?"

I felt my throat tighten and my face redden in the dark. "I don't know—why?"

She shrugged. "It's just, I picked up the phone to call the sitter earlier this evening, and I didn't realize Dad was on. And I heard this woman saying—in a very affectionate tone—something like '. . . already missing you . . . ,' and right away Dad said 'I'm on the phone!' and I hung up. Mom was out getting groceries."

"I don't know," I said. "Could be a patient. His patients love him."

"Maybe. You're driving too close to the shoulder. Maybe," she said.

"Does it bother you?" I asked.

She thought for a moment. "I don't even know if it's so. I hope not. But I think it would bother me more if Mom was doing it to him."

"Really?" I glanced at her.

"Just because she gives him so much crap."

"But you think it's okay for him?"

"Well, not okay, no. I don't know. They're weird. I just think it's a different set of rules for them now." She shrugged. "Whereas if you ever started stepping out with someone, you'd be in very deep water."

"I think that's 'hot' water."

"You'd be in very deep hot water."

I went ahead with the driving exam on Friday, passed by just one point, and stood waiting with Nell in a room full of sixteen-year-olds while a state trooper filled out a temporary license for me. He glanced at my shoulder boards and name tag afterwards and smiled. "Hope you're a little better at driving the ferryboat."

I was already embarrassed and couldn't help being a prick. "You don't drive a boat," I said, "boats are piloted."

His smile disappeared. "Whatever," he said, and he shoved the forms at me.

Saturday night Nell and I had some words about something stupid, unwashed dishes I think, and in no time it escalated into an argument that I welcomed, even provoked, I'm ashamed to say, as an opportunity to storm out of the house.

When I got to the cottage, Janice came to the door, all dressed up and behaving in a surprisingly civil manner. She gave me a sort of amused smile, asking if I'd happened to notice whether her car was blocked. Inside I discovered the source of her amusement: a rugged and mustachioed guy about forty wearing a blue polo shirt and seersucker pants—a suburban Marlboro man perched in the wicker chair. Janice's date, I hoped, but already I knew better. Margaret was nearby, kneeling over some pieces of fabric on the floor. She looked a little surprised and stood up smiling. "Well! I'm very popular all of a sudden." She was wearing her bathing suit—a red one-piece number like the local lifeguards wore—with an unbuttoned work shirt. I glanced at the guy in the chair, who smiled and smoothed his mustache as if waiting to see what would develop here.

"Sorry," I said, "I should have called. Bad time to stop by?"

"No, of course not," she said, "come on in." She had a thin layer of green sunblock on her nose and looked as if she'd been outside all day.

Janice stood in the kitchen doorway, running a piece of dental floss through her teeth while Margaret introduced me to Jerry. He was an architect and a friend of her ex-husband.

Hygienic Janice, clearly relishing my sudden awkwardness, emerged from the kitchen with a sweater around her shoulders. "Wish I could stay and visit, but I'm already late. Good night, men," she sang out, giving a certain emphasis to the last word that she no doubt considered witty. Margaret rolled her eyes and went to get me a beer.

"So, Michael, are you in school?" Jerry asked.

"No," I said, "I work for LCT."

"Oh, really, on the ferry?"

I nodded. "The *Ethan Allen* mostly."

"I did that for a summer back in high school."

I wasn't sure whether or not "back in high school" was a slight. From the kitchen Margaret called out, "Yes, Jerry, but you were a deckhand, I think; Michael's a captain now."

"Really?" he asked, looking at me again.

"One bar," I said, holding a limp finger up. "And only on the small boats."

"Still, they were all older guys when I was there."

"It's kind of a new crowd. Not just guys anymore, either. Just got our first woman skipper."

He mentioned the names of several captains he'd worked for, and it turned out he'd known my father.

"I saw in the paper where a whole wedding party spotted Champ recently," he said. "That wasn't your boat, was it?"

"No, unfortunately. They chartered one of the big boats."

"So you think they really saw something?"

"I don't doubt it."

"Maybe," he said.

Margaret came back with my beer and a bowl of pretzels. She'd pulled a pair of jeans on and wiped the sunblock from her nose. "Sounded convincing to me," she said.

Because of Ethan's new passion, I'd recently read a book on the subject, and I mentioned that Samuel de Champlain and his Abnaki guides had described a similar creature in 1609.

Jerry nodded. "Be pretty weird to be the only one of a species left behind like that," he said. "What do you do for a social life? You'd have to start hanging out with other kinds of fish." He laughed.

I nodded. "Or spend your life looking for your own kind."

"They think the one at Loch Ness has offspring, though," Margaret said. "Or a partner, at least. Anyway, they think there's more than one there."

"Well that's a little better," Jerry said. "Still sounds grim."

We each had another beer, and by ten o'clock I was thinking about leaving, convinced that Jerry was settled in for a long visit. But then he rose to his feet and said he had to be up early to play tennis.

I got up to shake his hand, and Margaret walked him out to the steps, giving him a neutral sort of kiss. I wandered back to look at the pieces of fabric she'd spread all over the floor. The one time I'd been to her apartment in town, she'd shown me several quilts she'd made. And Janice, before she learned I was an unfaithful wretch, had mentioned there were others at a gallery in Middlebury.

Margaret came back in and set her hand on my shoulder. "What do you think of those colors—a little too busy?"

"No, I like the blue," I said.

"You like everything blue," she said, flicking at my navy T-shirt. "What about the design?"

"D'you already get Jerry's opinion?"

"Michael, you're not going to do that to me, are you?"

"Okay, I'm not. But did you?"

"No. And he only arrived an hour before you got here." She sighed loudly. "What am I doing," she said, "justifying him to you—you with a wife and son at home. You're really something, you know that, Michael?"

"Okay, I'm sorry. Forget it. What were you asking me?"

"The design. What's it look like to you? What do you see?"

"Is this supposed to be a Rorschach quilt or something? An inkblot blanket?"

She shook her head, grudgingly curling a weary smile. "Forget it." She took my beer and drank from it.

"Okay, okay, I'm thinking." I leaned over. "Actually, it looks like pinwheels."

"Oh, *now* we're getting somewhere," she said. "Very revealing." She pulled the square back a little. "Now what's it look like?"

"Still pinwheels. Maybe a bunch of windmills, I don't know. A real sickie would say that part's sort of an abstract swastika. I'll stick with the pinwheels."

"Look at the whole thing, not just the pieces."

I stepped back, squinting, and all at once the center image appeared, its outline emerging from the margins of the other shapes. "Oh, a yellow, um, rose."

"Got the color right."

"Tulip."

"Very good," she said. "Trace of arrested development on shape identification, but he's got his primary colors down."

I glanced at the chart above the sofa. "So, yellow tulip. Symbolic of . . . ?"

"Well," and she winced. "Hopeless love, as a matter of fact."

"Hopeless love, wonderful, is that tonight's aphrodisiac?"

"No, that's tonight's quilt project," she said, and she kissed my mouth wetly. I could smell coconut sunscreen on her, and began maneuvering us toward the sofa.

"Wait," she said, "wait, I've been crouching over that quilt all night, I need some air."

* * *

It was cooler down on the beach. We strolled arm in arm past several small groups seated around bonfires: a nagging fat woman with kids in pajamas roasting marshmallows, couples drinking beer and staring after us.

Down by the point there was a rubber life raft at the bottom of a long stairway, and I went to untie it.

"What are you doing?" she said. "It's *dark* out there," but she was slowly rolling her pant legs up.

I had the brace on, and my rowing was stiff and awkward. Margaret leaned back against the stern with her long legs dangled over mine. "I hope you realize it's stupid to do this with your back," she said.

"Should I try it without my back?"

"You should try *going* back. Or else let me row."

"I'll be careful. Anyway, if I get laid up I'll have a great excuse to spend the night."

"Forget it," she said, "you're not getting laid *or* laid up."

I rowed a few more strokes, watching her. "You know," I said slowly, "there's a name for women who—"

"Frigid? Are you trying to tell me I'm frigid, Michael?" Beneath the serious tone there was vague evidence of a smile.

"No, that wasn't the one I had in mind."

"Cock tease?"

I nodded.

"You know," she said slowly, "there's a name for an amorous guy with a wife and kid at home."

"Yeah?"

"Red bet," she said, "it's a banking term. It means bad credit risk. You, Michael, are a red bet. Neon red."

I continued rowing and snorted as we stared at each other. "What's the big risk—your maidenhead?"

She poked me in the chest with her foot. We were out a good ways now, the water almost placid, and I stowed the plas-

tic oars against Margaret's thighs. Someone rang a bell outside one of the cottages, a signal for their child to come in. I
took Margaret's foot and set it in my lap. "Sasquatch," I said,
examining her long slender toes.

She wrinkled her eyebrows in mock annoyance. "Don't
look at my big feet."

She did have big feet, almost as long as my own, though
they had a certain delicacy. "I like them," I said. Her toes,
when she stretched them, had the odd knack of splaying wide
apart. I fit my fingers in between each of them and squeezed.
"I'm holding hands with your feet, Margaret."

"You're very weird," she said.

"You're very pretty."

"You're very seductive."

She flexed her toes and we were quiet for a bit, just drifting. Further out a motorboat roared past, and in a little while
its waves were rolling beneath us, making the raft seesaw.

"Careful," she said, "there's a reef over there."

I managed to turn us about with a deft little maneuver I
hoped Margaret might admire, but she was plucking distractedly at one of the circular rubber oarlocks. By the time I
stowed the oars again she was resting her head on the bil-
lowed edge of the raft.

"Where do you think this'll end up?" she asked finally.

"Us?"

"Yes. I mean, last week you told me things weren't that bad
at home, and then yesterday you tell me you love me."

"You don't believe me?"

"I be*lieve* you," she said, the words coming out in a puff of
exasperation. "I believe you. But you can't have both of us,
you know."

I nodded once, but it was fully dark now, and I wasn't sure
she could see me. "I know that." I also knew that treating Nell
the way I was—the only way I seemed able to deal with her
lately—couldn't continue much longer. "What if I left Nell?" I

said, aware that the question was as much for me as for
Margaret.

"Do you want to?"

"I want to be with you."

"That's not much of an answer."

"Okay," I said, "I'm not looking forward to telling them.
But I do want to be with you."

She touched my calf where it rested against her. "You
know, even if that's not how things end up, you're not bound
by something that happened in high school."

I'd tried that on for size recently, but it seemed like a
forced fit. Hearing Margaret now, it felt a little more comfortable. I leaned back and dropped my arms in the water, staring
at the low constellation of lights back in town. "No," I said, "I
guess not." And I tried to picture a life in this town with
Margaret. The two of us. And Ethan, of course, one way or
another. Nell would despise me. I'd lose a family all over
again, Jack and Louise.

Margaret was now working her foot up the loose leg of my
shorts. I squirmed a little, and she pressed on. "Don't tell me
you're ticklish. Relax," she said, "you're going to drown us,"
and in a little while I began slowly growing against the soft
probing touch of her toes. I was slow to think of reciprocat-
ing, but once I did she began pushing back against my careful
rubbing foot, her head lolling on the raft. Her own foot
slacked off, and every few seconds I heard a quick expulsion
of breath. I kept trying to estimate our little craft's potential
for grander activities, but it seemed unlikely, even apart from
my back.

By the time we reached shore, the only other people on the
beach were a few dim figures at a bonfire several hundred
yards away. We made a small blanket of our clothes, and I
remember thinking, lying in the sand later, that I might as
well have been a virgin—twenty-three years old and I felt like
I'd just discovered sex. Even so, I'd been unable to bring

things to the usual conclusion. What did me in, I think, was that at one point Margaret let out a terrified little yelp, and I thought, *Christ, what have I done?*

Something had bitten her, she said, something under the clothes, but when I reached under and pawed around, it was only a little metal matchbox car, a yellow checker taxi with its tiny sharp trunk stuck open. Margaret quietly cursed the thing, but later tucked it into my shorts, saying I should give it to Ethan. I carried it home, but felt too superstitious to ever pass it along to him.

Driving home that night, I began to realize what it was I was after with Margaret. And it wasn't just sex. Not just sex, or love, or friendship, though it was all of those, too. It sounds silly and juvenile now, but what I wanted, really, was more *life*. The same thing Ethan wanted once he'd mastered the lake's small mysteries of minnows and perch and catfish, and learned there might be something big and rare in those waters. Something more. That's what my son and I wanted that summer.

Sitting at a stoplight I lifted my hand to my face and inhaled coconut—coconut and the salty fish scent of Margaret's sex. I kept breathing the two all the way home.

Sunday afternoon I drove over to my brother's house to take his pick-up truck and help Jack. The damn thing felt incredibly wide on the road—an old Chevrolet monster with huge rounded fenders—and I was sorry I'd ever agreed to do this.

"You sure ride the clutch a lot," Jack said after several miles.

"I'm still getting used to this thing. I like our little Nipponese number a lot better."

"I'm just giving you a hard time," he said, scratching at the shadow of whiskers on his chin.

We were headed for Colchester, on the far side of the bay.

When we got to the Heineberg Bridge, with its lanes the width of bicycle paths, a half-dozen cars were coming from the opposite direction, all of them doing about fifty, close enough to touch as they whizzed past. I slowed to a near crawl, and the driver behind me honked.

"Just ignore him," Jack said. "These people are crazy, driving so fast over this bridge."

My arms locked rigidly into place on either side of the steering wheel until the solid green girders of the bridge sloped to an end, the pavement widened again, and what little traffic there was spread out. Jack toyed with the dial on the radio, but finally switched it off and sat back. "I guess you saw me at the diner out here this week."

I glanced at him and felt my face redden. "Yeah," I said, "I did."

He nodded slightly. "My friend recognized you."

I kept my eyes on the road, waiting.

"I'm not going to lie to you—it was what it looked like," he said. He paused. "Straight through this light here." He'd begun slowly twisting his pipe; every few seconds the stem let out a little squeak. "I hope you don't mind, but that's where we're going now. Clair Coleman's. I think she met you at the house once, years ago."

"That's okay."

We were silent for a minute, just sitting there with it.

"Are you and Nell having problems?"

"No, not really." I waited. "You mean the person *I* was with?"

"Well, I guess there was a woman with you," he said, more question than statement.

I nodded.

"I don't want to make you talk about it," he said, "I'm just concerned."

Driving home the night before, I'd thought it might all be in the open before long. But by the time Nell and I had finished our Sunday morning bed-wrestling match with Ethan, I felt a little less certain. *Red bet.* "It was nothing," I said, "just stupidness. Secret lunch date." I shrugged. "Stupid."

He nodded and mumbled something more or less agreeable sounding, setting his pipe on the dashboard. Then picked it up again. "I'm afraid I'm the one who's been stupid. Clair was just a good friend and we . . . " he shrugged, "let things get a little out of hand. Anyway, she's taking a job in Minnesota this month, so . . . there's an end to it at least. That's why we're getting this furniture. Some she doesn't want, the rest I'm gonna store for her."

I nodded.

We were both quiet for a bit and he drummed his fingers softly against the window frame. "Take a left up here," he said finally, pointing with his pipe. "The Realtor's sign."

Clair Coleman came around from the backyard in jeans and a patterned Hawaiian shirt, carrying the detached spray nozzle of a garden hose. She was about forty-five, pale skinned and attractive. She wore a kerchief over dark red hair that may have been natural, but probably had greyed and was hennaed.

She waved at Jack and stopped at my side of the truck as we got out. "Hello, Michael," she said, and held up a pair of muddy palms to show that I wouldn't want to shake her hand. "We met about five years ago. You were occupied with a baby at the time."

I smiled. "Probably so."

Her cheeks and nose were sunburned, and she had a curiously attractive tracheotomy scar, a perfect reddish pink circle centered in the hollow recess of her throat.

Jack came around and briefly set his hand on her shoulder in greeting. She tapped the pistol-like nozzle against his arm and gestured at her garage full of furniture. "You sure Louise won't mind jamming up the carriage house with this stuff?"

He glanced vaguely at it and shook his head once. "It's no problem."

We walked to the garage, which was crammed with dark, heavy-looking furniture, and suddenly I remembered my back. There were two antique bureaus, a small rolltop desk, and a solid-looking oval table with claw feet. As if he'd suddenly read my mind, Jack said, "Jesus, Michael, I forgot about your back."

"I'll be fine," I said.

"I can help you lift this stuff," Clair told him. "I got half of it out here alone."

"No, no, I can help," I said, and went to back the truck up.

But Jack insisted I not lift anything, and I didn't argue. He and Clair started with the smaller of the bureaus, and I began pulling drawers out of the larger one to lighten it. When I got to the bottom drawer there was a big oval wooden frame with an ancient portrait photograph: a grimly solemn couple in their forties, though at first glance they looked much older. "Did you know this was in here?" I asked Clair.

"Oh, God, my great-grandparents," she said. She cleaned the glass with her shirttail and showed Jack. "Notice anything odd about this picture?"

He tilted it nearer. "No, not really."

I didn't either.

"Their pictures were taken years apart," she said. "Notice how the background's a little lighter behind him? They got divorced in 1865 and never spoke to each other again; the photographer's date on here is 1871."

Jack raised his eyebrows. "Pioneers of divorce. What was their, uh, problem?"

Clair shrugged. "Who knows. I guess he was supposed to have been something of a . . . philanderer, maybe."

I glanced away, avoiding Jack's eyes. He grunted and began tamping his pipe.

"Anyway, their children didn't have a picture of the two of

them together. They got a photographer to work his magic on this one." She set it on the slats of an old sled, and I helped them get the next few pieces onto the truck without too much aggravation to my back.

Afterwards, Clair invited us in for a beer, but Jack said we had to get going. Still, we stood talking in the driveway for another twenty minutes, and I noticed Jack seemed especially youthful in Clair's presence, bouncing an old golf ball he'd found in the garage, springing onto the bed of the truck to tighten the ropes one last time.

We started back for town, and I thought about the picture of Clair's ancestors, how quaint the word *philanderer* had sounded when she used it. More innocuous sounding, probably, than what the reality had been. We drove past lakeside cornfields, and then along the narrow winding road beside the bay, and Jack was quiet, except to mumble once, almost to himself, "We just get stupid sometimes, I don't know."

I didn't know either. Despite the occasional tedium, I felt fortunate and generally content with Nell and Ethan, and yet I'd been all set to pursue a life with Margaret that for all I knew could lead to still more tedium—and maybe worse—somewhere down the line. Of course, I doubted that, but who could say? Margaret and her ex-husband had once doubted it, too.

We were back at the narrow Heineberg Bridge now, and looking at Jack gazing down on the wide stretch of river below, I felt a little sorry that he'd be losing Clair Coleman. There was no oncoming traffic this time, and I wasn't nervous about the bridge. I glanced out the open window at the water, and in a flicker saw something jump—a small dark shape, a splash, the sudden growth of concentric circles. I thought of Champ, but it wasn't anything so rare, more than likely a bass feeding, lunging out of his element, there and gone.

"Watch the road," Jack said.

▼

THE ORTHODOX
BROTHER

▲

"So," Adam said greeting her in the driveway, "we finally lured you away from the goyish hinterlands."

"I guess," she laughed. "What's this supposed to be, Tel Aviv-by-the-Turnpike?"

"Wait and see," he said, and winked. He had a cloth diaper thrown over one shoulder, a green suede yarmulke fixed to his hair with a bobby pin. He took one of Laura's duffel bags from the back seat and led her into the house.

In the cluttered sunny kitchen, Shira was emptying the loaded strainer while toting the baby on one hip. Tzippy, the five-year-old, sat on the floor tying her own shoelaces together. "Hey, look who's here!" Shira said, and Tzippy let out a whoop, scrambling to her feet and hopping into Laura's embrace.

When the three adults had sat down with coffee, Shira glanced around and said, "We should probably explain the dishes and things." She pointed to the cupboards and drawers flanking the big double sink; the left side, she said, contained plates, glasses, and silverware for meat meals, the right side held the same items for dairy.

Tzippy sidled up beside Laura and slid onto her lap.

"If it helps," Shira said, "the red glasses are for meat, the blue glasses are dairy. Same with the sponges," indicating four small sponge racks behind the faucet, "except for the yellow, which is *parve,* and the orange, for *trayf.*"

Laura nodded, nuzzling Tzippy's soft hair to mask her amused smile.

"I'm sure it's confusing," Adam said, "—you'll get used to it." He was straddling his chair backwards, the way he'd sat as a teenager, those nights at the kitchen table, tutoring—torturing—her in chemistry and algebra. Actually, his patience then had been exemplary. He'd wanted to share with her the mystery and mastery of his numbers and formulas, insisting that if the knowledge existed in him, it was there in her too.

"You'll get used to it," he repeated now, and tapped her wrist with Tzippy's plastic drinking straw.

Tzippy, she noticed, was staring at her, then glanced at Adam and back at Laura again. "I don't see how come you two are twins," she said.

Even as fraternals, they didn't look much alike. Adam was always considered more striking, with his dark and unmistakably Semitic features that blended handsome ruggedness and a sort of boyish sensitivity. Their mother insisted he looked like no one so much as his namesake, Adam Gladstone, a dashing uncle of hers who had died, heroically by all accounts, in the Warsaw ghetto uprising. Laura's looks were somehow less compelling, an impression underscored by the fact that she was short. From early adolescence, though, she'd been quietly content with her plain freckled features—the face of a generic redhead, more nearly Celtic than Ashkenazic. With a last name like Miller, it was rare that anyone even guessed she was Jewish.

"I meant to ask," Adam said during dinner that first night, "how's, ah, what's-his-name dealing with your move?"

She'd been seeing a man—a high school history teacher—for much of the past two years, though Adam had only met him a few times.

"Mom didn't tell you? That's over," she said, her tone suggesting it had been a mutual decision, though in fact she'd been ever so gently dumped when the teacher's former girlfriend returned to Portland.

"Oh, I didn't . . . No, nobody mentioned. Huh. How are you doing?"

She shrugged. "I'm a survivor. Lots of practice. Anyway," she said, "it's already history."

History, as they took to calling the ex-beau, had never much sparked Adam's interest. But then, he wasn't Jewish, and for Adam, especially in the six years since meeting Shira and embracing Orthodoxy, being Jewish was key. Of course, one or two of the women who'd marched in Adam's preconversion parade had not been Jewish—Shira's immediate predecessor, with whom he lived for over a year, was a pretty blond computer engineer named Jill O'Connor—but it was generally understood that Adam now dismissed all that as so much youthful folly.

They'd finished dessert and were sitting around the table drinking tea when Adam and Shira mentioned the names of several friends they were eager for Laura to meet. She was curious and flattered, but after a minute realized they had it in mind to fix her up with a nice Jewish boy. Which might have been fine, except she knew that the only Jews in Adam's social circle now were Orthodox. Somehow, the idea of an Orthodox man had about as much appeal as a membership in the Jerry Falwell Dating Service. On a scale of fun, it was up there with Islamic fundamentalism.

Shira set her teacup down and widened her long-lashed eyes with inspiration. "You know, we should have Yossi Glaser over for dinner some night. He's *very* interested in art—always going to galleries."

Laura smiled appreciatively, her head tilted at an odd angle

while Tzippy, who'd once again climbed into her lap, attempt-
ed to braid her hair. "You know, I really appreciate it, but I'm
just not sure I'm ready yet. I think I still need some time to,
you know, put History behind me."

Adam nodded, wiping a fleck of tuna fish from the edge of
the table and onto his dessert plate. "Eighty-six the match-
making, right?" He smiled, a bit disappointed she thought.

"Well, maybe just for now. Besides, wouldn't your friends
find me a little on the *trayf* side? I mean, I ate a BLT this afternoon."

Tzippy, her bony little bottom now rooted to Laura's leg,
swiveled around and asked, "What's a bealty? What's a bealty?"

Shira rolled her eyes and said, "A sandwich. It's just a sandwich." Her refusal to elaborate confirmed for Laura that she
had uttered the gastronomical equivalent of obscenity. She
watched Shira sit smoothing the edge of the tablecloth as if to
maintain her composure. She was a pretty, pale-complexioned
woman, slender and much taller than Laura, with a straight
nose and high forehead that reminded Laura of Renaissance
portraits.

Adam shrugged at Laura and said, "You never know. Some
visionary meshuggener might see potential in you." Then his
smile faded and he leaned toward her, speaking more quietly.
"They're not all complete nerds, you know."

"Adam, I know that," she said, feeling chastened and defensive. "I know that. And I do appreciate your thinking of me,
it's just, *you* know . . . Maybe once I've settled into the job and
all."

He nodded. "I understand."

Michael Westgate was not Orthodox, was not even Jewish as
far as Laura could determine. What he was, according to
Trish, the associate art director, was a young editor who'd
taken an increased interest in the covers of his authors' books
since Laura had arrived.

Laura liked to think so, but she wasn't sure. She knew that her confidence had recently been jarred, but she also suspected the jarring simply afforded her a more clear-eyed view of herself. She'd be thirty soon, and it was probably time to accept that this was who she was: a woman not so unappealing that handsome and intelligent men didn't occasionally ask her out, but not someone those same men ever remained with in the end. There was a carpenter/boat builder she'd dated off and on in Maine one year, a well-read but slightly rough-edged man, who had told her it pissed him off that her inclination was always to agree with people, even when he knew that her true feelings must be to the contrary. "I don't know if it's a twin thing or what," he said, "but I think your you has slipped its mooring." For weeks afterwards the thought had come to her unbidden—*My me's unmoored*—though she wasn't sure just how, or what to do about it.

Today Michael Westgate had stopped by the art department to invite her to lunch. It was probably just a simple professional courtesy, but walking beside him amidst the noisy lunch-hour buzz of lower Fifth Avenue, she felt the distracted and anxious sensation she remembered from first dates.

Michael was also a New Englander—from western Massachusetts—though he'd been in the city for seven years. He'd started with this same publishing house after graduate school, then left to work for a book club, recently returning as a senior editor. He was tall and courteous and generally soft-spoken, though earlier in the day she'd overheard him throwing a small fit—and a large manuscript—in the office of Midge, the division publisher.

The incident, Laura suspected, was still on his mind; walking to lunch, he said a bit sheepishly that he was worried he'd begun to believe New York was the center of the world. He waited for her to respond, but she only smiled and dipped her head in what she hoped was an understanding nod; she hadn't been here long enough to decide otherwise.

"I mean, it's a pretty common attitude," he said, "but it's

also just . . . metropolitan provincialism." He shrugged. "I don't know, maybe it's the only way of rationalizing all the indignities of the place." A gust of wind flipped his tie over his shoulder. "I go up to New England now, and everyone looks so *healthy*," he said. "I mean, it's crazy, here we are breathing visible soot every day when there's oxygen to be had. The thing is, this city's too seductive." He clammed up suddenly, his face reddening, and she wondered if he was unaccustomed to voicing such mildly personal thoughts.

Then she realized. That's nice, she mused. That's sweet. Blush, you bad boy. Seduce me.

"It's the next block here," Michael said, skirting a line for a pretzel cart. The throng of pedestrians thinned out again, and she noticed two Lubavitcher men in black suits and hats. They were standing beside a small motor home with a Star of David banner; two speakers propped on the curb played a scratchy version of the cheerful, nasally horn music she remembered from youth group gatherings. Passover, she realized. Passover was next week.

One of the men, she saw now, was actually a boy: eighteen going on forty-eight. At least Adam still looked more or less his actual age. At least he hadn't gotten in with these fanatics.

The older of the two Lubavitchers, perhaps in his forties beneath the mass of mossy beard, took a step toward Michael. "Excuse me, sir," he said, "are you Jewish?"

Laura turned to Michael.

"No, sorry," Michael said. "Some of my best friends, though," he added with a smile, and at first she missed the joke, thinking maybe he meant her.

The Lubavitcher nodded. "Everybody's a comedian," he said pleasantly. "Have a good day, sir."

Michael looked at Laura as they turned down 18th Street. "I've always wanted to say 'Yes, I am' and go into one of those things, you know," gesturing back at the bannered vehicle.

"Really?" she asked. "Why?"

"I don't know. Just to see what they do in there." He shrugged. "Check out the inner sanctum of the Passover-mobile. At least I think Passover's this month. I'm Episcopalian myself. How 'bout you?"

A bicycle messenger in black Lycra squeezed past them carrying a wheel. Laura pretended it had rubbed against her suede skirt and leaned over to brush at the leather. "Oh, I'm not anything really," she murmured distractedly.

Michael nodded, glancing at her as if he expected her to continue, and she felt a light blush come to her cheeks.

In college she'd met kids who responded similarly to such questions. At first their answers had sounded implausible to Laura, but she soon realized they really did lack any sense of religious identity or tradition. Eventually she had begun appropriating for herself that same unaffiliated status. On the one hand, she didn't entirely believe you could be born Jewish and honestly claim no religious affiliation, whether you were a religious Jew or not. Then again, why should the disclaimer be any more legitimate for a gentile?

"You sounded a little uncertain at first," Michael said. They'd settled into a wooden booth at the Old Town. "Sure you didn't have other plans for lunch?"

"No, not at all. Well, to tell you the truth, I had an appointment to see an apartment, but I canceled it. I can go after work."

He seemed mildly flattered by this revelation of priorities. "Where are you looking?"

"All over the map. This one's on Mulberry Street."

"Fun neighborhood."

Was he teasing? She had fond memories of once strolling through the area during a festival honoring some saint.

"Where are you living now?" he asked.

"New Jersey. My brother's house."

"Older brother?"

"By about forty minutes."

Michael looked puzzle for a second. "You're a twin?"

She nodded.

"Amazing," he said, "I'm a Gemini."

She was so high-strung—afraid now that mentioning the canceled appointment seemed too forward, wondering if she should tell him that one strand of his tie was still blown over his shoulder—that she heard the remark as earnest enthusiasm, thinking, *Oh God no, he's an astrology freak.*

Her disappointment must have been apparent, because all at once Michael's expression changed. "I'm joking," he said, "I'm only joking. I mean, I am a Gemini, but it was a joke."

"Sorry," she told him, "I'm a little slow on the uptake sometimes."

He shrugged, smiling, and she decided that if things went well she'd ask if she could draw him sometime, try to capture that delicious dimple to the left of his handsome mouth.

The waitress came and handed them each a menu.

"So does he look like you, your brother?"

"No, not really," she said. "Not at all, in fact. People used to think we were lying."

He smiled. "When I was little," he said, "there were two sets of twins on our street. The Jensens and the Soodalls, identical and fraternal; my father used to call them the Genuines and the Pseudos."

She laughed, nodding. "That's what it's like. Other kids hear you're a twin and they want the full freak experience, you know? Something like double vision. But they didn't get it with us."

The waitress approached, and he shook his head, indicating they weren't ready yet. "So are you and your brother close?"

"Mmm, we used to be." She paused. There was an anecdote. How when Adam was being delivered, the obstetrician had glanced up and mumbled through his surgical mask, "Getting a little resistance here—I think the other one's got him by the foot." Within the family it had been a combination of punch line and prophesy, because for years they did almost nothing except as a pair. Even in high school, a girl in Laura's art class had once innocently—and rather enviously—asked how long she and Adam had been going together. But relating such trivia just now seemed somehow inapt. "We used to be," she repeated. "Less so now. He's become . . . sort of . . . conservative."

Michael nodded, the earnest green almonds of his eyes finally meeting her gaze without ricocheting off to her shoulder. "I'm a lefty myself," he said, "in everything but golf. But I don't golf."

She laughed.

Walking back to work later, she mentioned that if he had the patience to pose, she'd like to try sketching him sometime.

His mouth opened slightly, but he didn't speak.

She was being too forward, pushing it again. Christ, why didn't she just shut up? Then she realized he must have thought she meant a nude sketch.

"Your face, I mean. Just your face."

"Oh," he said. He smiled. "Oh, sure."

Seeing the apartment on Mulberry Street would have to wait until Monday. She'd forgotten it was Friday already, or at least had forgotten the new meaning of Friday; if she didn't get home before sundown, Adam and Shira would be annoyed. Her watch read 6:28 as she wheezed her way up Adam's street; sundown was at 6:24 today. Every taxi at the train station had been taken, so she'd jogged the mile home in her black pumps. There was a four-inch run in her new stockings; her blouse was wet with perspiration. Turning up the driveway, she spied Tzippy gazing out the screen door. "Shalom you're home!" Tzippy said. "What's that you've got?"

"Flowers—for your mother." She knew that Shira had had a rough week—an oven fire Wednesday night, a fender-bender at the market the next morning. Not to mention it being that special time of the month when Adam and Shira's king-size bed magically became twin beds pushed apart and made up separately. ("One for meat and one for dairy?" Laura had asked.)

Inside, Adam and Shira were sitting in the living room playing with Isaac. Laura glanced at the clock over the piano: 6:31; no one seemed to have noticed. She handed Shira the flowers and settled onto the sofa, puzzled to see Shira's expression go from gratitude and delight to a sudden distracted confusion. "Adam, Laura brought me flowers."

Adam dandled Isaac on his knee and smiled. "That was nice, Laura," and he winked in appreciation for her rushing home.

"*Flowers*, Adam," Shira repeated. "They're all wrapped up."

"Yeah," he said. Then, "Oh," and his smile became awkward.

Laura glanced back and forth between them. "What? What is it?"

"Well, it's Shabbos," Adam explained; "we can't tear paper."

"No problem," Shira said, "we'll just put the whole thing in a vase of water until tomorrow night."

"Well," Adam winced, "that's not really . . ."

"You're right, I forgot," Shira said.

"*What* is going on?" Laura asked.

"We can't put them in water," Shira told her. "We can't *water* them."

Laura felt her face getting hot. "You're kidding. I mean, you're not farmers irrigating crops, for Christ's sake. Isn't that what the original law's about?"

Adam tried to catch her eye as a gentle admonishment, but she wouldn't allow it.

Then Shira hit upon a solution: sliding each rose through the inch-wide opening in one corner of the wrapping. Laura stood and watched as, one by one, ten perfect, expensive, red and white roses became slightly mangled, Shira inserting her slender fingertips and tugging each flower up through the unsealed corner. Finally, she folded the wrapping paper with the trimming still inside and handed the wad to Tzippy to throw out.

"Oh, before I forget," Shira said, "you had a call a little while ago. Michael someone."

"Michael Westgate?"

"Yeah, I think so. He tried to find you at work, but you'd already left."

"Did he leave a message?"

"It's on the table. I think he wanted you to call back, but . . ."

"But what?" And then she realized. "Don't say it: I know. Forget it. I'll call him tomorrow night—it's not important."

She had a small desk phone packed with her bags on the third floor and had noticed there was a jack in one corner of the bedroom. She wasn't about to make a Sabbath sacrifice of Michael Westgate.

Upstairs, she unpacked the phone, fussed her hair into place, and dialed his number, but it was busy. Over the next ten minutes she tried four times more. Finally she slid off her skirt and the ruined black stockings and pulled on a pair of jeans. When she dialed Michael's number again she got a ring, but this time there was no answer.

Shira had placed the roses in a green vase on the dinner table—sans water—and the injured ones didn't look as if they'd make it through the Sabbath.

"Remember this?" Adam said. He was standing over Isaac in his high chair, bobby-pinning a navy-blue yarmulke to the boy's curls. Seeing the thing, she felt a sudden sweet nostalgia, and then a distinct unpleasantness. It was the yarmulke she'd crocheted for Adam's bar mitzvah seventeen years ago. Its outer rim was embellished with a thin white zigzag design that formed his initials—AM—linked and repeated around the circumference. She'd spent a month or more secretly needle-and-hooking yards and yards of the thin, tightly spun cotton, finally presenting it to him just before they'd left the house for the synagogue. Later that night, when their father had offered to take them all out for sundaes, they'd piled into the car, Adam still wearing the yarmulke. Parking outside Howard Johnson's, their father had glanced at him and said, "I think it's safe to take your *kippah* off now, Adam."

"That's okay," Adam said, "I'll keep-a it on," and Laura had felt delighted that he so liked it.

Their father's smile was forced. "Come on, you don't need it on in here."

"David," their mother had whispered, "Laura *made* it for him."

"Dad, does it bother you or something?"

"It doesn't bother me at all, I just don't think you need to go overboard just because you've been bar mitzvahed."

She didn't remember exactly what had happened after that. Adam snatching it off and throwing it into the car? Adam wearing it into the restaurant in glum triumph? Each seemed true.

Shira now lit the candles and Adam recited the kiddush. Tzippy led them through the short *hamotzi*, her Hebrew nearly flawless.

"You're going to fit right in when we live in Israel," Adam said.

Laura looked at him. "You're moving to Israel?"

"Just for ten months or so. If I can manage a leave next year."

Tzippy dipped a piece of challah into the tiny glass of Manischewitz Adam had poured for her and turned to Laura. "Have you been to our homeland?" she asked.

"Your homeland."

"*Is*rael," Tzippy said. "Dad, isn't it Laura's homeland, too?"

"Yes, of course," Adam said.

"No, I've never been to Israel," Laura said.

"Don't you *want* to go?"

"Oh, I suppose," Laura said, poking at a piece of kugel. She knew she should stop right there, but sitting opposite the bouquet of half-mangled roses, her reserve of diplomacy seemed to have run dry. "I don't really think of it as my 'homeland,' though. To me, America's my homeland." She avoided Adam's eyes.

"But you're Jewish, right?" Tzippy persisted.

"Uh-huh," Laura said.

"Then it's your *home*land. Right, Dad?"

Adam nodded. "That's right."

"Well, I know what you mean, Tzippy, but I think of it as the homeland for people who were *born* in Israel. I was born in America."

"But you're Jewish," Tzippy said, her tone both question and statement.

"Yes."

"I'm glad you'll concede that much," Adam murmured.

"Come on," Laura said, "I just don't see any point in claiming a connection that's not . . . real."

Adam raised an ironic eyebrow. Meeting his glance, Laura thought she could guess what he was thinking. For a moment she felt herself back in her college dorm room, winter of 1981.

Their father had died that fall—two days before Thanksgiving. Several weeks after the funeral, on a Friday in mid-December, Adam had surprised her by showing up at her dorm in Waterville. She'd come back from the library one afternoon, and from down the long hallway spied him sitting on the floor outside her door with a small duffel bag. When

they embraced, all the emotion she'd contained since returning to school was suddenly unleashed and she began crying
into his shoulder.

"Sorry," she said after a moment, and summoned a smile as
Adam patted her back. "I'm okay, really." She unlocked her
door, grateful to find that her roommate was out.

Adam glanced at several charcoal nudes scattered on the
floor and lowered himself onto the nearest bed. He'd taken
his exams early, he said, because he wanted to come home
and be with the family. En route, though, he'd decided to
detour and see her first. He leaned back on his elbows and
glanced slowly at the bed's headboard, outlined in tiny, unlit
Christmas lights, then at the bed across the room, similarly
decorated. "Is this your bed?" he said.

She nodded, plugging in a hot plate for tea.

He widened his eyes slightly and turned to examine the
nearest wall: a black-and-white photograph their sister had
taken of Adam and Laura tightrope-walking the split-rail
fence in the yard at home; a watercolor landscape Laura's
instructor had liked, stubbled cornfields along a dirt road of
crooked telephone poles; and a tattered antique print called
"Bringing Home the Christmas Tree."

He glanced again at the headboard lights and turned to
her. "Did *you* put these up?"

She shrugged. "Both of us."

"But why?"

"Oh, Adam, it's just decoration, it doesn't mean anything. I
like that old print, it's a great piece of Americana."

"I don't mean the print, I mean how can you, these
lights . . ." He glanced around, noticing now a single bough of
mistletoe draped over her wall mirror from home. "Does your
roommate know you're Jewish?"

"I suppose," she said. She tore off a paper towel to wipe two
mugs clean.

"Does she?"

"Adam, I'm not hiding it. God, they're just lights. It's just a piece of plant. I mean, Christmas, big deal, it's practically a secular holiday. I'm just helping my roommate celebrate."

"But, Laura . . ."

"What?"

Adam shook his head. "I don't know, I just didn't realize . . . how much he'd gotten to you."

"What?"

"Dad. This is all Dad. You know that, don't you?"

"What are you talking about?" she said, prying the lid from a tin of tea bags.

"Come on, Laura, the man's life mission was to assimilate. He hated everything Jewish. Christ, he hated himself. He spent more time passing than a goddamn race-car driver. Why do you think he changed his name to Miller?"

"He took his mother's name 'cause he felt closer to her."

Adam closed his eyes and shook his head. "Jesus, Laura, give me a break." He was quiet for a moment, then gazed out the window, slowly pushing his hand through his hair. "That is not why." He glanced at the watercolor again, releasing a slow, sibilant sigh. "Gotta give him credit, though. Perfect death for the self-hating man."

She froze, dangling a tea bag over one of the mugs as if she'd forgotten what to do with it. "What do you mean?"

"You think that was an accident?"

"Of course I do. Dr. Draper said he must have gotten his medication screwed up. How can you *say* that, Adam? You don't know that."

"Laura, if you don't want to believe it, that's fine. I understand. But don't fool yourself about the rest of this," and he flicked at one of the lights on her headboard.

"Well don't you lecture me. God, they're just a bunch of lights. I know perfectly well who I am, Adam, whether or not you happen to like the decor."

He'd sat silent, not moving, suddenly looking weary.

Laura busied herself collecting sketches from the floor, then took her coat off and sat on the other bed. "We're *all* upset about Dad, Adam—please don't take it out on me."

"That's not . . ." he began and then left off, shaking his head. "You don't—" and he stopped again. "Fine," he said finally. "I'm sorry. Enough said."

And he didn't say anything more about it. He spent the night on a cot in her room, and the next morning toured the campus with her before catching a bus for home. She felt, though, that their visit—maybe even their relationship in general—had never quite gotten back on track after those first unpleasant minutes. Three years later, when Adam met Shira and came to embrace Orthodoxy, the derailment was as good as confirmed; the person she'd been closest to in the world had become a stranger.

After dinner she tried Michael's number again, this time with success. It was the first time they'd spoken by phone, and his voice was nicer than she'd remembered—deep, but rather tender. He apologized for the short notice, but wanted to invite her to a dinner party he was hosting for one of his authors on Saturday night. He seemed happy to chat, but she was worried Tzippy might come up any minute, so she thanked him, twice, and said her brother was waiting for a call.

Later, wondering what author the dinner might be for, she pulled out a catalog from work. Most of Michael's authors were biographers and historians. His titles on the spring list were *A Life of Andre Maginot, The Other Berlin: A Memoir,* and *The Ironic Curtain: Soviet News Media in the Eighties.* The dinner party would no doubt be made up of the kind of people who'd see through her ignorance in a moment. Christ, the Maginot Line—was that World War I or II?

*   *   *

Saturday evening as Laura was changing, Tzippy came scuffing up the stairs in her slippers. "Are you going out?"

"Yes, in a little while."

"You look pretty."

"In my slip?"

Tzippy giggled. "Sure." She settled into the desk chair and watched as Laura tried an olive linen skirt, then a rayon floral print she'd bought in SoHo. Between appraisals, Tzippy examined Laura's wallet photos on the desktop. "Is that you in this picture?" she said, holding up an ID from work.

"Uh-huh."

Tzippy leaned over toward the desk lamp and drew the card close to her face. "It doesn't really look like you."

It didn't actually, though Laura rather liked the way it made her look about twenty years old, her hair in the wide black headband she'd chosen that first morning of work, her smile somehow the easy, confident grin of a person she didn't recognize. "So who's it look like?" she asked.

"Um . . . Mima." Mima was Tzippy's imaginary friend.

"Oh, that's interesting. I always wondered what Mima looked like."

"That's kind of what she looks like," Tzippy said. "Excep' younger." She paused, chewing on her lip. "You know, someone at school said Mima's just a . . . a fig, um, a fignant, um . . ."

"A Fig Newton of your Maginot Line?"

Tzippy smiled uncertainly. "Something like that."

"Oh, they're just jealous," Laura said. "It's actually a very good thing to have a Fig Newton like Mima."

Tzippy was giggling now.

"As long as you know where to draw the Maginot Line. *N'est-ce pas?*"

Tzippy scrunched her face and laughed again. "You're being very kooky tonight."

"Can't help it, Tzippy. People talk about Fig Newtons, and I just turn into a kooky."

Tzippy chortled again, then, looking suddenly inspired, called out, "Fig Newton! Fig Newton!" and Laura, with a third rejected skirt around her ankles, began hopping in a wild spastic dance, her arms waving and her tongue dangling in absolute kookiness. Tzippy shrieked with laughter, finally clutching at her pants as she rocked back and forth and warning, "I'm gonna rainy! I'm gonna rainy!"

When her happy delirium subsided, she moaned a slow, weary *nnnnggg* sound, sliding off the chair to her knees. "Can't you stay home tonight?"

The door at the bottom of the stairway creaked open, and Shira called out, "Tzippy! Are you up here?"

"She's with me, Shira."

"I hope you're not bothering Laura," Shira said, starting up the stairs.

"Oh, she's a terrible nuisance," said Laura, winking at Tzippy.

Shira was still wearing the blue beret she'd donned when one of Adam's friends stopped by. Laura wasn't sure if her refusal to buy a *shaytl* was a matter of vanity (Shira's real hair was lustrous) or an uncharacteristic streak of independence. Seeing Laura dressed up—or nearly so—Shira widened her eyes. "Are you going out tonight?"

"Yes, if I can just stop changing."

"A man?"

"Uh-huh."

"The Michael guy?"

"Um, no, someone else." Lying seemed ludicrous, but if she said yes, Shira would probably suspect the illicit phone call.

"Ahh." Shira raised her carefully plucked eyebrows and smiled. "Is he Jewish?"

"Well, no." She couldn't help taking a certain secret delight in disappointing Shira's parochial expectations.

Standing in the doorway, Shira nodded, her sincere and indulgent smile shrinking only slightly. She bent to pick up a stray barrette from the rug and looked for a place to set it, casually surveying the room: duffel bags with clothes spilling out of them, stacks of art magazines and book catalogs, the phone balanced on top of a grey suitcase. "I didn't know you had a phone up here," she said. And all at once Laura could see it dawn on her. Shira's mouth pursed in annoyance, and Laura felt her own eyes reluctantly admit the truth.

Shira glanced at Tzippy, who was peeling the edge of a Band-Aid from her arm, experimenting with various agonized expressions. "Tzippy, Daddy was looking for you. Will you please go down and see what he wants."

Tzippy stood up, smoothed the Band-Aid back into place, and scuffed her way down the stairs. Shira stood twanging the metal barrette with her thumb until the door to the second floor had closed. "You went ahead and used the phone yesterday, didn't you?"

"Yes, but I don't see that it matters. I'm not Orthodox, Shira."

"But we are, and you're living in our house."

"I appreciate that. I do. Okay, from now on I'll do it Yahweh." Shira glared.

"Come on, Shira. I really don't think my phone call interfered with anybody's Sabbath." She slid the linen skirt on again.

"You're really trying to make things awkward for us, aren't you?"

"Shira, you're making things awkward for yourself. Just ignore me, for God's sake."

"We can't ignore you! We can't even have friends over," she said, her voice nearly breaking.

"What are you talking about?"

"We usually have friends stay over for Shabbos."

"So?" There was still a spare guest room.

"Most of them have kids. They don't want their kids seeing you coming and going all day, carrying your work, taking the train. It's hard enough getting kids to observe Shabbos."

Laura's hand had begun trembling, and she clutched her hairbrush tighter. "I didn't realize I'd turned your social life upside down."

"It's not just that. It's Tzippy, too. Don't you think she notices you doing things differently?"

"Shira, this is America—a lot of people do things differently. You think it's so bad for Tzippy to know her aunt's not Orthodox?"

Shira leaned against the door frame and shook her head. "You just don't understand, Laura."

"Don't understand *what*?"

"What a difficult position we're in." She blew a purse of air in exasperation. "We had to go to the rabbi about you living here."

"What?"

"Well we did. And don't let Adam know I told you that," she said in a petulant voice, "he'd kill me."

"What do you mean, you went to the rabbi? What on earth for?"

"Because we were worried—about Tzippy, about how to deal with you . . ."

"How to *deal* with me? What did he say?" Her voice had squeezed to a thin reedy sound.

"He thought as long as you kept kosher and observed Shabbat, there shouldn't be a problem. And there wouldn't have been."

She was determined not to cry in front of Shira. "Well I'm sorry it *has* been such a problem," she said, her voice barely audible. She sat on the bed and pulled on her black pumps, concentrating on the smooth leather of the toes, trying to keep her eyes from clouding over.

"If you can wait till six-thirty," Shira said, "I'll give you a ride to the station."

Laura shook her head. "The next train's too late."

Shira's mouth tightened and she turned.

Downstairs, they could hear Tzippy at the piano, slowly picking out a simple scale Laura had taught her.

"Tzippy," Shira called out, "not yet!"

Michael was an anxious host, rarely settling for more than a minute. Scrupulously attentive to empty glasses and anyone left on the sidelines of conversation, he seemed everywhere at once. His neck looked raw and recently shaved, and he smelled of the same mentholated shaving cream Laura's carpenter boyfriend had used.

His apartment consisted of three small rooms in an upper West Side brownstone—the sort of tasteful, pleasant place she'd given up hope of ever finding or affording. There was a small brick fireplace in the living room, and around the doorways, oak molding with scrollwork. A dozen black-and-white family photographs filled one wall, the oldest an oval portrait of a mustachioed Union army officer.

The half-dozen other guests who'd arrived included Maddie Epstein, a slender, urbane-sounding editor from the History Book Club; a fiftyish man with an eye patch whom Laura recognized from work; and his quiet, expensively dressed wife. Michael kept glancing at his watch and jumping up to check on things in the kitchen.

"Can I help with anything?" Laura asked, following him out.

"Oh no, I'm just being frantic," he said.

On the sideboard, a huge bowl of sea scallops sat soaking in milk. Michael lowered the flame beneath a battered-looking wok, stirring at a glistening array of vegetables. "I got carried away with crushed red pepper," he whispered, "so I tried to drown it with wine. Too much wine." He shook his head. "What you see here is a culinary disaster in the making." "It looks great."

He scowled, then smiled, glancing at the doorway. "It'll be okay." He opened a drawer, grabbing a single chopstick. "Tell you the truth, I was mainly worried you'd think I'm a fuckup. Now you know, so I'm off the hook. It's very liberating."

"You're no fuckup," she said.

He scraped a pepper seed to the rim of the wok and plucked it out. "I'm no Craig Claiborne, either," and he scraped again, his eyes darting to her face. "Awfully glad you came, you know."

By eight-thirty everyone had arrived. The guest of honor was Inge Kelnop, an East German memoirist of about fifty. According to Michael she had escaped, rather dramatically, across the Berlin Wall in 1963. She was a handsome, athletic-looking woman with short chestnut hair and an oddly attractive scar across her right cheek, a feature Laura couldn't help associating with her escape.

Michael summoned the nine guests to dinner, and a young editor whom Laura didn't know sat beside her. He'd heard her mention Maine, and began quizzing her about the Portland area, where his lover had recently inherited a small parcel of land. He seemed surprised that Laura had lived nearly all her life there but was unable to tell him anything useful about either property taxes or the tenor of gay-straight relations. She tried generalizing for a minute or two, finally welcoming the distraction of an increasingly urgent-sounding discussion across the table.

"On the contrary," Inge Kelnop was saying, "it does not at all mean I condone the atrocities of the Third Reich." Her English was generally excellent, though she spoke with a thick accent in which *th* sounds were variously pronounced as *z* or *s*, as in *ze Sird Reich*. "But the acquiescence of so many Jews in their fate," she continued, "is not something one can altogether ignore."

Michael looked uncomfortable. "Well, Inge," he said solemnly, "that's a rather sweeping generalization—"

"You think the Israelis themselves don't recognize this?" Inge Kelnop asked. "Consider the hyperaggressiveness of the Jewish state: it is in re*action* to this. The famous military zealousness of Israel—what they call 'muscle flexing'—is not just a reaction to having been persecuted; it's a reaction to having *accepted* their persecution. That is what the slogan 'Never Again' really means."

"But, Inge," Michael began, "I really don't—"

"Wait and see if they don't overreact to what has happened in Jerusalem today, this business outside the Knesset. They are still compensating—overcompensating—for their complicity in the Holocaust."

"Oh, 'complicity'—please, Inge," Michael said.

Inge Kelnop cocked her head like a little girl, shrugging as if to say, "What, then?"

Maddie Epstein, sitting on Laura's left, was worrying a small hoop earring between her thumb and finger. "And is this an argument you make in your book?" she asked. "That the Jews made a mad dash for the ovens?"

Inge Kelnop smiled, touching at a drop of soft wax beneath one of the candlesticks. "No, this is purely personal observation."

"Ah," Maddie Epstein said. "I was just wondering—you didn't happen to personally observe the Jews in the French Resistance, did you? Because I think maybe the word 'complicity' is losing a little something in translation here."

"Excuse me, but I think I have spoken English quite as long as you. Yes, a handful of Jews may have fought in the Resistance, no question; their participation does not disprove my point."

"Your point," Maddie Epstein said, "is too bizarre to merit rational debate."

Inge Kelnop's calm expression suggested that, on the contrary, she viewed any reluctance to engage her in debate as merely a concession of her point's validity. It occurred to Laura that in the same situation, Adam, the former high school debate-team captain, would have pursued this argument, would easily have marshaled specific evidence to refute the woman's claims.

"Inge," Michael said, "with all due respect, I think maybe your family's immediate experience, which some people here might not—"

"No, Michael dear, you needn't make excuses for me. I stand by what I am saying. I stand by it. Quite independent of anything else."

To her horror, Laura realized that she was about to speak, that her left heel, a cartoon of nervousness, had begun chattering against the floor. "What about the Warsaw ghetto uprising?" she heard herself say. Her own voice was strange, like the muted sound a swimmer hears from beneath the surface.

"Granted, yes," Inge Kelnop said: "the ghetto in Warsaw *is* an exception. Still, why were there not *more* Warsaw ghetto uprisings? This is the very question I am asking."

Laura was silent, her chest pounding.

"The problem," Maddie Epstein said, "is that it seems like a very short step from the way you're asking it to insisting six million Jews felt they . . . *deserved* annihilation."

"No, deserved is your word, don't put it in my mouth," Inge Kelnop said. "Also," she added, "the figure is nearer to five million."

"Pardon me?" said Maddie.

"Five." She held up the splayed fingers of one hand.

"Well, that's in dispute," Michael said.

"Actually, she's right," a young man sitting near Inge Kelnop replied. He looked like an academic, though he wore a tiny gold post in one ear. "Most historians agree six million is slightly exaggerated. Not that it changes anything."

"No," Inge Kelnop said, "the ugly fact remains. But tell me also this," she said, turning toward Maddie and Laura again: "Why is Nazi Germany always portrayed solely as a *Jewish* tragedy? And don't misunderstand me—the Holocaust was, by all means, a major Jewish tragedy. But the Nazis annihilated many more Christians than ever they did Jews."

"Is that true?" asked a buxom woman from the sub-rights department. She wore a heavy gold necklace with industrial-size chain links.

"Certainly," said Inge Kelnop, and the hip young academic nodded. "Twelve million people they destroyed; of those twelve million, *seven* million were Christians."

"I didn't realize that," the sub-rights woman said.

"No, you didn't," Inge Kelnop said, "and most people do not. Why? Because the Jews have given the impression they have sole title to the suffering of World War II. They have this ownership mentality about tragedy. 'It is our hurt, not yours. You just stand back and feel guilty.' "

Laura's mouth was cotton; she needed a sip of water, but knew her hand would be shaking too much. "But no other group," she said, "was singled out the way Jews were. If they had been, other ethnic groups would commemorate the Holocaust too."

"Exactly," said Maddie Epstein, and Michael nodded.

"I am not criticizing the commemoration," Inge Kelnop said, "only the absolute exclusiveness of the martyrdom." Then, inclining her chin at Laura and Maddie, she asked, "You are both Jewish, I suppose, yes?"

Laura swallowed, saw the candle flame before her weave a small swaying motion. "Yes," she said, "I am." To her right, she was dimly aware of Michael's puzzled gaze.

"Yes," said Maddie, "you'll have to forgive us—we're not wearing our yellow stars tonight."

"Cute," Inge Kelnop said, "cute," her glance traveling from Maddie to Laura, "but it's all too apparent who you are."

Meaning what? That she'd had Laura pegged as Jewish all along? Or that she saw more deeply: beyond the rational rebuttal to the history of evasiveness and denial?

Michael looked distraught and awkwardly suggested a change of topic while Laura sat rigidly, her heart pounding and her breath coming from beneath a weight. She could barely focus on anything anyone said the rest of the evening.

Later, when people began leaving, Maddie Epstein offered her a lift to Penn Station. She'd been planning to stick around, to offer Michael some help cleaning up and finally to be alone with him. But Inge Kelnop was bending his ear and seemed in no hurry to leave. "Thanks," Laura said, "if you're really going that way."

Sunday morning she got up late. When she went downstairs, Adam was sitting in the kitchen feeding the baby. Isaac grunted a greeting, twisting toward her in his high chair.

"Where is everybody?" she asked.

"Shira went over to her sister's house with Tzippy." He wiped a drop of applesauce from Isaac's chin. "You have a good time last night?"

"No, not really." She'd have liked to unburden herself of the lingering unpleasantness, but she was still angry at Adam for what Shira had told her. Besides, she could too easily imagine him suggesting it was the kind of thing that came of getting involved with gentiles.

He nodded slightly, holding a yellow cup to Isaac's mouth. "I guess you and Shira had a bit of a talk?"

"Yeah, a bit." She took a glass from the cabinet and stood swishing her finger under tap water. On the windowsill in front of her was a small assortment of silverware—forks and knives she'd used inappropriately, now awaiting some mysterious purification process.

"Well, that's my fault, I think. I should have made things a little clearer when you first came."

"You mean my so-called 'coming and going all day' on the Sabbath?"

"Well, you haven't been quite *that* bad about it."

Laura rolled her eyes.

"But if you *could* try to stay in until sundown. Or on Friday nights, just to get here before Shabbos starts. You know?"

"Adam, I've got a job that doesn't always make that possible."

"I know, but last night, for example? And the phone . . ."

"You're right, that was wrong. I'm sorry about the phone. It's just, my social life has been almost nil lately." She rinsed the glass and set it in the proper strainer. "Of course, I guess yours hasn't been too hot either."

He stirred the tiny spoon through Isaac's jar of applesauce and glanced at her. "What do you mean?"

"That was also part of our little talk last night. How you and Shira can't have friends over because they wouldn't want their kids ex*posed* to me?"

"That's not . . ." He shook his head, letting the remark trail off.

"Not what?"

"It's not true."

"Sounded convincing the way Shira told it. I mean, after all, if you had to check with your rabbi about even letting me stay here."

He'd been about to say something and stopped with his mouth partly open, finally releasing a small sigh. "Okay, so I talked with the rabbi. That's not such a big deal. I talk with him about a lot of things." His cheeks, above his neatly trimmed beard, were flushed now; his ears too had suddenly gone red.

"Adam, I'm your *sister*, since when do you consult a rabbi to know whether I should stay in your home? I can't believe it."

"That's not what happened, Laura. It wasn't about *whether* you should stay here, it was just about . . . accommodating everyone's needs."

"Oh, that's it, do a semantic number on me."

"It's the truth. We just thought we should talk to him about what we could reasonably . . . " he shrugged, "expect of you."

"You couldn't decide for yourself? Jesus, Adam—"

"Laura, come on, you know that I wanted—"

"Sometimes I think you didn't just get circumcised, I think they snipped your balls off too. I really do."

"Laura, take it easy! It was not about you personally. We had Tzippy to think of, we had—"

"Oh brother, what does that mean?" She folded her arms, toeing at a wooden Hebrew-alphabet block with her bare foot.

"Tzippy idolizes you, you know that, she notices things; we've got to think about what influences her."

"Sippy!" Isaac said gleefully. He tugged at his bib, straining to look behind him. "Sippy!"

"So you're going to hide her from a whole world of people who are different? That's democratic. That's really broad-minded."

"Laura, you don't understand."

"Well I'd like to understand. Are all your Orthodox friends like this? A bunch of fucking xenophobes?"

He set the jar down with a smack and Isaac started, then grimaced and began crying. "You know," Adam said coldly, "you've got some pretty curious attitudes. I hate to tell you, but for a Jew you really sound like an anti-Semite at times." He rubbed absently at Isaac's chubby forearm.

"Oh, that's rich—I'm an anti-Semite?"

Adam leaned back and stared at her, fidgeting with Isaac's tiny spoon.

She let out an irritated sigh, but could feel herself trembling. "That's terrific, Adam," she said, and his name caught deep in her throat.

"Laura," he said a little less coldly, "you haven't exactly shown much respect for what we're doing here."

"It's not a question of respect. I just don't think religion's supposed to erect barriers between people."

"It doesn't exist without barriers. And it *is* a question of respect. You come back from Manhattan and rave about the wonderful ethnicity of the place—all the bilingual Hispanic kids, women wearing saris, Little Italy. You think it's so damn terrific they're all embracing their ethnic heritage; well what the hell do you think we're *up* to in this house?" He gestured at the walls in general. "I think what you really like is the tourist version of ethnicity. Something entertaining while you stroll by, a little local color. But it's more than that for us."

He grabbed a damp washcloth from the sink and wiped at Isaac's face; the boy squirmed, his eyes shiny with the residue of tears. "What you and I grew up with was half-baked, that New England assimilationist bullshit. Halfhearted attempt at being observant two or three times a year. We didn't know who the hell we were. And when we did, we weren't so sure it was anything to be proud of. I want Tzippy and Isaac to *know* who they are. Because I wish *I'd* been certain fifteen years ago. I could have used some of this back then." He wiped his hands brusquely on the washcloth and twisted a lid onto the applesauce jar. Isaac, his face red and clean, slapped his arms on his tray. "So let us at least try to keep our home consistent. Is that really so much to ask?"

Standing there leaning against the sink, she lowered her eyes and twisted at the wide silver band on her index finger. She'd never realized Adam had ever felt any uncertainty. From day one he'd seemed to know exactly who and what he was. She watched as he bent to lift Isaac from the high chair, the white tassel of a single *tzitzis* snaking out from beneath his T-shirt.

The phone rang and Adam shifted Isaac to one arm and

answered it. "Sure, just a moment please," he said, and held it out to Laura. "Michael Westgate."

She waited a moment while Adam pushed the sliding glass door open and carried Isaac out to the backyard. "Hello," she said quietly.

"Hi," Michael said, "I wanted to apologize. I feel awful about last night."

"It's okay," she said, "it really wasn't your fault."

"I should've been a little tougher on Inge, though. Shouldn't have let her go on."

"Well, being the host," she said, "I'm sure it was awkward." She stood in front of the refrigerator, where Shira had taped a sonogram of Isaac at three months, and slowly traced her finger along the picture's grey swirls.

"Yeah, but still." He paused. "The thing is, there are, in a way, some . . . extenuating circumstances. Sort of."

"Oh?" she asked. "Are you . . . involved with her?"

"Oh no, not at all." He seemed vaguely amused.

"Well, I just . . ."

"No, no," he said. "And of course I don't condone what she was saying. But I thought you might not know her parents and sister died at Buchenwald. Not that it really changes anything."

"She told you that?"

"I've known for a while. She's written about it."

Laura nodded, silent. "I suppose she's also half Jewish, right?"

"No," he said slowly, "she's . . . not . . . Jewish," and Laura knew he was recalling her dissembling answer the day they'd walked to lunch. "Actually," he said, "they were hiding Jews."

"You're kidding."

"The SS found out about a young couple her parents had in their cellar. She thinks her father was involved with the wife. Anyway, the whole family was sent off in a cattle car."

"She too?"

"She was visiting relatives in the country at the time. Her aunt kept her through the war."

Laura was silent. Out the window she could see Adam balancing Isaac on a seat of the swing set. "I guess I wish I'd known that," she said.

"Well, she was shameful, and you and Maddie were right to call her on it. I thought it might put a different edge on things, though." He paused. "I don't know," he said, "I guess the other reason I'm telling you is so you won't think I'm some kind of anti-Semite."

She blew a puff of air. "No, of course not. I was hoping you wouldn't think the same of me."

"Why would I?"

"That day we were talking about religion? Walking to lunch, the Passovermobile?"

"Yeah?"

"I wasn't exactly candid with you."

"Well, I wondered about that . . ."

"Also, when you asked me about my brother and I said he's sort of conservative?"

"Uh-huh."

"What I meant to say, what I should have said, is that he's very religious—he's Orthodox."

"I thought so."

"You did?"

"When I called to invite you to dinner the other night. Your sister-in-law said, 'Can I have her get back to you after the Sabbath?' I figured they must be pretty religious."

She shook her head. "I must have seemed awfully shallow then, being evasive about all that."

"No, but I wondered—especially since you were so open last night—why you weren't more . . . that way before."

"I don't know," she said. "It's hard to explain. I'm sorry, though."

"It's okay, I just . . . it's okay."

They were silent for a moment.

"So," he said, "any more confessions?"

She leaned her forehead against the sliding glass door. "Well . . . Just that I'm fond of you."

"Fond of you, too," he said. "I'm glad you got that off your chest."

Out in the yard, Adam sat on the swing with Isaac in his lap. He glanced up and noticed Laura leaning against the glass, lifted Isaac's wrist and waved.

She pressed her open hand against the window. "Michael?"

"Yeah?"

"Maybe sometime you could come out here and meet my brother."

"I'd like to," he said. "I'd like that."

When they hung up she sat down in the kitchen and watched Adam carry Isaac to the small plastic pool. Even from here she could make out her brother's prematurely greying hairs. Their thirtieth birthday was less than a week away. She wasn't especially eager to be a year older.

She leaned back in her chair opposite the sonogram hanging on the fridge. It was little more than a blur, a dark satellite photograph of the cosmos. Locating the strange grey planet that was her nephew, she imagined for a moment that she could actually remember that early morning in May thirty years ago, when their nine months of womb time had come to an end. Suddenly Adam was sliding away from her, toward all that noise that lay beyond their little sac of water and warmth. Closing her eyes, she could almost believe she remembered the awful solitude of her forty minutes in there without him. And then, finally giving in to it, she'd shunted along the watersmooth walls, let the crimson contractions carry her along to him, emerging wet and cold into all that brilliance of light.

▼

INFATUATED

▲

Alone in Roanoke with a one-semester job he couldn't refuse, McNeil hasn't written to Shushie in three weeks, has phoned her only once in all that time, but he quickly crumples one more attempt at a letter, landing it in the kitchen wastebasket with little more than her name—a simple salutation he cannot proceed past. Midway through the spring semester he's fallen for one of his students, finding, to his dismay, that it's a full-time preoccupation, this business of being infatuated. Emotionally, he's regressed ten years in as many days, though he's also aware of a welcome sense of rejuvenation. God knows he's been acting juvenile.

The letter a lost cause, he caps his pen and removes his reading glasses, rubbing his eyes and summoning in the sudden dark the wonderful trace of whitish down that runs below Susan's ear and along her jaw line. Strange how the stuff can be so blond on a brunette. A tennis star from Florida, her fresh-off-the-court features beam health and wealth: a freckled patrician nose, prominent ruddy cheekbones, and, more uniquely, almond-shaped, almost Asian eyes. At five ten, she's

just a few inches shorter than McNeil, but with the endearing-
ly soft, shy voice of a more diminutive woman, especially, it
seems, when they talk on the phone.

"By the way," she'd said quietly when he called her last
night, "I think I left my *um*brella in your car," emphasizing
the first syllable in a way he's never heard in the north. The
slight trace of a Southern accent is sweet, but it also nettles
him, because he hasn't forgotten his last night in New York
with Shushie. She had taken his hand as they walked home
from a movie, and McNeil had concentrated on holding her
fingers firmly, for often he would ease his grip and uncon-
sciously let his hand slide free. Then she would say, "You
don't like holding hands anymore, do you?"

This time, though, she had simply pulled their cold joined
hands into her big coat pocket, smiling a little ironically and
asking, "You won't get distracted being at a women's college,
will you?"

"Oh, I shouldn't think so," he said, and Shushie had squeezed
his hand, hard, until they both heard his knuckles crack.
Watching her perfect white teeth revealed in a smile, he had
rather missed the slightly buck teeth she'd had in high school,
and tried to remember her face as it had been then, with
braces. The first time he'd ever noticed her, she was a pretty
tomboyish type, playing the fiddle and tapping her foot in a
school production of *Oklahoma!* The next day he'd had a
friend who was in the show introduce him to her. She was
friendly and polite, sitting alone peeling an orange in the
cafeteria, her violin case resting on the table. He had noticed
a faint stubborn trace of stage eyeliner still showing beneath
her lashes. And there were the braces, oddly charming, which
he hadn't seen from his seat in the auditorium. They'd chat-
ted about a local university production—*Man of La Mancha*—
and even after his friend left they sat talking, drinking
chocolate milk from half-pint cartons. When they stood up to
go to class, he realized he'd been right about the tomboy bit:

she wore jeans with hightop Converse basketball sneakers (not yet fashionable in the seventies), her bony elbow jutting outward as she carried the leather instrument case across her shoulders.

It was a more cosmopolitan Shushie—black wool skirt, black tights and pumps—who'd smiled bracelessly while crossing Sixth Avenue in December, saying, "I can just imagine those Southern private-school girls fawning all over you." And then, in a drawl, clasping his hand to her breast, "Wouldn't y'all lack to come an' visit ma daddy's horse fom, Professa McNeil? Or can Ah call ya Caleb? That's such a nass name— Cay-lib. Y'all ahn't *really* serious about that girl up in New Yoak, ah you? What's her name? Shushie? That sho' is a strange name."

He had laughed, even as he slowly recognized that the silly sidewalk parody was also intended to have the power of jinx; that Shushie, if only as an afterthought, hoped it might later make a dead end of any real scenario that might resemble it.

But it has not dead-ended Susan. And although she told McNeil at lunch that she has to finish a paper tonight on Hobbes' *Leviathan*, he wonders, sitting in his kitchen, if she'll leave it aside and join him for a drink. Maybe she's finished by now. He gets up and digs out the student directory, then changes his mind and tosses it on the kitchen counter. Instead he begins a stack of essays from the class in which Susan sits in the second row, abandoning them gratefully when the phone rings.

It is Shushie. She misses him. She knows it's silly to call an hour before the rates go down, but she couldn't wait. She had hoped for a letter from him today. She understands, she says, how busy he must be, but she needs the sustenance of his letters.

It's a word he's heard her director use more than once, sustenance. He is jealously alert to every new phrasing adopted in his absence.

Shushie, oblivious, mentions that the new *Village Voice* has a piece on Garrett Ripley, which may prolong the run of the otherwise unknown production she's rehearsing. Ripley is her sustenance-spouting director, a handsome young Irishman who has been successful with shows in Dublin and London, but is still considered unproven in New York. McNeil liked Garrett when they were introduced backstage after an Off Broadway show, first because of his irreverent wit, but also because he'd remarked, as others had over the years, that McNeil and Shushie could pass for brother and sister, they looked so much alike. For some reason this observation always pleased McNeil. Then again, perhaps it was only Ripley's wishful thinking. Maybe the man has designs on Shushie.

Who reminds McNeil once again that the play opens in two weeks, that she's counting on him being there for opening night. It may not even run for more than a week, she says. Her nervousness is evident to him in the anxious way she taps her teeth. It's her first substantial role in an Off Broadway production.

He is suddenly surprised by a perverse impulse to mention Susan, not so much as a guilty confession but because, well, because she's on his mind. But he summons his sanity and assures Shushie that he will manage, one way or another, to get to New York for the opening.

"I'm really missing you, kiddo," she says.

"It's pretty miserable without you, too," McNeil says, worried that the words ring as falsely to her as they do there in his kitchen.

That false tone echoes in his ear, and to mute it he continues talking. Shushie is not a particularly social creature, always more prone to privacy, and he asks if she's gotten to be friendly with anyone in the cast.

"More or less," she says. "I've gone out for dinner a few times with that girl Carla. She plays the gay guy's first wife? You didn't get that letter yet? Oh, guess where she went to school."

"Our very own alma?"

"No, Hollins."

"Huh. What'd she say about the place?"

"That it's full of girls."

"Perceptive woman."

"I'm not sure you're really safe there. Safe for me, that is."

"I'm safe."

"Really, though. Sounds like that quaint little campus has student-teacher affairs in academic proportions."

Lockjawed, McNeil does his best to grunt appreciatively. "I'd say she's exaggerating a little."

"Only a little?"

"Shush," he says, "come on."

"Are you saying my name, or telling me I should shut up?"

"Yes," he says.

"Well, you watch yourself," she tells him.

He assures her that a letter is on the way, and when they hang up he's left wondering at his perverse impulse of confession minutes earlier. Grabbing a fresh toothpick, he settles down at his desk and mumbles out loud, "Lot of good that'd do her." He's begun talking to himself since he and Shushie have been apart.

With less effort now, he writes a letter to her, not just one of recent trivia concerning his jovial alcoholic landlord— helping old Sinclair adjust the basement plumbing one night, McNeil dropped a wrench on the man's hand and quickly apologized, at which Sinclair held out the two amputated stubs of his middle fingers and said, "That's okay, young fella, you just knocked my fingers off!"—McNeil writes not just of Sinclair and the factious faculty and stud-farm students he deals with each day, but a letter to offer some real, yes, sustenance.

This time he feels slightly more sincere.

The letter left in the mailbox on his corner, he grudgingly returns to his pile of papers, where Susan's is fourth from the top. He would like to read her essay first, but something, superstition or strange ethics, compels him to read them in their random order. Two B-pluses and an A-minus later, he is there.

REALITY AND ILLUSION IN *DEATH OF A SALESMAN*
Susan Bentley Barnes

He examines the sheets of her essay, front and back, for any subtleties addressed to him, but there is nothing: no note, no scent, no self-conscious scribblings. He reads it, slowly; another A-minus. Nothing especially dazzling or new, but a smart analysis and a more than competent prose style.

And now he has to be with her. It is nearly eleven, but she will be up. He'll ask her to go for a drink, though already it seems futile. He feels a bit ridiculous, dialing a girls' dormitory at eleven o'clock. At any time, really. The phone, he knows, is in the hallway, not in Susan's room, so the chances of her answering are slim. A voice that is not hers manages, through stifled laughter, to ask, "Hello?"

He asks for Susan *Barnes* (there is another Susan on the floor, who last week let him get so far as inviting her to lunch before clarifying the confusion), and hears in the background, "Susan! Su-san!" And then the conspiratorial silliness of "You have a male *call*-er."

When she picks up the phone and answers, it is that shy voice, the vulnerably uncertain tone that so suddenly puts him at ease, at least until he sees her. "You have a male *call*-er," McNeil says.

"Hey! Caleb. Yeah, don't remind me. Really, I can't help living here."

"Sorry, I know."

"What time is it?"

"I think about ten-thirty," he lies. "How's the Hobbes paper?"

"Oh, I'm having a whale of a time."

He laughs, a little too hard for such a modest pun, feels his face warming. "Listen, you want to take a break and get a drink—or some coffee? I'm all out of beer here," he says, staring at an extra six-pack of Rolling Rock in the corner.

She says softly, "Oh . . . wow," but the tone is not promising. He thinks she says "wow," "like," and especially "I mean" too much.

"Oh wow no?"

"What?"

"You mean Oh wow yeah, but oh wow you can't?"

"Yeah, kind of. I mean, I'd really like to, but I haven't taken this paper very far yet."

"Okay, that's cool," he tells her. McNeil has never in his life said "that's cool"—except in childhood, as an expression of admiration and awe—but it is another of the recurring phrases in Susan's vocabulary, and lately the words come to him almost involuntarily, especially in conversations with her.

"What about tomorrow night?" she says. "You said there was a film . . . ?"

Heartened, he scans the schedule taped to his refrigerator. "I think it's a double feature. The second one's probably better. Or do you want to see both?"

"Sure," she says. Then, with great girlish gaiety, "Yeah, let's," and McNeil, bolstered by her enthusiasm, strives to keep her on the phone, clinging to her voice and even happy to hear about tennis practice and shoulder injuries; happy too to answer her questions about his day (grading papers in solitary, then a departmental meeting that was nasty, brutish, and interminable, ha ha), until on her end there is a pause. McNeil hears a voice in the background, and then Susan saying, "I'd better get off, my roommate's got to make a long-distance call. How 'bout if I call you around five tomorrow, when I get home?"

"Yeah. I'll be here."

"All right. Pleasant dreams, then. And thanks for calling me, Caleb."

He loves the deliberate way she occasionally tags his name onto the end of sentences. His first night with her they had sat in a bar full of students, McNeil foolishly thrilling to the gossip of that's-the-visiting-professor-in-English-with-Susan-Barnes that he sensed all around them, thrilling also at the pleasure she took, with him at her side, in returning the greetings of friends. For McNeil, unmarried but many years monogamous, there was the additional pleasure of dusting off old anecdotes for someone who hadn't heard them ad nause-am. She asked about his once considering the priesthood, which he'd mentioned, and then regretted, during a class discussion of *Saint Joan*. McNeil evaded the question by saying something like, "Yeah, I've never dated a Wasp before." And Susan laughed, insisting she didn't believe him, to which McNeil only nodded and said, "It's true." Which it was, though he didn't bother mentioning he'd been seeing a Jewish woman for more than a decade.

"Caleb's not a very Catholic name, though, is it?" she asked.

"There's a Yankee Wasp connection," he said. "My father's side. But not so much that Protestants haven't always seemed a little bit 'other,' you know what I mean? Or didn't you grow up with those prejudices?"

She shrugged a vague acknowledgment.

"God, the Episcopalian kids in my town used to hate us," he said. "Called us 'Cat-lickers.' Wanted to know what we were doing 'up on the hill' anytime we rode our bikes through their neighborhood. We called them 'Piss-pickles.' Beat 'em in church-league basketball every year. Most of them were more interested in skiing, though. And tennis, of course," he added with a wink.

The two of them had compared and contrasted Catholics and Episcopalians, deciding guilt was the major difference, McNeil not mentioning money. She asked how early the obsession with guilt began, and he said that at age eleven he realized he'd willfully done enough dubious things that heaven was hopeless and he was going to fry in hell. Her face had furrowed sympathetically and she said, "That's terrible, Caleb," the first time she'd used his name, her hand inching nearer his on the table.

She had described, in turn, the heritage of privilege—private schools, private clubs, courts, coaches—McNeil granting silent absolution for the elitism of it all, acquiescing in the boyish buoyancy washing over him, even when he imagined Shushie sitting at the next table and shaking her head.

Inside the foyer of Susan's dorm, it was partly her height that kept him from kissing her, he suddenly found slightly intimidating the fact that she could almost look him level in the eye. Instead he touched her wrist as he left, and she briefly set her hand on his arm. Home at two-thirty, too giddy for sleep, he fell on the bed fully dressed, nuzzling his pillow like some teenager.

He woke early the next morning, his blood pulsing with possibility. It was a Saturday, but he felt so invigorated he considered rising to tackle the fearsome stack of essays on the floor beside his desk. Instead he had lain back to think of her, the sheet over his head, holding her.

His ear now numbly warm from the phone, he chins himself ten quick times on the metal bar that spans his high kitchen door frame. It occurs to him that he should be as righteous as her roommate, performing the pieties of long-distance calls, but he abandons the thought, heading upstairs to finally get some real work done. He places a four-foot plank of plywood across the arms of his easy chair, rests his feet on the bed, and continues with the ABC-ing of papers. He had begun to worry that maybe he was more pursuer than pursued in this little drama, but the adrenaline coursing through his legs now suggests otherwise.

He was a teenager the last time he felt quite so vital. Pathetic:

thirty years old and already a stranger to romance. Then again, wasn't this only the novelty of someone new? A novelty that will no doubt wear off in time, given the chance. And what would he be left with then? Not, he suspects, a woman he could spend the rest of his life with.

But even knowing the impossibility of Susan, and that Shushie is inevitable, he falls asleep in his chair creating scenes with the girl, later dreaming that he is tonguing a mouth lined with the dry leather grip of a tennis racket.

As he drives his dying Datsun through Thursday morning, every tall girl with long brown hair is Susan, every girl in a knee-length denim skirt. But each time he is wrong. He decides to detour through the tennis courts, where Susan is bound to be hitting, and is, with some curly-haired blond bastard, who splays the fingers of his left hand to accent the follow-through of his oh-so-perfect technique, the two of them laughing over lobs lost in the sun, strings of their rackets outlined in perfect letter *P*'s. If she turns and sees his car he'll later have to explain being here, but she is concentrating too intently on returning the blond brute's nasty serve.

Spitting his splintered toothpick out the window and pushing the accelerator to the car's rusted-out floor, he flies past other drivers until the man in the red Audi on his right is the department chairman, and McNeil behaves himself at thirty miles an hour. The car stalls at the parking lot entrance, as it has whenever he's given Susan a lift, McNeil each time blush-mumbling the embarrassed apology that would never be necessary with Shushie.

By the time he reaches his office he has forgiven Susan her tennis partner, but cannot concentrate on the remaining papers he must read, nor on the students who come to see him, each stopping in the middle of some sentence until his eyes wander back into focus. At twelve-thirty he sneaks away from his office and rambles across the main campus, looking purposeful, but in fact only looking for Susan, aware that he is making himself a fool for this girl, who would seek him out, after all, if she really wished to see him. But somehow it is always he who seems so intensely urgent when he leaves her at her door with a kiss and a question: What are you doing *tomorrow* night?

Before he knows it he has spent a full hour foolishly searching among the blue jeans and backpacks. He must collect his thoughts for a two o'clock class.

It is the class in which Susan sits in the second row, and McNeil, despite the difficulty of concentration, has prepared a brilliant lecture on Samuel Beckett. Susan is not there as he runs through the attendance, and though he stalls so that his brilliance will not be lost on her, he is forced to begin without her. Ten minutes into class, she slips through the rear door of the room and sits in one of the last rows. McNeil acknowledges her presence with a nod, and she raises her eyebrows and winces in apology.

At three-fifteen there are questions, comments, and comely young women about the lectern. Some advance aggressively ("Don't you think it's reductive for critics to equate Godot with God?"), others hang slightly back, waiting to pose their questions more privately. This was Susan's routine earlier in the semester, often accompanying him back to his office or to the parking lot. Now she does not seem to see him as she gathers her books and bows into the hallway.

Not at five, but at five-thirty she calls. She doesn't mention his lecture, except to apologize for being late. He asks if she'd like to get some dinner with him before the film. She would, but she and her roommate just polished off a bag of chocolate croissants, and after an almost-all-nighter, she needs to nap for an hour. "How 'bout if I pick you up at seven?" she asks.

"You don't trust my driving anymore?"

"No, no, it'll just be easier, since you have to go out of your way for me."

"What are you gonna do," he asks, "borrow a car?"

"No, I've got one."

"From where?"

"I have a car."

"You *own* a car?"

"Yeah," she says, almost reluctantly.

"Oh." It occurs to him once again how little he really knows about her. He also wonders why it has always until now been he who has gone out of his way, her car a secret even when his was lent to a friend, McNeil that night hoofing several miles home in the rain after walking Susan to her dorm.

"Caleb? I think I'm going to need directions."

Which McNeil provides before hanging up, sitting down, the day's mail before him with a bottle of beer that says twist-off cap but leaves deep marks in his thumb and forefinger and won't come off until he covers the damn thing with a dish towel. He is not hungry, his appetite lost lately in the constant and adolescent anxiety of his stomach. He reads the latest letter from Shushie, which he would not open while waiting for Susan's call. It is rife with I'm yours I love you please try to come to New York some weekend soon I'll send you the money if you need it is only ten o'clock now but I'm going to bed to dream about you.

But McNeil tells himself this is only the language of long distance, not of daily life together, and he won't let her passion off the page.

Susan knocks, and when he goes to the door they do their affectionate arm-touching thing. Her blue Honda Accord, apparently new, sits in the driveway, and she is an excellent driver. She wears perfume, which he has always automatically dismissed as a silly sort of vanity—Shushie never wears it—yet it flatters him to think of this girl so consciously preparing for him, and in fact the scent is pleasant, even stirring. Like Shushie, he has noticed, she's never pierced her ears, which seems surprisingly unconventional for Susan.

Their conversation tonight is cumbersome, full of awkward pauses and unnatural rhythms, and while he tells Susan what he knows about the director Lina Wertmuller, he sounds to himself like he is lecturing still, feels old and stuffy, except for his legs, which are once again full of unreined adrenalin. It occurs to him that it's ridiculous to go to another movie; nearly all of their dates have been to this or the campus film series, and they've probably spent more time sitting next to each other in silence than actually conversing.

Susan cuts off the engine in the theatre parking lot and reaches across his lap for the glove compartment. "I'd better not forget my glasses this time," she says almost into his chest. McNeil can't decide if there is something more to this maneuver or if she really is only getting her glasses. It's encouraging, in any case. He has begun to open his door, and the interior light briefly reveals the lovely white down of her jaw and upper lip. He figures it's probably an annoyance to her, something she considers unfeminine, although to him it is strangely attractive.

He is unable to concentrate through most of the first film, thinking only of Susan's hand, which he takes soon enough, giving it a small squeeze that she firmly returns. When *Swept Away* begins, she leans against McNeil's arm. At one point she removes her hand from his to adjust her glasses, and his hand slides onto her thigh. During the sex scenes his left hand looms large on her leg, and McNeil is certain that people on either side of them are watching it, but to move it is equally awkward, and it stays.

Her eyes are glassy with unshed tears when the film ends. McNeil sets his hand on her shoulder, asking, "All right?" as they file out, as if anything would be wrong with her. She smiles and nods, a bit embarrassed, and outside McNeil knows it's too late to suggest going for drinks, his wretched refrain, decides he will let her take him home; perhaps it's the privacy of his own house that has made her insist on driving.

At a red light Susan says, "They should never have left the island," and McNeil agrees, which leaves little to say, so he disagrees. Shushie is in the back seat, shaking her head again. He considers flattering Susan with the information that he cannot concentrate these days for thinking about her, but he knows such a line would be pushing it at this point.

When she pulls into McNeil's driveway and switches off the ignition, it's a good sign. "Will you come in?"

"No, I have to sleep. I have to be up early."

"Just for a bit. I'll make sure you get home soon."

"No, really, Caleb."

"Okay." He forces a smile, but his chapped lips crack and prevent it, reminding him to wet them this time before kissing her. Somehow he's felt like a complete novice each time he has kissed Susan good night: the alignment is never quite right, or he makes a ridiculous smacking sound, or parts his lips more or less than her own. As she often does while they say good night, Susan toys with the end of his wool scarf. She's never noticed his initials embroidered in small letters in the corner, and on the other end the words *from your most lover*, which was what Shushie's little sister, at age six, had once called McNeil. He half hopes Susan will discover the embroidery and ask, though he's also relieved that she overlooks it. Neurotically insistent, ever the planner, he knows Susan is traveling with the tennis team tomorrow night, and in spite of himself asks, "When can we get together again?"

Susan straightens. Dropping her hand from his scarf, she stumbles over "umm's" and "I mean's" before announcing that, well, she thinks a relationship should be "defined."

And McNeil's heart sinks.

"I really enjoy being with you," she says, "but I liked it when things were a little more casual. I just think I'm too tense with you. Something's not right. Don't you think?"

He rubs at the unfastened buckle of his seat belt. "Yeah, I guess," he says.

"It's not that things are that bad. It's just, I mean, I can see where it's going, and I think you must, too. Or you will."

But McNeil already does see, and has seen, despite his persistence, and realizes she is only being more honest than he. Which still does not mean he wants to hear her say: "I just don't think we should see each other so seriously."

He stares out the windshield at the wooden swing swaying on his front porch. "Yeah, you're right," he manages. Adolescent in this to the very end, he summons his old high school ethic of never allowing a girl to think she's devastated him.

He realizes what a pitiful little boy he must nonetheless seem to her when she tells him, "I know you'll find the right person eventually."

"No, it's not—I'm not . . ." He begins, but is unable to tell her that he already has.

And Susan blushes for reversing their classroom roles, mumbles, "No, well, I didn't mean to sound . . ."

"It's okay," McNeil nods. "Really."

"I'd still like to go to the film series with you . . ."

"Okay," he tries to say agreeably, but he's sure he'll never call her again. Still, he leans over to kiss her as he had planned, wondering if he is already transgressing her new directive. But she does not avert her face, only kisses him back automatically and evenly. With a final, subdued "Good night," he is out of the car and walking slowly up the creaky stairs to his porch, steadying an arm of the swing with his hand, aware that he is somehow only playing at solemnity as he turns to wave once from the door. But once inside he finds himself smiling. Chins himself on the bar in the kitchen doorway, swings into the kitchen and hungrily tears open an orange. He is free. Shushie's number rushes at him like a song.

▼

O SOLE MIO

▲

My son is at that self-conscious stage of adolescence. It's not just the hours I know he spends before the bathroom mirror. Or that Monday morning, as Maggie later told me, he changed shirts three times before leaving for school. No, I can see it in the way he will stride across the kitchen in his tight Levi's and blue turtleneck with rips at the collarbone, to take down from the cabinet a can of tomato paste his mother cannot reach. It's the way he now appears in the kitchen as I get three eggs for the girl next door, shirtless, his hair dripping in stringy brown points from his shower, nothing but a pair of white gym shorts covering his slender buttocks and the gentle swinging motion at the front. He has become acutely aware of his body in recent months, and takes pride in it. I notice that the neighbor girl, on departing, takes in the sight of this indifferent fellow once more with a covert sweep of the eyes.

Humming to himself, he stands profile in the adjacent laundry room, a single grey sock draped over one damp shoulder, left hand scratching the sun-browned skin of his hip red. He leans over the noise of the dryer tumbling through its cycle, affecting an expression of concentration as he sorts through unmatched socks. He knows I am watching him; he must not let on.

I gaze at the glistening golden hairs on his finely toned legs—legs a girl might be happy to have—and remember bathing him sixteen years ago, musing over his tininess, his dependence on us, yet his utter indifference to us. Somehow envying then his having dwelt within Maggie's womb.

I try to recall all the things I told myself at his age to be sure to remember as a father. And I don't remember anything. To be more like my mother, perhaps. I don't know.

He finds the other grey sock and swings by me with the grace of a dancer as I get up and move to the refrigerator. It's almost as if he is mocking my sprouting waistline with his tight, tanned body. I watch him fly up the stairs and decide not to have a second beer.

"Dry your hair!" Maggie admonishes as she passes him on the stairs, and I smile as she enters the kitchen laden with a wicker laundry basket. I tug on the faded red ponytail that is just long enough to rest on her shoulder, and say that I am going to my office at the university, that I have work to do. She asks me, can't I even spend Saturday around the house, and wasn't I going to help her with the storm windows? Frankly, she is much better than I at such handyman activities. For instance, we finally bought a small piano last week for our daughter's lessons, and once we got it up on the front porch, it was clear that I would have to remove the door. I went to the basement and got my father's old toolbox, took out a screwdriver and began to remove the hinges. "Don't be ridiculous," Maggie said. She scooped up a hammer and a tenpenny nail and nudged me out of her way. Placing the nail against the hinge pin, she tapped the pin loose in two deft motions and easily plucked it free. I stood coping with my incompetence while Maggie, crouching, repeated the procedure on the lower hinge.

She now looks at me somewhat peevishly to say, "I thought after we got the windows in, baby would be awake, and maybe we could drive to Chittenden's." It is a lovely fall day, the foliage is at its peak, and retrieving pumpkins from Chittenden's Cider Mill has been an October weekend routine since Nick was a baby.

And yet I tell her that I have forty-four papers to read. There is next weekend, I tell her. Halloween is two weeks off.

"Okay," she says, and retreats just like that. She picks the wicker basket up from the arms of the high chair and walks into the laundry room.

I can't decide if this is genuine or tactical on her part, but either way it hardly matters. I tell her okay, that I can do the papers tomorrow. "Are we ready?" I ask.

I expect at least a smile for my compliance, but Maggie takes my impractical spontaneity and turns it inside out with mature responsibility. "Let me get another load in and dry these things. I'd rather not have to wake baby."

I tell her all right, but can't help adding that there's no sense in going if she's planning to be like this, aware that it's a rather clichéd thing to say. My son has lately launched a personal campaign against clichés, and I, it seems, despite my red pen marks noting "stale syntax" on students' papers, am one of the great offenders.

"No, we'll go, we'll go," Maggie says nodding, forcing a smile that doesn't quite manage to curve her mouth but merely stretches the straight line of her lips wider.

Nick has not accompanied us on our weekend rides for several years now, but Chittenden's is an exception, and I call up the stairs to ask if he will come with us.

He doesn't think so, he says.

I sense I might coax him into it, and put on a Pavarotti record while Maggie finishes with the wash. Perhaps it will perk her up. Pavarotti has that effect upon us. Mainly, though, the record puts me in mind of the Italian operas my father would listen to and explain to me when I was young. His familiarity with something most Americans deemed dauntingly high culture surprised me, and he would tell me that just as I went to see Tom Mix or Hopalong Cassidy every weekend, in Italy he would go to the opera on Saturdays.

It upsets Nick that I never learned Italian from my parents. He thinks I've ignored a valuable part of our heritage, and of course he's right. I don't dare tell him that I was older than he is before I stopped being embarrassed by my father's accent and poor English.

And yet Nickie doesn't much care for Pavarotti. Though he likes the song "O Sole Mio." And "Funiculi Funicula." He asked me recently what the words *o sole mio* meant. I told him and he nodded, apparently pleased. As I do, he often wanders through the house singing the first lines of the song in a sort of mock tenor, although he is sometimes embarrassed to find that I have a student visiting, or that Maggie is in the kitchen having coffee with a neighbor. He is in good spirits now, having tied for second this morning in a cross-country match against sixty other boys. Pavarotti brings him downstairs with a burst of, *"Che bella cosa 'na iurnata . . . ,"* which Nick uniquely renders as "no you are not-a." Life's complexity in a nutshell. He pours himself a glass of grape juice and begins thumbing through the phone book.

Maggie sets the washer, which sounds like some giant watch being wound, and comes to sit in the kitchen with a sigh. Intended to make me feel indolent, or merely to evoke sympathy? It manages both. "So I guess we'll get the windows later?" she asks.

"Yeah. Unless you'd rather do them now."

"I guess not," she says. This may mean just the opposite, but I choose not to consider that she is being ambiguous. Half of the trick to marriage, it seems to me, is learning how to interpret one's spouse as one is meant to when he or she does not say what she means. I realize, of course, that I am responsible for divining her exact meaning, and I'm prepared to accept any consequences for this self-serving interpretation.

I have been studying the snug-fitting running pants she's wearing—navy-blue stretch nylon—part of an outfit I bought for her last birthday, now with cat hairs all stuck to the front. Last year they were loose on her. Since the baby was born, she has taken to wearing the pants almost daily. "You like those pants, huh?" I ask.

She has been scraping the excess peanut butter from a knife onto the inside rim of the jar, and looks up quickly. She does not so much ask as accuse, "You think I look too fat in them?"

I do my best to look offended. "No!"

"Judas priest, Mom," Nick says half laughing, "he asked a harmless question about a gift he gave you."

Maggie pinches at the excess flesh on her waist and says, "This is the gift he gave me, and it wasn't a harmless question."

It would be a pleasure to have our son on my side for once, but instead I feel slightly guilty because he has misinterpreted the remark in my favor. For I do think the pants tend to highlight her present heaviness, and they're a bit sloppy to be part of a daily ensemble.

"You guys are too much," Nick says, resting his foot on a chair to tie his sneakers. He has recently said that we bicker too much, and he can see just where we go wrong in every argument.

Maggie appears to be sulking now, flipping through the paper as if she's alone in the room, and then standing to briskly wipe toast crumbs from the table into her hand.

I say that I just thought she might want to wear some other pants in case we stop anyplace else. I notice that Nick looks a bit surprised, realizing that maybe he did defend me unnecessarily.

"What else do I have to wear," she asks, "that I can decently fit into?"

"What about the stuff my sister sent you?"

"I'm not so big that I have to wear that still."

"Okay, you're fine as you are."

"I'll change," she says, and I see that I've turned her earlier tactic upon her.

In his black T-shirt that reads NO NUKES, the letter *o* a flaming golden circle, Nick rolls his eyes. "You guys need a new script," he says, and springs up the stairs again.

Fortunately, his remark gives us the benefit of having a common critic, and I can see a mellowing in Maggie's face when she turns to me, brushing crumbs from her hands at the sink. "Really, it doesn't matter to me," I say in a more sincere tone than I could earlier have conjured.

"Of course not," she says, and pinches my arm. "I'll change and get the baby. Will you call Gail? And see if you can get him to come with us, too," she says, gesturing her head at the ceiling.

I step out the back and call Gail, who seems to be talking to a cobweb in the woodpile. "Go to the bathroom and get a sweater; we're going to get some pumpkins and cider."

A cry of "Goody!" and a cartwheel, which gives me greater confidence in venturing into the distance-running marriage counselor's room.

He is lying on the bed reading *Runner's World.* His radio blares a program called "Songs of the Sixties." He senses he was deprived of an important decade, having only been born in 1964. He loves to look through old *Life* magazines in the library or in people's attics, or at any television documentary dealing with that decade. He is a strange one for the past. Nick looks to our small city as I once knew it with respect, nostalgically. He likes to take the Volkswagen for dates, but he thinks we would be better off with trolleys.

He rolls over onto his back. "You going now?"

"Soon." I glance from the pictures of Frank Shorter tacked to his bulletin board, to the grey-and-red Indian blanket on the wall, to the poster of Peter Fonda advertising *Easy Rider.* My brother gave him that. "You know," I say, "it smells like running shoes in here."

"I'm immune to it."

There's a jar of Vaseline on the table by his bed. I try to remember whether he came in alone last night. I must be staring at it, because he says, blushing, "It's for breaking in my new running shoes."

Oh, I think, slightly relieved, but I innocently ask, "What?"

"Mom's Vaseline."

"Oh." On his desk there is a graduation picture of a curious-looking dark-haired girl. I don't recognize her. I would like to see what is written on the back. "Who's this?" I ask.

From behind the magazine he answers, "Mm, nobody special."

"What's her name?"

"Helen," he murmurs. "The face that sunk a thousand ships."

"Sank," I say, "past participle."

"Sank, sunk, whatever."

"She's not so bad looking. 'Nick, you're a great kid, and I feel lucky to have known you. Good luck in everything you do.' " He looks up from his magazine, but sees I have not turned the picture over. "Close?" I ask.

"Close enough."

There is a pause, and he half turns back to his magazine in the awkwardness of our exchange, avoiding my eyes without committing the rudeness of actually reading.

"Who was that girl with the red hair today? She put her hand on your back after the race."

"That's Dana."

"The girl you went out with last night?"

"Yeah."

"She's very cute. You seem to be susceptible to redheads." And then, before I can stop myself, I have said it. "Like father, like son." And in the campaign he has launched against clichés, I am now under attack.

"Dad, for an English teacher, it's amazing how many clichés

you toss around. I mean, I know you were kind of joking, but you do it all the time."

I tell him he's right and apologize. I'm not a Little League parent, but I say that if he wins next Wednesday's meet, I'll cut down drastically on clichés. He ran a fine race today, and I cherish the image of him crossing the finish line with an upraised hand clasping the hand of his best friend, but I know he had enough kick left to have won the race. Still, I don't want to seem anything less than abundantly proud, and I tell him how good Maggie and I and his little sister felt watching him, and squeeze his knee, singing teasingly with the radio, *"Sonny, thank you for the joy that you've given me-e-e . . ."*

But my sentimentality embarrasses him, and he points out, "Dad, it's not 'Sonny' boy, it's 'Sunny' sunshine, with a *u.* "

I have heard the song for probably fifteen years and never realized this. "Oh," I say. I carry my sideswiped sentimentality out the door with me like an ignominious wound, remembering to call back to him to come with us.

Never failing to surprise me, he now replies, "Okay, Dad."

In the kitchen we are all together getting ready to go. I check the stove: off, off, off, off. The oven: off. Nick looks vaguely surprised to see me draw a metal comb from the breast pocket of my corduroy jacket and pull it through my hair. He doesn't expect a man my age to be concerned with his appearance.

I know that he is still full of this morning's race, and I prod him with a question so that we are both reliving its glory. He tells me his friend Mouse probably would have taken second place alone except that his jockstrap malfunctioned during the last half mile. Understandably, in view of the many spectators, he didn't care to risk the consequences of a vigorous final kick. Last week it was Nick and Mouse and Cubby all tying for first place in a dual meet against a small rural school. I envied their camaraderie at hearing how, in the last half mile, just before emerging from the woods where they had agreed to tie, Nick told the others, "I changed my mind—see ya later," and burst ahead for several seconds at an impossible pace before slowing to rejoin his laughing teammates.

He is now interrupted by his sister, who comes from the living room where she has stopped the stereo in the middle of a repeated "O Sole Mio." She asks what is that song about that Nick and I always sing. Here is my chance to impress him. Despite the little Italian I know, I am able to sort out the few words of this song I have heard all my life. I tell her it's a song a man sings to his lover, exclaiming, "What a beautiful thing is a day of sunshine!"

Nickie looks up from his seat at the kitchen table. "What?"

"Yeah," I say, encouraged, and I go on.

> *Che bella cosa 'na iurnata è sole!*
> What a beautiful thing is a day of sunshine.
> *N'aria serena dopo 'na tempesta!*
> A clear blue sky after the storm.
> *Pe' ll'aria fresca pare già 'na festa!*
> As though the fresh air were in festival.
> *Che bella cosa 'na iurnata è sole!*
> What a beautiful thing is a day of sunshine.

Nick looks annoyed. "I thought it was 'O s-o-n of mine'?"

"No," I say. "*Sole,* as in solar," and I point at his T-shirt.

"Yeah, yeah, I get it," he says.

"Now we're even. Sonny." Our eyes meet briefly.

"How the hell can anyone sing so passionately about the damn sun?" he asks, cleaning his thumbnail with the prong of a fork.

Gail tells him not to swear, and poses another dangerous question before we leave. Can we stop by Holliday Murphy's house so she can invite her friend along with us? A precocious nine-year-old and the daughter of two psychiatrists, Holliday Murphy once sat with us watching a television show in which two children vied for the affections of their parents, and uttered in a cool and analytic tone, "Sibling rivalry." She is a cute girl, forever in a baseball cap, perhaps always too ready with an opinion for one so young. And I don't think we really need her company today.

I tell Gail I think it would be nice if we were together just as a family this afternoon, but apparently Maggie has told her earlier that it would be fine to invite Holliday along. "She hasn't seen Holliday all week," she now adds ever so tactfully in front of Gail.

I tell Maggie I agreed not to go to the office so that we could all be together this afternoon. "Let's just have it be the four—the five of us for a few hours."

She says I know damn well that between the baby and everything else, nobody's going to pay enough attention to Gail, so why not let her have a friend along? Why, she asks me, do I have to be so exclusive about these outings?

And I, in turn, ask how I am to have any influence with our children if she's going to undermine me each time in front of them.

"*You* undermined?" she shrieks, tugging baby's pants on fiercely. "I told her she could invite Holliday half an hour ago. You're contradicting what *I* told her."

From behind a half-peeled banana, my son asks, "Come on, do we have to have this again?"

"Don't talk with your mouth full," Maggie tells him.

"Look," I say, "I'm not trying to contradict you, and I think Holliday's a nice kid, but it would be nice to have it just be us this afternoon. *Famiglia solamente.*"

"It doesn't matter," Gail says, somehow the ever calm product of Irish and Italian tempers.

"It does so," Maggie says. "You wanted her to come, I told you she could, and you still want her to come."

"But, Maggie," I say, "if it doesn't matter to her."

"It does matter to her. And it matters to me not to be con-
tradicted when I tell her something."

Nick stands up, tosses his banana peel into the sink, and
announces, "I can't take an afternoon of this. You can go
ahead without me," and he moves to the back door.

A few years ago I could grab him by the arm to prevent
such a departure, but he is not now of an age or size so easily
approached. "Nickie, don't leave," I ask him. "We're not
going to argue. Come on."

"Dad," he says, "I'd just rather be alone than listen to it."

"Come on. If Gail wants Holliday to come, that's fine. Let's
all go, at least. We always go to Chittenden's together."

"Look," he says, "I know you guys have been going to
Chittenden's every fall since I was a baby, and I know I always
go with you, and I know I'm going to hear about the time you
rode the tandem out there and got a flat and how Mom had
to fix it, and I know baby's going to puke or something, or
Dad's going to run a stop sign and you guys are going to bicker, so I'm just not going to come along. I'll be thinking about
you. I'm sure I'll be able to imagine it all perfectly."

I never realized we'd so overdone the story of the flat tire.
"Come on," I say, "nobody's going to bicker. Besides, I want to
hear more about the race."

But he is quickly out the back door. I stand at the kitchen
window and watch him crossing the yard, then scaling the
fence. In a moment he is hopping the stream and striking out
across the golf course that borders our backyard. Shoulders
hunched, hands thrust deep in his pockets, he looks almost
fragile as he strides across the lush green fairway in the day's
full sun.

My friend Caswell has written a poem to his son. "Icarus,
Come Back," it is called. And although Nick is on no particularly perilous course, that title occurs to me repeatedly now.
As I watch him head for the woods where we once walked
hand in hand together, I know that eventually, as all sons

finally do, he will come back. He will return when the stock of stories he has heard about us are not just the tiresome anecdotes of nettlesome parents, but the cherished moments of two lives. Yet it will be some years more before he realizes. He doesn't realize that he is himself compiling right now the little narrative boredoms that his son will one day hear a stranger recite.

▼

CHEATERS

▲

If it kept up he'd have to cancel lunch with Mackenzie, the old Canadian lawyer. Brendan couldn't tell for sure yet, but sitting hunched over his desk, sifting through an unlikely accident report from Aetna, he recognized a familiar blossom of pain in his lower abdomen. One thing he knew by now, if he was about to go into labor with a kidney stone, he wanted to be home in bed. Not sitting across from Mackenzie in some restaurant, or driving frantically across town, and not gasping on the little sofa here in his office, but in bed, with the door shut against his wife and daughters so he could moan and thrash with dignity.

He'd already passed two painful stones, the first about ten years ago, at twenty-seven. He'd been a little bit awed by the fact that each had occurred immediately after an affair. To anyone else it might not seem like much of a coincidence, but after the second round of urinating blood in the wake of great infidelities, he was half convinced there was more than an excess of calcium causing his intestinal grief. As if guilt alone wasn't enough, his body had worked out its own private penance for him.

Still, he'd been on the fidelity wagon for nearly three years now. Since the thing with Poppie Hansen, he'd hardly looked at another woman. Somewhere between kidney and conscience, important signals had been crossed. He pulled the black desk phone nearer and could feel the pain building slightly, though it hadn't moved at all. Kneading delicately at his right side, he dialed Martin Mackenzie's office to cancel their lunch, but the old Canuck was not in. The secretary asked if there was a message, and Brendan told her his daughter was sick at school, that he had to pick her up right away. Somehow he didn't think a young PI hobbled with kidney stones sounded especially promising, particularly to a health nut like Mackenzie.

He pushed the phone away and watched helplessly as it nudged a yellow legal pad off the other edge of the desk. The pain still hadn't shifted, it just grew more intense, and he began to wonder if it might be his appendix. That wasn't the sort of thing you could sit around and wait to pass. If the pain would only move toward his groin, he'd know, but he also knew that was when it turned nasty. He rose gingerly and shuffled over to the coatrack. But after pulling his jacket on he slumped back down at the desk, breathing heavily and trying to remember just what side the goddamned appendix was supposed to be on.

A jingle sounded from the old strap of sleigh bells attached to the outer office door. Not Mackenzie, he hoped. He leaned over his desk to peer out, causing his side to throb. A rugged-looking guy about his own age, in corduroys and a worn suede sports coat, stood with one hand still on the doorknob. "Uh, Brendan Kellogg?"

"Yes!" He rubbed gently at his stomach beneath the desk. "Sorry, but I was just on my way out—I've got kind of an emergency."

"Oh. Oh, no problem. You be in tomorrow?" The man had advanced as far as the doorway connecting the tiny outer office, and stood scratching at his shirt with a single silver car key. He was handsome and tastefully disheveled, with a short growth of greying beard. Like Brendan, he was tall enough to have to dip his head in approaching the office doorway.

Brendan stood up, grunting lightly with the effort. "Yeah, if you could come in a little earlier tomorrow morning?"

"I c-c-c-can't make it tomorrow morning," the man said, squinting his eyes tightly on the stuttered word.

Brendan peered more closely at the face. Something about him, the stutter, or the green eyes behind wire-rimmed glasses, was vaguely familiar. One of the many half-remembered faces from high school, maybe. "Well, if you'd like to leave your name and set up a time tomorrow afternoon. I'll be back by three." He was breathing through his nose now, trying to suppress involuntary groans as he spoke.

"Sure, sometime around three'd be good," the man said, nodding slightly.

Brendan sat down again and reached for his pen. "And you're Mr. . . . ?"

"Dan Truax." He stepped closer and extended his hand, the back of his fingers stained with varnish or brown paint.

"Truax," Brendan said aloud, jotting the name. Yes, Truax, that was it. Junior year of high school, the end of baseball season. The rawhide webbing on Brendan's old first-baseman's glove had begun to fray; a throw from the shortstop finally tore half the pocket right out of the glove, though he'd somehow managed to hold on to the ball. They were playing Winooski that day, and Truax was Winooski's first baseman, the only other lefty on either team. When it became obvious in the game's delay that no one on Brendan's team had a glove he could use, this Truax, bearded now, had come jogging from his team's dugout chewing a fat wad of bubble gum. "Here you go," he'd said, tossing the glove from several yards away. "You c-c-can leave it on the bag after." It was a fine new glove, a Wilson, with the name TRUAX neatly engraved on the long thumb with a wood-burning pen.

At the top of the final inning, with two out and a mouthy

kid from Winooski on first, Truax had come to bat. He swung
at the first pitch and hit a high pop-up that soared above his
team's on-deck circle. Brendan lurched forward, then side-
stepped and backpedaled as the wind carried the ball behind
him, Brendan finally slamming against the visiting team's
dugout screen and snagging the ball at shoulder height. There
were shouts of "Ingrate!" and "Try that one with your own
glove!" from some of the Winooski players behind the screen.
Truax came walking over to first, actually smiling, and said,
"Nice c-c-catch" as Brendan handed him the glove. It was the
most gracious gesture Brendan could imagine, though all he
could think to say was, "Yeah, sorry. Nice glove."

Should he remind Truax of that? Better to wait. The pain in
his side had let up slightly, but he knew it could start in again
any minute. "And what was it you wanted to see me about?"

"Well . . . I understand you do surveillance work . . ." His
cheeks, above the beard, were reddening.

Brendan could already guess. "Yeah, I do *some* surveillance
work."

"I don't know if you take this sort of job or not, but uh, it's,
it'd be my wife." He made a slight shrugging gesture.

Brendan nodded and said, "Uh-huh," waiting for him to go
on, trying to affect the sort of indifference that would assure
Truax he wasn't being laughed at as a cuckold, that this was
not an uncommon request. He was glad now that he hadn't
mentioned the glove incident. A man in Truax's position
wasn't looking for recognition.

"You suspect that she's . . . ?"

"Having an affair," Truax said quickly, not quite looking
Brendan in the eye.

"Yeah, I see." He gestured Truax to a chair. "Uh, I don't
really take that kind of case these days. I can tell you the
state's had no-fault divorce legislation on the books for years,
so if that's what's in the picture, my services aren't even needed. You don't have to *prove* anything for a divorce."

Truax was unmoved. He sat patiently shaking his head. "That's not what I'm after. I don't want a divorce." He paused, glancing at a pigeon settling on the window ledge outside. "It's just that something's g-g-go-go-going on, and I want to know." His big stained hands were set in his lap; he clicked the car key against his thumbnail, waiting for Brendan to speak.

"Have you confronted her with, uh, your suspicions?"

"Yes, but of c-c-c—" And here he stopped. Sitting in the chair, he raised his left hand to shoulder height, index finger extended, almost pointing at Brendan. He smiled faintly, almost apologetically, and slowly lowered his hand about six inches, drawing it across in front of himself in an L shape. ". . . course she denies it," he said in a calm, slow expulsion of breath. Then, "Sorry, it's part of the therapy for my stutter."

Brendan nodded.

"She denies it, but I wouldn't have c-c-c—I wouldn't want to hire you unless I thought there was something there. Look. I'm not gonna go out and shoot anybody. I'm not gonna beat my wife up if it turns out I'm right. It's just, I just c-c-"—again the L in mid-air, a sort of half blessing—"can't . . . con-cen-trate on my work these days," he said with great deliberate-ness. Almost whispering he added, "I need to know." He stopped and stared at Brendan, his mouth collapsing into a scowl. "The signs are all there, you know? I mean, suddenly all these long lunches and nights out with girlfriends that I c-c-can never really verify, all that, but little things, too. Stuff a husband can tell. Brushing her teeth eight times a day, always shaving her *legs* these days, you know? She even seems to dress a whole lot more self-c-c-c-"—the index finger—"con-scious-ly," he said slowly. "It's not like a woman who's been married ten years. Not the one I've been married to, anyway. I know something's going on."

"I'll tell you," Brendan said. "I've got this emergency I've gotta head out for right now. Think about it tonight. If you

still want me tomorrow, I'll meet you here at three and we can
go over things."

Truax stood and solemnly extended his big hand again.
"I'll see you tomorrow, then."

From the window, Brendan watched him leave and then
rushed out to his own car. The pain had moved forward and
down now, and he drove straight for home, running two red
lights. The urologist had told him that when the pain began
he should drink water and try to stand erect as much as he
could to facilitate the stone's quick passage. Stand erect. That
was what got him this way the other times, it seemed. "If you
can," the urologist had said, "you should even go jogging."
The man clearly had never passed a kidney stone.

At home Brendan stood in the kitchen drinking water,
then groaned his way from room to room as long as he could,
until finally the pain was too much and he got into bed.
Rachel wasn't home, probably tutoring at the grade school;
Beth and Addie would still be there, too. He pulled a pillow
over his face and couldn't help picturing the jagged brown
bitch of a stone tearing away at the soft narrow tissue leading
to his bladder. It had to be a big one. After a while he hobbled into the bathroom and took a Vicodin left over from
Rachel's ear infection, but the pain persisted on and off for
nearly two hours. When it finally stopped, he fell into the sort
of exhausted, sweaty sleep of release that he associated with
spent sexual energy.

The next morning, standing at the toilet with a paper cup,
he watched a tiny, reddish-brown calculus, the size of four or
five grains of beach sand, float into his urine. "Little fucker,"
he said, and washed it off before sealing it into an envelope.

Truax would be back in the afternoon, and though Brendan
had turned down a dozen similar jobs, he would agree to take
this one on. There was only one other licensed investigator in

town, a less than reputable character, which meant Brendan could rely on enough corporate work and retainers from law firms without having to take on what he called "motel jobs." The independence was a distinct improvement over his days as a police detective—his income was better, too—but it could be dull labor at times. He'd taken on two or three truly "private" cases in the past, jobs that had been interesting in a gossipy sort of way; but usually he was just hustling around the county interviewing witnesses for upcoming court cases, running checks on car accidents, gun registrations, character references, writing up piddly reports for the boys in three-piece suits.

Checking Truax's wife out to see if she was really getting it on with someone might actually be a welcome diversion. And aside from that, he'd have a hard time saying no to the former first baseman.

Truax was there at three-fifteen; he was prepared to spend what it took. Brendan got out a yellow legal pad and suggested they make a schedule of Liz Truax's activities. He tried to sound casual, but already there was something unpleasant and inappropriate about the arrangement that made him feel awkward.

Truax and his wife ran a furniture-building business, a fairly prosperous one Brendan remembered having seen in a cluster of new shops across from the old Maltex factory. Liz Truax kept books and assisted in the shop three mornings a week. She swam at the Y most Tuesday afternoons, was active in the League of Women Voters, which met twice a month, and attended an art history class at the university on Monday and Wednesday afternoons. Otherwise, Truax said, at least three afternoons a week and most Saturdays she was on her own, ostensibly either home, shopping, at the library, or visiting with friends. Truax suspected her friend Paula was sometimes prepared to cover for his wife. They had no children; a young son had died two years earlier of heart complications.

After putting it off for several days, Brendan decided on Monday—*First Day of Spring*, his calendar said—to start dusting Liz Truax. He'd never seen her in person, but her husband had provided two recent photographs.

The art history lecture theatre was on the lower level of the university museum. Brendan wandered through the collection upstairs until students began to arrive. Picking Liz Truax out was easier than he'd expected. In the corridor downstairs, she stood in the midst of a flock of undergraduates, a tall, chestnut-haired woman, thirty-five years old. Less stunning than the two color snapshots indicated, and slightly heavy in the legs, but rather attractive nonetheless. Even surrounded by twenty-year-olds, she didn't look exactly out of place. She wore blue jeans and a handsome leather jacket, and stood by herself while students from the previous lecture filed out of the theatre.

In a few minutes the corridor had emptied out in a mass exchange of backpacks coming and going; Brendan read notices by the bulletin board and peeled open a package of Certs. A moment later a short handsome man wearing pointy cowboy boots with jeans and a drawstring tie came trotting down the stairs. He carried a leather briefcase and, in his other hand, a carousel of picture slides. He nodded curtly at Brendan, slowed at the double doors and tucked the slides under his briefcase arm, then quickly combed his hair with his fingers. When he swung the door open, Brendan tried to get a glimpse inside, but there was no telling where Liz Truax sat. He grabbed the door before it closed and held it open a few inches. The professor character had stopped at one of the aisle seats, setting his slides on the wide cement step while he spoke with a student. He balanced the briefcase on one leg, opened it and withdrew a magazine, which he handed to Liz Truax. Then he hurried down to the front of the room.

If nothing else, the little guy was certainly a candidate, though Brendan half hoped he wasn't going to solve things so quickly.

He walked up to the student union and, with a view of the museum's exit doors, sat sipping coffee in the dimly lit snack bar, adolescently amazed at the number of perfect female bodies gathered in one room. A few girls glanced interestedly at him, but he couldn't get over feeling irreparably aged and out of place. He'd done two years at this same school in the late sixties, until one impoverished summer he took an exam that got him a scholarship to the Police Academy in Plattsburgh. Since then, he hadn't set foot in any of these buildings. Occasionally he regretted not going back to finish his degree, but right now it was the sheer sexuality of the place that made him half mourn all he'd missed. Still, his last affair had left him leery of anything outside his marriage.

Liz Truax emerged from the museum an hour later. Wyatt Earp was a few yards behind her, but she seemed to be walking alone, he flanked by two other students. Brendan followed her across the campus to the library parking lot and watched her stop at the passenger door of a green Volvo. She removed a stack of books from the front seat and started across the sidewalk toward the fine arts library. It was a small two-story building Brendan had never been in, and he sat on the railing outside the dairy bar for half an hour until she came out empty-handed, heading back toward the Volvo. His own car was in a lot behind the theatre. He jumped off the short ledge beneath the railing and dashed across the wet grass and melting snow beside the main library, almost losing one of his shoes in the muddy suck of the earth there, trying to keep Liz Truax's departing car in sight.

He finally caught up with her at a light beyond the mall on Route 7. There were two other cars between them, and he kept it that way for another mile, though he knew he couldn't expect much now; the development Truax had given as their address was off the main road ahead, and her turn signal was flashing. He followed at a distance for another half mile until she turned into the driveway of a big modern freestyle house, natural wood with lots of angles and windows overlooking the lake.

He parked down the street in case she came back out, but ten minutes later tuned the radio to an old Supremes song and headed back to the office.

Unless Truax called with some spontaneous information likely to produce results, there was nothing on his wife's schedule worth pursuing until her Tuesday afternoon swim. Brendan went to the Y after lunch on Tuesday, and from the observation window near the squash courts watched her crawl and backstroke steady sets of laps for almost forty-five minutes, still unaccompanied, occasionally chatting with men and women she seemed to know. In a bathing suit her legs were tauter and more shapely than he'd guessed from seeing her in blue jeans. In fact, she was rather athletic looking—a slightly older version of the classic broad-shouldered Olympic swimmer.

From the Y he followed her downtown on foot to a number of the nicer clothing stores, venturing into one of the larger ones, but otherwise waiting outside. He was sure she hadn't noticed him that first day, but he'd been stupid to stand there in the corridor as he'd done. Eventually she bought an Orange Julius and walked back to her car, then drove to Tree Spirits, "the shop," as Truax referred to it.

In his log book Brendan jotted: *Swim, Downtown, Tree. $2\frac{1}{2}$ hours. Wasted.*

Back at the office he washed his face and hands before settling down to other work.

* * *

Wednesday he followed her from the time she left the shop, just before noon. She met two other women downtown for lunch, but afterwards her routine was the same as Monday's: class at the museum, walking unaccompanied to the fine arts library, emerging alone with her leather satchel, then driving straight home.

Her days were almost as dull as Brendan's own. Maybe Truax was simply paranoid. Still, after ten years of living with the woman, it was likely enough the guy could sense something unusual in the works. Maybe the lover was out of town this week. A business trip. Maybe Brendan wasn't tagging her at the right times, although Truax was supposed to call, even at Brendan's home, if she went out at night, or under dubious circumstances. Truax had to come through with something, too.

Thursday afternoon was another zero. Then Truax called to say she claimed she had a meeting that night. So Brendan followed her—to a session of the League of Women Voters.

All in all, he'd begun to feel a little slimy about the whole thing. Suppose someone had done this to *him* three years ago, when he was falling in love with Poppie? He was a professional investigator, hired in a perfectly legal capacity, but somehow he felt as if *he* were the offending party, tagging this woman all around town, carrying her photographs and a schedule of her life.

But then, couldn't some good come of it? Truax was already certain she was cheating on him; it wouldn't exactly be news Brendan would provide. Maybe some specific information could help save the marriage, if Truax could just approach her with the facts in hand. There was that side to it, after all. He was doing this decent guy Truax a favor, wasn't he?

But what good would it really do? And what kind of favor was that, charging the guy thirty dollars an hour to tell him

he's a cuckold? A c-c-c-cuckold. Fuck it. He was better off running errands for some douche-bag lawyer.

For the rest of the week he let up on Liz Truax, deciding he'd
be doing himself and Truax both a favor if he waited until the
man could give him something more concrete. He spent the
next three days pursuing a list of leads and interviews for
Mackenzie concerning the murder of a banker in Stowe.

But even with other distractions, in a few days his thoughts
began to circle Liz Truax again. He'd followed her for nearly
a week, albeit a rather lazy one, and had seen absolutely nothing noteworthy. And yet her husband seemed so certain.

Thursday night, after Brendan and Rachel had put the girls
to bed, he opened a beer and sat down in the living room,
rubbing the smooth side of the bottle against his cheek, wondering if maybe it was the little cowboy art professor after all.
He heard Rachel's newspaper close across the room and
could feel her eyes weighing on him. "What's up, anyway?"
she asked. There was a vaguely accusatory tone to her question that hinted as much of suspicion as of sympathetic concern. When he glanced up, the set of her mouth confirmed
it; not so much accusation, perhaps, but a defensive pre-
paredness for the worst.

Less than three years ago he'd moved out, when Beth was
seven and Addie was five. He'd had a short, superficial affair
early in their marriage, which Rachel had never known about,
but the summer she and the girls flew out to visit her parents
in Minnesota, he'd ventured into deeper waters. It was the
year Brendan had been elected to the board of aldermen
from his ward, pursuing, practically on a whim, a latent political interest.

As an alderman he'd discovered a previously unrealized
ability to speak spontaneously and persuasively before large
groups. Eventually he was spearheading a drive to prevent

construction of a wood-chip power plant on the city's waterfront. Local reporters were calling the house and often
stopped him as he left City Hall on Wednesday nights. One of
them was a twenty-six-year-old woman named Poppie Hansen,
polite and pretty in a plainish way, with an accent that wasn't
quite British but was somehow more formal than American. It
was because of her that Brendan had moved out of the house
that September, after Rachel and the girls had returned from
Minnesota. The three months he'd spent in an apartment of
his own were gradually seeming to have been some other life
he and Rachel had lived, and occasionally she could even half
joke about it now. But he also knew that her dreams were still
haunted by those days, even though Poppie had long since
moved away.

"What's up, anyway?" Rachel asked.

He smiled briefly and flipped his bottle cap like a coin in
her direction. "Nothing, sorry, just tired." He waited for her
to return the smile. She still had what Brendan had always
admired as typically Midwestern beauty, especially with her
wheat-colored hair drawn back in a ponytail, as it was now.
Her eyes were beginning to reveal some faint creases—each of
which she claimed dated back exactly two and a half years.
Maybe she was right. His own dark eyebrows had each sprout-
ed several long white hairs at about the same time. Bodies
told stories after all.

She was still holding the same straight face, watching him.

Banjo, the cat, wandered into the room and rubbed against
Rachel's leg until she received him into her lap, stroking the
full length of his spine as he settled. "Did you get a letter or
something?"

"No, no letter. It's just a new case. Something's got me
stumped."

"Phone call?"

"Rachel, we're not going to hear from her anymore. Jesus, I
thought you'd stopped with that. I wish you'd finally forget it."

"I wish it had never happened."

"Well so do I." But that wasn't quite true. Sometimes it seemed almost true, but never completely. As much as he loved Rachel and regretted hurting her, he also regretted at times the fact that he would never know a life with Poppie.

"So what's this new case?"

"I'm not even sure it's anything, really. Just some guy."

"Oh, well don't bore me with all the details."

"Sorry, I'm just not sure it's even worth talking about." He didn't want Rachel to think he was getting into slime work, kicking down motel room doors with a Nikon handy. And aside from that he just didn't have the energy to tell her the whole story right now. There wasn't much to say, and yet trying to express everything there *was* to say about Truax was more than he felt up to. That was getting to be a familiar feeling, that sort of lethargy of the larynx. He and Rachel had always communicated pretty well, but in the last five years or so he'd certainly backed off; there was a lot he just didn't bother to share anymore. Maybe especially since that crazy September. And there were certain details of his days, even now, with Poppie back in Washington, or in her parents' hometown in Wales, or God knew where, that he felt a desire to share with her alone: the gems and tidbits and minor triumphs of his job, for example; the artistic talent Bethany was beginning to show, sketching Brendan's face with great accuracy while he slept on the couch; or something funny Addie might say, sitting on his lap and munching Saltines.

He flicked his thumb in the mouth of the beer bottle and made a careless *thock* sound. "It's a guy I remember from high school. He didn't recognize me, though. He played baseball for Winooski." He sighed, and shrugged. "He was really desperate, he thinks his wife's running around, and I agreed to do some . . . 'surveillance' work for him. And now I kind of regret it, even though nothing's turning up."

Rachel had never liked him taking on the domestic jobs

that came his way. She respected his work, was genuinely interested in it, but she thought most domestic jobs should be left to the parties involved. It was an issue she could be more than a little emphatic about. So he was grateful for the fact that she only nodded now, even looked sympathetic, when she might have frowned and compounded his unhappiness.

"See, it's nothing for you to worry about," he said.

"Well, I doubt I'm ever going to stop worrying, so don't get your hopes up." She paused. "Anyway, I'm sorry to be such a nag, but the oth—oh, never mind."

"The other what? The other day something happened? What?"

"Nothing, forget it."

"I want to know. What happened the other day? A letter came?"

"No, it's stupid, nothing."

"The phone rang and somebody hung up?"

"No."

"Well tell me!"

"Okay. The other day I saw this tall girl downtown who I thought for a minute looked just like that little bitch, not that I ever got a very good look at her. This girl was kind of slender, though. What's her name wasn't very slender, was she?"

It was a rhetorical question; Rachel knew perfectly well that Poppie was a big woman, though she wasn't at all overweight. He knew Rachel wanted him to say, "No, she wasn't slender, she was a big fat ugly bitch," but he wouldn't say it, even as a lie to soothe Rachel's battered loyalty.

"Rachel," he said, "she went off to Washington, or Wales or someplace, and I'm sure she went for good, so you don't have to keep carrying that cross. Jesus, it's been almost three years." He rubbed an itchy spot on his wrist against the stubble on his chin. "I know it was foolish, it was mean, but I wouldn't make that mistake again. Christ, I regret it as much as you do."

She tilted her head and treated him to an expression of extreme skepticism, which he knew he had coming. "I'm just glad you care about Beth and Addie as much as you do, or I doubt we'd have seen you again." She dropped a clump of Banjo's loose fur to the floor.

"Rachel, that's really unfair. I don't know why I can't convince you."

"Because I know what's true. I wish you could convince me, but I think I know what's true. I know you love me. I just think I know other things, too."

She still maintained that if it hadn't been for the girls, and for her own reports of the way Bethany would cry seeing his empty chair at dinner every night, he would never have returned at all. But reluctant as he had been to break off with Poppie, he knew Rachel was wrong. Nights in Poppie's little apartment on Buell Street, her big wooden easel gathering dust and dominating a corner of the living room like an abandoned tepee frame, the two of them had agonized over his waverings and final decision. By the time it came, he knew he'd have returned to Rachel even if they'd been childless. Their lives were that inextricably bound up after fourteen years. He couldn't escape Rachel, and, even for the wonder of Poppie Hansen, didn't want to when all was said and done.

But Rachel wouldn't be convinced. Or maybe her failing to be convinced was just a tactic she'd opted for, so that he'd be forever proving himself to her now. Either way, it didn't matter. They were together, and she'd found it within herself to summon a forgiveness he could never have located in his own love.

He made a disappointed *dit* sound with his tongue and drained the rest of his beer, the bottle making a little bird-whistle noise as it emptied.

Rachel watched him, stroking Banjo's forehead. "So what are you going to do about your baseball player?"

"I don't know. Call him tomorrow and tell him there's nothing to worry about, I guess." He stood up and crossed the room. "Everybody's so goddamn suspicious." He stopped and rubbed at the cat's smooth forepaw. "You know?"

Friday evening Rachel had asked him to pick up Beth and Addie after their dance lesson. He'd come close to calling Truax a few hours earlier to say the whole thing was seeming pointless and maybe they should call it off. But then he remembered that Liz Truax was supposed to be in the shop on busy Friday afternoons, and he didn't want to make things any more awkward for Dan.

He sat in the car outside the dance studio and toyed with the radio until he could see Beth and Addie come pushing out the heavy glass doors, chattering earnestly about Addie's awkward arabesques, or how Mona, the instructor, must have permanent PMS she's so grouchy, or why did Sharon Seaver even bother to keep taking classes, she was such a space cadet—never paid attention and had all the coordination of a broomstick.

Beth took a quick stride ahead of Addie to claim the front seat, her silver cross bouncing on a thin chain at her neck. "Hi, Daddy, sorry if you had to wait for us." Their cheeks were flushed; wispy brown curls had formed about Addie's round forehead.

"Nope, just got here," he said. "Good lesson?"

"It was okay. Addie's real sore. Mona *worked* us today. Her boyfriend was there. I think she was showing off for him."

"Is *that* why we kept doing those things?" Addie asked. She pulled her ponytail around to the front and untied the pink ribbon she wore strictly for dance classes, slumping tiredly in the back seat. Aside from being two years younger, she seemed to have less endurance than Bethany, was less sleekly athletic. Brendan figured it was just baby fat, but it sometimes added to his worries that Addie was going to be forever frustrated trying to emulate her older sister's graceful successes through life.

They drew up to the traffic light in front of the police department, and he glanced up at his old office window. He didn't know who sat there these days, although he still kept in touch with former colleagues. Marcie, at the information desk, had a stack of his cards in her drawer and occasionally directed potential clients his way. He'd have to stop by with Beth and Addie some day and show them off.

Bethany was hunched over now, rooting through the Capezio bag at her feet, and finally drew out a red plastic hairbrush. She pulled down the mirrored sun visor and began brushing out her hair, a little tip of red tongue curled at the corner of her mouth in concentration.

Addie loosened her safety belt, leaned forward from the back seat and said, "Daddy, do you believe Bethy dreams cartoons?"

"What?"

"I do," Bethany said. "Dad'll tell you. I dream cartoons all the time."

"Bethy says she dreams cartoons at night. I never dream cartoons. Do you think she really dreams cartoons?"

He looked at Addie in the rearview mirror. "Yeah, I think she does," he said, "but they're only in black and white. She can't get color."

"Nuh-uh," Beth said, shaking her head quickly, but Brendan winked and she stopped, smiling knowingly at him over their private understanding.

He hoped Addie hadn't noticed the wink. He looked in the rearview mirror again and told her he thought her posture had become quite graceful with all this dancing.

"It oughta be," she said sluggishly, and he laughed, glancing up at the light and just then noticing the Volvo—Liz Truax's green Volvo. It pulled up to the intersection opposite them, came to a stop, and abruptly turned left on the advance

signal. But in the front seat with Liz Truax, laughing and rais-
ing something, an apple, to her mouth . . . Poppie? His heart
took off, and his hands were damp on the steering wheel. He
leaned over the dashboard and quickly flipped Beth's sun
visor up to get a better look.

"What's wrong, Dad?"

"Nothing. Just thought I saw someone." He could only see
the back of their heads now. If it was Poppie, she hadn't
noticed him; he'd only managed the briefest glance, but he
was almost certain it was she. After two years he was, at any
rate, well past the point of mistaking every woman who looked
remotely like her for being the real thing. Maybe Rachel *had*
seen her the other day. And then he realized it had to be
Poppie, that Truax had practically told him so when he'd said
his wife had a friend named Paula . . . god*damn* it! What the
fuck kind of investigator had he dwindled into, anyway? Truax
had said Paula, plain English, Paula, and Brendan hadn't
even bothered to ask "Paula who?" Just when he'd managed
to stop howling at his own private moon every time he heard
the names Paula, or Poppie, or Cardiff, Wales, someone
referred to the only Paula he knew in the world and he
missed the connection completely.

The Volvo was out of sight now; Addie was tapping his
shoulder from the back seat. "We've got the go, Dad. Dad,
we've got the go."

The light was green. He was tempted to follow them, but
they were too far away now. Besides, the girls were with him,
and what the hell would he do if he caught the car? If Poppie
was in town he'd find her soon enough. That couldn't be too
tough, even for the incompetent slouch he'd apparently
become. But the coincidence of her knowing Liz Truax was
unsettling. As he drove home, his momentary glimpse of the
two of them hung there just beyond his windshield like some
morsel of meaning he couldn't comprehend. Or was he
investing the coincidence with more than it deserved? Maybe
coincidence itself was the only lesson here.

He still had to stop at the store for ice cream and then collect Beth's friend Lisa, whose parents were in the middle of
an ugly divorce and had asked if she could spend the night;
but when he got home he checked the phone book for a listing. Nothing. He closed the door to the den and dialed information while Rachel prepared dinner. Yes, they did have a
listing for Paula Hansen, and an address at 24 Dodge Court,
wherever that was. He asked the operator if she could tell him
how long the number had been in service, but she couldn't
say for sure.

He sat restlessly through dinner, and afterwards asked
Rachel if she'd mind his going out to take care of some things.

"Is this still about your suspicious baseball player?"

"No, no, it's something for Mackenzie. I'll tell you about it
later." He forced a smile and kissed her quickly on the lips,
his adulterous talent for swift deception emerging dusty from
the wings. Two years and more of almost total virtue, and it
took only one look at Poppie Hansen to set him off lying
again. Still, he felt somewhat calmer about lying now, more so
than in those other reckless and deceitful times; now he
wasn't concealing anything that had to be hidden with constant care. Nothing much, anyway. Not yet.

He grabbed a jacket and got into the station wagon, Rachel's
car, because the Toyota was almost out of gas. He decided to
swing past Truax's house first, just to see if the Volvo—and
maybe Poppie—was there.

The evening had grown dark enough for headlights as he
turned into Truax's neighborhood. From the end of the
street he could make out the green Volvo in the driveway.
There were lights on in an upstairs room, and on part of the
first floor. If he waited for the last bit of light to seep behind
the mountains he could Tom the ground-floor windows. He
parked further down the street and sat in the car until the
trees in Truax's yard were vague silhouettes.

At the split-rail fence he stepped quickly up the side yard

to the rock garden at the back. There was a deck spanning
almost the entire rear of the house; the kitchen window shed
a small circle of light near the top step. He edged across the
boards, trying to control the leathery creak of his shoes,
wishing he'd worn sneakers. A vibration of footsteps from
inside the house, and suddenly Truax appeared in the
kitchen in an untucked white shirt. He took a knife from a
drawer and sliced something, cake, from an aluminum pan
on the counter, then went back into the other room, out of
sight.

Brendan edged along the deck until he came to another
set of windows and another room, this one visible only in the
flickering light and shadows of an unseen television. A few
steps further and he could see Truax in a big easy chair,
drinking from a coffee mug. Brendan stepped back down to
the yard to check the upstairs windows. The second-floor light
went off, and in a moment another came on in the large
room where Truax sat. He crept back up the deck and saw Liz
Truax standing beside Dan holding a clear plastic plant
spritzer. She was wearing jeans and a long Indian-style shirt
that came to her knees, a maroon scarf tied around her head.
She set the bottle on the floor and spoke to Truax with her
hand on his shoulder. He patted her wrist and said something
without looking up. Liz glanced at the television and spoke
again, Truax looking up at her and nodding, and suddenly
Brendan realized she was leaving. He heard the door close at
the front of the house, and saw Truax jump up and dash to
the kitchen telephone.

He still wanted to find Poppie, but if he followed Liz Truax
now, he might finally manage what he'd been hired for.
Inside, Truax stood with the phone at his ear, tapping his fingers anxiously against the wall. Brendan heard the Volvo's
ignition catch and sprinted across the neighbor's backyard to
his own car.

She'd driven only a half mile north on Route 7 when he

caught her. He'd never tailed her with the station wagon, so he felt less conspicuous now. She signaled a turn at the mall and drove straight across the wide parking area to the liquor store. Brendan parked in front of Sears and watched her get out, a Mexican wool bag hanging from her shoulder. Through the plate-glass window he could see her at the register buying a bottle of wine.

Ten minutes later, with just a puttering red Volkswagen between them, he watched Liz Truax hang a right onto Henry Street, an older residential neighborhood several blocks from the downtown business district. The houses here had been built early in the century, most now broken up into apartments. The Volvo's brake lights lit up, and he slowed to a stop as she backed into a space at the corner. She had quickly gotten out of her car and was heading away, so he pulled into a spot beside a fire hydrant and left the car at a peculiar angle several feet from the curb.

She'd already turned down a side street, a narrow cul de sac, apparently. When he reached the corner he could see her almost a hundred yards away, disappearing up the front walk of a house with a motorcycle parked out front. He slowed to a walk now.

The mailbox on the front porch had two typed labels taped to it; the lower one read *Paula Hansen (2nd Floor)*. He stared for a moment and then touched at it.

Through the front door's low beveled window a green carpeted stairway led to the second floor. The door was unlocked, and he stepped inside, but the apartment door to the right was ajar, and a man called, "Bonnie? Is that you?"

He'd been dangling from the first fat limb of the oak tree for only a few seconds, his shoes about five feet from the ground, wrists and forearms all scratched to hell—feeling perfectly ludicrous—when a boy carrying a motorcycle helmet and a

can of beer clomped out of the house across the street.
Brendan tried to slow the momentum of his swing, but the
noise of his shoes scraping against bark drew the boy's attention. He stopped at the curb and looked around, then settled
his gaze directly on Brendan and laughed out loud. "Howdy!"
he said, then drained the beer, pulled his helmet on and
straddled the bike. He revved the engine a couple times,
looked up at Brendan again and waved, then gunned his way
up the street.

A few moments later Brendan had managed to throw one
leg over the limb, where he was safely obscured from anyone passing by. His wrists were rubbed raw, and he'd half
destroyed his shoes. He slowly eased himself into an awkward
clutch-and-straddle position, only now recalling just how
much he disliked heights. A queasy, clenching feeling twisted
his bowels as he stood to reach the next higher limb. The one
above that, jutting out at an odd angle, poked up close to the
two lighted second-floor windows.

In a few minutes he was straddling the final branch, sitting
just six feet away from the kitchen window with a clear view
inside: Liz Truax sat flipping through a magazine, a box of
crayons and a glass of wine on the table in front of her.
Across the room, Poppie stood talking on the telephone. She
was prettier than he'd remembered, but her hair was much
shorter, almost boyish, in one of the more tolerable new-wave
styles. His breath shortened and his heart began racing
again, as it had when he'd seen her in the car earlier. She'd
lost a little weight, and though he wasn't sure he liked the
haircut, she was still striking in some peculiarly European
blend of plain and pretty. He'd almost expected her to have
aged in some tangible way, as his morning confrontations
with the bathroom mirror constantly confirmed he had done.
But Poppie looked wonderful. If anything, the haircut made
her look younger, though somewhat less feminine.

As she talked, she wrote on a piece of paper taped to the

wall. She was wearing an embroidered white blouse and black corduroys. After a moment, she set the pencil down and began twisting one of her earrings. It was a long flat silver piece, which he remembered, remembered taking into his mouth once while she had worn it, lying in an apartment not far from here. He said her name quietly to himself and shifted on the branch.

Liz Truax set her glass down and carried the magazine into another room. What was the connection here?

The wind let up, and edging closer to the window he could catch now and then the familiar polite notes of Poppie's voice, though he couldn't make out what she was saying. "Don't worry"? "Don't hurry"? A few other sentences, mostly unclear, and then, "Bye-bye, Louise," and something in Welsh. Louise. Her older sister. She set the phone down and sat at the head of the table, facing almost directly out at Brendan as she toyed with the cork from the wine bottle. She filled her glass, leaned her head back against the chair and closed her eyes. He could hear Liz Truax calling out from another room of the apartment, and Poppie said loudly, with her eyes still closed, "Yes, next month she believes." She opened her eyes for a moment, hunched her shoulders and covered a yawn, slumping deeper into the chair. Watching the creamy skin of her throat, he thought of the first time they had slept together—Poppie, amazingly, still a virgin at age twenty-six—how innocently surprised and yet pleased she had been when he'd come onto her soft white belly. Without taking her lips from his, her fingers had gently, almost tentatively, explored his semen shot across her stomach, and then she had clasped him to her gratefully, as if he had presented some cherished and unexpected gift.

Liz Truax returned from the other room adjusting the long tail of her shirt. She stopped behind Poppie's chair and placed her hands over Poppie's eyes, like Addie did when she wanted to take Brendan by surprise. Now she slid her thumbs

over Poppie's eyelids, Poppie smiling and tilting her head
back, reaching up and linking her hands around the other
woman's neck. He gripped at the limb beneath him and
watched Liz Truax bend over and kiss Poppie's forehead. His
breath came short now, as if one lung had stopped function-
ing. Poppie reached for the glass of wine and brought it to
her mouth, then to the smiling mouth above her. Still standing, Liz Truax sipped at the glass and slid her hand into the
top of Poppie's blouse and beneath her bra. She was caressing
Poppie's breast with her open hand, kneading lightly at it
until she finally took Poppie's wrists and pulled her to her
feet, drawing her to another room.

Brendan shinned backwards on the limb until he could
lean against the tree's rough trunk. From a nearby branch an
unseen owl moaned a solemn *woo* sound.

The bedroom light was on at home, but he wasn't up to facing
Rachel; he parked quietly and went for a long walk up the
street, the smell of spring mud in the air, a few crickets shreep-
ing out a song. Then back down the street and across the playing fields of the middle school. He let himself in through the
garage door and sat in the den with a single reading lamp on.
Rachel, in her flannel nightgown, came in to ask if everything
was okay, and he said yes, that he just wanted to catch the news
and get a little more tired before coming to bed.

"Dan Truax called for you a couple hours ago," she said. "Is
that the baseball player?"

"Uh-huh."

She turned the television on for him and switched it to the
twenty-four-hour news channel. "Come to bed soon," she said.
She stopped by the doorway. "Okay?"

"Uh-huh, soon," he said, and smiled at her, grateful for the
routine, and security, and sane and steady love in their lives.

"You won't fall asleep out here?"

"No, I'll be in soon."

Rachel made a kissing sound and padded barefoot back to bed, her bony frame almost shapeless beneath the nightgown.

He wasn't focusing on any of the news stories, and after a while he just wanted to climb into bed with Rachel and feel the flesh and flannel warmth of her as he drifted off. He checked the back door and went upstairs to look in on Addie. She was lying on her side at the outer edge of the bed, a red wool blanket pulled over her shoulder. Banjo was stretched across the bed widthwise, taking up three-fourths of the mattress between Addie and the wall. He gave Brendan an indifferent glance when he stepped into the room, then made a throaty grumbling sound as Brendan shifted him against the wall and rolled Addie onto her back.

In Beth's room there was an empty cot made up in the middle of the floor, but Beth and Lisa were cramped onto the tiny painted wood-frame bed that had once been Rachel's in Minnesota. They were half covered by a sheet, each wearing underpants and a T-shirt, one of Beth's long legs slung across Lisa, who looked uncomfortable. He bent down to lift Beth over to the cot, but she woke and mumbled, "Wait, it's not ready yet."

Brendan paused, then snorted, amused. "Yes it is."

"No-o," she murmured, but then she closed her eyes again and he decided to leave her there.

Rachel was sleeping, and once in bed he scrunched up close behind her. But even as his eyes gave in to the tug of exhaustion, he could see Poppie and Liz Truax feeding each other wine at a kitchen table.

Shaving at the bathroom mirror Saturday morning, he felt as if he'd only half wakened from a bad dream. But he hadn't shaken the compulsive urge to talk with Poppie, and by ten o'clock he was down on Dodge Court. She came to the door in jeans and an oversized white T-shirt, taller than he'd remembered, even though she was barefoot. She held the door in one hand and shook her head slightly. "I had a feeling," she said, smiling and biting her upper lip for a moment before reaching out and kissing him lightly on the cheek. She took his hand and said, "Don't look so put out, Brendan," drawing him inside and leading him through a simply furnished living room. In the kitchen she offered him a seat at the table by the window.

"I saw you yesterday in a car," he told her. "Kind of threw me. I didn't know where you were. Certainly didn't think you were right here."

She touched his hand and pulled her chair in. "Only since February," she said. "I came back from Wales last fall and stayed with Louise for a few months. I sold a couple of paintings, so I had some money. I'd been feeling a lot better, really better I thought, and then things just got . . . grim again. So I decided . . . "—she shrugged slightly—"to come back."

"For . . . ?"

"How do you mean?"

"Come back for what?"

"You," she said, as if it were obvious.

"That's why you've been here since February? For me? And I only got a look at you yesterday—as a matter of chance?"

She frowned, pulling at a loose green thread in the table-cloth. "Things didn't happen like they were supposed to. It's a little complicated."

She seemed different to him now, a little more "American" somehow. For all the familiar and tentative feminine gestures, the habit of biting her upper lip, the slight shoulder shrugs with an uncertain dip of her head, she was more sure of herself now, seemed to leave him less in control.

"How complicated?" He lifted the glass salt shaker, rubbing his thumb along its smooth surface.

"Complicated."

"I'm all ears, Poppie." He'd never been this way with her before, cool and aloof. They'd never even had an argument, really. The only problem had ever been whether or not he'd go back to Rachel.

"You can probably guess half of it."

"You've found true love with someone else," he said a little mockingly.

Poppie sighed. "Yes, more or less." She pulled his hand from the salt shaker and laced her fingers with his. "Brendan, I honestly came back here to be with you. I decided, even if you won't leave Rachel, we're going to be together. I thought I'd just . . . wait for you and have you when I could. That we could be together whenever you'd manage. That was the plan, anyway."

He shifted in the chair.

"But when I got here it didn't seem so easy to call you. And then things happened, this other person. Out of the blue, really. I mean, it's someone I knew before, but not like this. I don't know. And I didn't want to just be a home wrecker again. Then this other thing just . . . began . . . developing." She set her hands down flat on the table, chewing her lip and staring at him. "You don't look like you believe me."

"I believe you," he said dully.

"Louise knew I was coming back here to be with you. She kept saying, 'Don't you have any pride? He already threw you over once.' She was fed up by the time I left."

He picked a sliver of cork from the tablecloth and creased it with his thumbnail. "So what would she say about you and Sappho?" He surprised himself; he hadn't planned to say anything.

Poppie stared for a moment—blankly, then bitterly. "Let's not play games—why don't you just tell me what you really know. Do you already know everything?"

"No, I—"

"How long have you known I've been back?"

"Since yesterday, like I said. And I don't know *any*thing else, I just saw you and made a guess. A wild guess, but correct, I'd say."

"Saw me where?"

"Downtown."

"Where downtown?"

"Poppie. I know you, isn't that enough? I could tell."

"You're really quite the detective."

"Yeah, I'm a bona fide dick."

"Sure you haven't been following me?"

"Poppie, come on, Jesus Christ."

"Okay. Okay, I'm sorry."

They were silent for a moment.

"So where are you working—or are you?" he asked. "Haven't seen the Paula Hansen byline lately."

"Oh, the university. I picked up some crazy hours at the fine arts library. Afternoons and nights."

"Jesus," he whispered.

"What do you mean?"

"Just . . ." He shook his head. "That you've been right here and I haven't known. I don't know. I wish I had. So what's the story with your friend?"

"She's married," Poppie said, glancing up to register his reaction. "To a pretty nice guy, in fact. She might leave him, but I don't know. There were problems before me. I'm not sure she really knows what she wants."

He shook his head slightly. "How did this get started, anyway? I mean . . ."

"Are you so disgusted with me?"

"I'm not disgusted."

"Well you don't exactly look like you're fond of me."

"Christ, I fucking love you. The whole thing sort of threw me a curve, that's all. I don't know. I mean, think about it."

"Well I'm not ashamed, if that's what you're trying to get me to say."

"Okay, you're not ashamed, I'm not saying you should be. I just think it's so goddamned sad, Paula."

She unscrewed the silver top from the salt shaker and spun it slowly on the table.

"I do, really. I mean, I know you've had some bad luck a few times. But it wasn't because of you I went back. You know perfectly well that if it hadn't been for Rachel and the girls, you and I'd be together now. I mean, I'm not beyond being jealous of someone else in your life, but I don't think you have to turn your back on men altogether."

"That's not what I'm doing. It's not some conscious, deliberate choice, Brendan, it's love. I'm sorry to shock you, but it is. I didn't suddenly assess my situation one morning and say, okay, from this point on it's women only. It just happened. And I can't imagine even feeling this way about any woman other than Liz."

"All right; I'm sorry." He took the salt cap from her and twisted it back onto the shaker. "Well are you at least happy with her?"

"I'm happy," she said. She didn't sound emphatic, but he believed she meant it. He remembered a letter he'd received from her months after he'd returned to Rachel, in which she had written: *I know it sounds rather too jaded, but I think compromise will be part of anything either of us ever has in the way of happiness now. Don't you think?* At first he wasn't sure, but after a while he realized she'd probably articulated the main truth of his life since he'd left her. Or maybe it was true for everyone anyway.

The phone rang, and he could tell from the familiar way she said "Hi" in two pleasant syllables that it was Liz Truax. "Let me call you back in a bit," Poppie said, and Brendan stood up from the table.

"You don't have to go," she said.

"Yeah, I do. I'm supposed to take the girls shopping." He started slowly toward the door.

"Doesn't Rachel do that?"

"Yeah, well, both of us, I guess."

"Mmm. How are they? I mean, the girls *and* Rachel?"

"They're all fine. I hope you get to see Beth and Addie sometime. You probably will, I feel like a chauffeur some days, all over town."

"I'd *like* to see them. Guess I can't exactly pay a social visit to the Kelloggs, though. It'd be nice if I could. If we were all just friends, at least."

"Yeah, it'd be nice . . ." They stood by the door for a moment without speaking.

"I might be going to Wales for the summer. Or Liz and I might. I don't know. I'm not really expecting anything of her. Can we see each other again?"

"I'd like to."

"You don't sound very definite."

"Poppie, after two and a half years I'm still dreaming about you, for Christ's sake. Of course I'd like to. I'm just a little shell-shocked still, you know?"

"Just call me sometime. Anytime. Don't worry about who's here."

"Maybe," Brendan said. "I might," he added, but he knew the terms of their relationship had been permanently altered. And he still felt as if he hadn't fully wakened from an unpleasant sleep.

On Monday he was to meet with Dan Truax. By the time he got back from the city clerk's office at four-thirty, Truax was sitting in his pickup out front, fifteen minutes early. Brendan pulled in next to him and got out. "How you doing, Dan." They shook hands, Truax's palm a calloused history of untold hours of woodworking. Brendan remarked on the new cargo rack on the back of the truck, stalling now, feeling hopelessly phony, going through the goddamn motions when the man wanted a simple one-sentence answer for which Brendan hadn't yet devised a phrasing.

They stepped inside and Truax asked, "D'you get the message I phoned you Friday night?"

"Yeah, I did." Brendan gestured to one of the captain's chairs and went behind his desk.

"I guess you've got news for me," Truax said.

"Yeah, I think it will be news for you." He reached for a folder at the corner of the desk, but still wasn't quite sure how he wanted to start.

"Look, I don't mean to be rude," Truax said, "but I don't want to diddle around, okay? She's seeing another guy, isn't she?"

"I've gotta tell you," Brendan said. He looked Truax straight in the eye. "She's not." He indicated the folder. "I've put in quite a few hours on this. She's not seeing anybody else. She spends a lot of time with her friend Pop—Paula, the woman who works at the fine arts library. But there's no man."

"She's really spending all that time with Paula?"

"From all I see, she is. She's got other lady friends she's met for lunch. She seems to *know* some of the men who swim at the Y on Tuesdays, talks with them at the pool, but that's it. I mean, there's nothing."

"Hmm." Truax didn't look too satisfied. "I want to believe it, but . . . Friday night? When I phoned you? She didn't come home till the next morning. I mean, I don't c-c-care what kind of ingenious excuses, there's only one reason a grown woman doesn't make it home at night. It's not like I've never dicked around myself before."

"Yeah, I *followed* her Friday night. That's why *I* wasn't home when you called."

Truax sat forward, interested now. "So where was she?"

"Down on Dodge Court, Paula Hansen's house. The two of them. Putting a lot of wine away as far as I could see."

"Just the two of them? No men?"

"Right."

Truax winced skeptically.

"Hey, you see these scratches?" Brendan held his wrists up, each of them streaked with thin lines of scabs. "I broke my balls climbing a tree to see into those kitchen windows Friday night. I'm telling you, that's where she was."

Truax was giving in to a very slight smirk now. He nodded his head. "That's what she said when she called. About one-thirty, two A.M. Said she and Paula drank too much, that she was gonna c-c-c-"—he stopped and carelessly drew the L with his finger, twice this time before it worked—"crash there. Jesus, she was really at Paula's?" He let out an airy snort of amazement. "I didn't believe it."

"Believe it," Brendan said.

Truax was still suppressing an unenthusiastic smirk. "How'd you know she was going there Friday night?"

"A little luck, really. I was in your neighborhood. Saw her car and picked up on it."

"I'm impressed. You do good work."

Yeah, I'm a certified dick. "Thanks," Brendan said. He was embarrassed for Truax, the guy praising his lazy, lying services just because Brendan was telling him what he wanted to hear.

Truax nodded to himself. "Well, maybe I've been foolish then, I don't know. It's not exactly an A-number-one marriage these days, whatever she does with her time."

"Well, shit, we all go through bad times," Brendan said.

"Yeah, I guess. What am I gonna owe you, anyway?"

"Don't worry about that yet."

"Well, you can probably understand I don't want to pay you with a check. Liz k-k-keeps books for the shop and all."

Brendan wanted to quote a minimal figure—he'd put in few enough hours—but then Truax might reasonably question whether he could say with any certainty what Liz was up to. He pointed to the folder. "I've got some of it here, but my

log book's at home. I'll try to drop an invoice off in the next
few days. When you're alone."

Truax nodded and stood up, thanking him. He shook
Brendan's hand, looking a little distracted—a man who clearly knew his troubles weren't over.

Brendan stood by the window and watched him drive off.
He was through for the day, and what he wanted to do now
was drive out to the amusement park near Malletts Bay, slam
fast balls back at the automatic pitcher. Other cops, he
remembered, when a mood had them, used to go to the basement of the station house and bang away in the low-ceilinged
firing range; but Brendan's private therapy had always been
the automatic pitcher. During the thing with Poppie that year,
and especially in the weeks afterwards, he'd been a regular
out at the bay, sometimes dropping fifteen bucks a week on
baseballs. And all the time entertaining a perverse fantasy
he'd never given in to: standing on top of the plate empty-
handed, letting the machine, set at Major League speed, fire
away at him. Stupid.

Just as driving out there now seemed stupid. He walked to
the car and drove slowly in the direction of home, not wanting to go there yet, but not sure where else to go. At the light
in front of St. Anthony's, he stopped and watched a catechism
class emerge from the big double doors, remembering how
his father used to make the sign of the cross whenever they
passed a Catholic church in the car. For just a moment he
considered parking and stopping in for "a visit," as his father
used to call it, but decided he was just pitying himself and
being melodramatic, trying to soothe his guilty depression
with sudden piety and humility. Even so, he wasn't ready to
head home yet, and instead drove down to the lakefront.

The plan for construction of a wood-chip plant, which had
been such a hot issue with the board of aldermen a few years
earlier, had been defeated. There were still oil tanks and a
few unsightly coal banks off to the south of the ferry dock,
but there were also new bike paths and grassy areas with

swing sets and fountains, the sight of which often inspired in Brendan a surge of prideful vanity. For these had been *his* alternative proposals for the lakefront, projects he had helped realize in his final two years on the board.

His days with the board of aldermen were over, though. Everyone said reelection would be a breeze after the lakefront issues, but when it had come time to declare his candidacy in January, he'd let the deadline slip by. All those hours could be better invested in Beth and Addie, though he couldn't really say he was giving them the extra bulk of attention he'd once thrown into city affairs.

What he needed was the energy and idealism of his younger self, back when he was so damn sure he'd be a flawless husband and father. Or maybe he just needed to visit Poppie. That was the thought that had been hovering somewhere just short of a decision all day. But when he pictured her in the kitchen at her apartment, or behind a desk at the fine arts library, he knew that wasn't what he wanted either. He wasn't ready for a purely platonic friendship. Nor did he want to share her with Liz Truax. And yet neither was he willing to usher the confusion of a full-blown affair back into his life. He'd begun to see that in the years since they'd been together, Poppie had acquired an almost mythic status in his imagination. Maybe it was better just to preserve that.

He got out of the car near the ferry dock and watched some men adjusting a cable out on the breakwater. When they finished he wandered over to the big slabs of granite piled at the pier's edge and noticed a kid about Beth's age fishing nearby. He had an aluminum pail crammed with thin green perch still alive in water, each about five or six inches long. "Looks like you've done pretty well today," Brendan said.

"Yup, I guess." He was an urchiny kid, skinny, with a grubby white T-shirt and brown hair barely longer than a butch. "I don't eat 'em anymore, though," he said.

"Why not?"

"My teacher says these perches got mercury poisoning. You can't see it, but it's in there."

"Yeah, I'm afraid she's right." Let your vanity gnaw on that one, big guy. All that time spent worrying about the goddamn waterfront when the lake itself was dying. Hadn't seen the forest for the fucking wood chips. Barking up the wrong tree again.

"Uh-uh. He."

"What?"

"My teacher. It's a he."

"Oh."

"I'm gonna throw 'em all back in as soon's I get one more," he said, tugging gently at the line, his attention out on the water like a seasoned old angler. "Pulled in a rock bass a little while ago," the boy said. "But he flapped outta my hands as soon's I got the hook out."

"Rock bass? Big one?" Brendan pictured a heavy grey fish gliding along the lake floor with a stone in his belly.

"Big enough. Fourteen inches easy. Guess he knew I was thinkin' of keepin' him." The boy reeled his line in and plucked a thin ribbon of lake grass from the lure. "You know what time it is?"

"Yeah," Brendan said, "just about six." Across the lake the sun was edging down behind the Adirondacks. Time to get home to Rachel and the girls. His three women. "Oh, all these women in my life," he would tease when he found himself unable to keep up with their several simultaneous demands. But in the years since Poppie he had to be careful about such remarks. For a man who had held the opposite sex foremost in his thoughts since the age of twelve, it sometimes struck him as a divine and ironic intention that he should be charged with the upbringing of females only. As if someone were saying, See, these women of the world, not just your own little plunder garden, Brendan boy. Here are two you'll have to look at a little differently.

But it was fine with him. Two healthy daughters he couldn't have loved more. At times he had to wonder what a son might be like, but it was a mystery he could live with. Besides, girls were probably easier in the long run. And they were both fond of doting on Daddy, securing his seal of approval for every little thing, which in its own way could be as gratifying as the flattery of a grown woman's attentions. Not to mention a whole lot safer. To them he was still an infallible protector, still a little bit immortal, and it was a welcome role. The only problem Brendan could foresee was that someday he'd be exposed—standing there with his size-ten feet of clay mired in the mud. That and the fact that the doting would eventually focus on someone else, maybe even someone he didn't care for—a young man as selfish and irresponsible as Brendan himself. But that, he figured, was only how it had always been. For now he had to get his clay feet back home.

▾

FLAMES

▲

My brother the priest is home, which means our mother is utterly in her element. Since Martin has no woman, of course, not even the proverbial housekeeper to watch over him (his parish is a small and poor one), our mother will outdo herself this weekend, joyfully ministering to Martin's needs. Already she is a woman of renewed purpose. Tall, sturdy, and bespectacled, with classic Irish features that none of us olive-skinned offspring inherited, she darts back and forth across the kitchen, pulling trays of hot cupcakes from the oven while I open two bottles of beer and place one before Martin at the kitchen table. "Federal," I say, "why don't you sit down and relax?" A certain nostalgia, generated by Martin's presence, prompts me to resurrect the nickname by which I referred to our mother in high school, when she would greet me at the front door most nights with the same five words: "Let me smell your breath."

"Never mind me," she says, "you just take it easy on that beer. It's barely noon."

"I know, but Martin's got a head start on me," I say; "he had his first drink at seven this morning."

"Baloney," she says.

"Martin, am I right or am I right?"

"Afraid he's right, Mom," Martin says, and he sweeps his black bangs from his broad forehead.

She furrows her brow and bestows upon Martin an expression of puzzled concern.

"See," I say, "sun's barely risen and Martin's hoisting the old chalice. Couple more years of daily masses and you'll have a bad habit, my friend."

"Oh, is that all," she says, setting before us a plate of cooled and frosted cupcakes. "I'd hardly call that drinking."

" 'Is that all'?" I say. "Mother, we're talking about the Blessed bleeding Sacrament here."

"Well then," she says, "it wasn't wine at all, was it?"

"Touché," says Martin, and he peels a cupcake.

Federal smirks and leans over to finger Martin's Roman collar—not the plastic tab that most priests wear these days, but the older, more tasteful collar of heavily starched linen. "Remind me to buy some bleach later," she says, "that's looking a little soiled."

Martin nods and murmurs his thanks through chocolate crumbs.

"Which reminds me," she adds, "I saw Sheila and her son at the A&P yesterday."

A distinct flicker of interest dances across his eyes, though Federal doesn't notice.

"What's that youngest one's name," she asks, "Douglas? No, Gregory, I think." She pauses, laying an index finger over her lips. For all her commanding size and presence, our mother can be a rather silly sort of woman, much given to the distraction of insignificant details. "I always forget that child's name."

"*Any*way," I say.

From behind his cupcake, Martin smiles at me, but there is something gently admonishing in his eyes, as if to suggest, *Be patient with her.* Easy to be patient when she believes you're Christ incarnate.

"Well, whatever," she continues, "he looks just like his father, God rest his poor soul. Oh, what *is* her youngest son's name, Martin?"

"I think it's Gordon."

"Gordon," she says, "thank you. Anyway, I told Sheila, 'Father Martin's coming home this weekend!' "—she repeats this in the same cheery tone with which she doubtless related the information in the supermarket—"and she wanted to know all about your new parish. She said you wrote her a *love-ly* sympathy letter after the accident. I think it really meant a lot to her."

"You call him 'Father Martin' to Sheila?" I ask.

"Well certainly, dear. He's not 'Father Granotti' to her—my goodness, they used to date each other."

"That's what I mean," I say, "fifteen years ago he was copping feels off her—now she's supposed to call him *Father Martin?*"

"Patrick, that is disgusting." She snatches a pot holder from the table and returns to the oven. "Martin didn't fly up here to listen to that kind of talk."

His face impassive as he touches a napkin to his mouth, Martin winks at me.

Federal pokes a toothpick into the cupcakes still baking. "It *was* nice of you to write to her, dear—Lord knows she's had a difficult year. Still looks terrific, though."

My mother is right about that, for I too have recently run into Sheila, and frankly wouldn't mind getting a piece of her widowed action. But I, for one, have had action enough in the past week, which is why, at age twenty-four, I'm living at home for the first time in five years. Never having been blessed with Martin's taste for celibacy, I recently took up with a spritely and energetic girl who follows the local band I sing with, a young woman by the name of Vivian Tresser. Like me, Viv is a

drummer, but unlike me she is a high school sophomore, age
sixteen. As it happens, her golf pro father is a rather protec-
tive and volatile man, not to mention something of an alcoholic. After he learned she'd been seeing me—that is, after he
caught her sneaking back into the house one morning—he
phoned to say that next time he'd break every one of my fingers, noting that I'd be lucky if I ever played "so much as a
goddamn bongo drum again." By the second call, two nights
and one rendezvous later, he got right to the heart of the matter, telling me in no uncertain terms that if I ever speak
another word to his daughter, let alone touch her, he will personally see to having me emasculated. What he finally did, or
so I'm convinced, was set fire to my little rented bungalow
outside of town. I reported my suspicions to a desk officer the
next day, but the police won't even concede it was arson.

In any event, the important thing for me to do right now is
lie low. Keep my fingers and various useful organs at home
and intact. And the next time Vivian takes it into her head to
call me here, make sure I answer the phone before Federal
does. Because the look that woman gave me last night, standing in her nightgown and holding the receiver against her
leg, was by no means uplifting. "For you," she said in a chilly
monotone. Her mouth was pursed, and her eyes narrowed
just enough to convey both disappointment and disdain—an
expression of hers that I am barely less vulnerable to today
than when I was twelve.

The fact is, this has always been a decidedly matriarchal
family, which is, I suppose, appropriate for any good Catholic
home. After all, even Saint Joseph is but a simple and ineffec-
tual carpenter when stood beside the majestic mystery of Mary
the Virgin Mother. Our own father, who passed away seven
years ago, was by no means a wimp, but it was clearly always
Federal who wore the pants here. Since Martin Senior's death
she has become more solicitous of male opinions—of my
brother's, anyway—but she remains a veritable monarch of a
mother. We children—Martin and I and our two married sis-

ters—were suckers for parental approval, yet it was always our mother's acclamation that mattered most. Likewise, on those occasions when we committed some transgression or other, it was *her* disappointment we deemed most damning. And still do today, I suppose.

Federal now pulls a package of frozen whitefish from the freezer and runs it under warm water. (In recent years she has rarely felt compelled to serve fish on Friday, but Martin's being here is an exception.) "You two should take a walk while it's still nice out," she says. I suspect she's asked Martin to have a talk with me while he's home, and this is most likely his cue.

The two of us cut across the lawn and turn down the street toward the high school—the Catholic one, Martin's alma mater, which I was lucky enough to avoid. The sidewalk is littered with the thorny green casings of fallen chestnuts, which Martin scuffs at as we walk along. "D'you lose a lot in the fire?" he asks.

"Enough."

"All those books and tapes?"

I nod. The thought of the loss, still fresh, can prompt me any moment to tears if I dwell on it.

"I see you saved the pedal bass, at least."

"And the snare. Needs a new a batter head, though."

He nods, scowling slightly to convey his sympathy. "I've got some clothes stored in the attic, if you need anything."

"Thanks," I tell him.

We walk in silence for a time, somehow a little less at ease with each other than we were in Federal's presence.

By the time we reach the high school, someone's burly Saint Bernard has joined us, loping along at Martin's side. We cross the football field and the cinder track to the old cement grandstand. The dog takes off after a squirrel.

"Mom tells me you're thinking about going back to college," Martin says, starting up the crumbling steps.

"Not really, I just wanted her to stop hounding me about it."

"Oh." He stops at a row near the top, brushing a piece of broken glass from the seat and sitting down. "Still, you'd only have, what—thirty, forty credits left to do?"

"More than that. Anyway, a B.A.'s not going to land me a recording contract."

"No, but if you ever wanted to do something else, later, it could help."

"I suppose," I say.

For Martin, as for Federal, the highlight of my music career occurred eight or nine years ago, when I played guitar for several months at the Newman Center's folk masses. Still, any time the band lands a gig in Boston, or if we get a feeler, say, from some record exec in New York, it is most likely Federal I'll find myself calling with the news. As I say, she'd rather see me with an acoustic guitar singing "Michael, Row Your Boat Ashore," but she's still one of the O-Zones' biggest supporters, and every few months insists that I bring the other four band members over for dinner.

Martin is quiet now, lobbing pieces of cinder onto the track, and I wait to see if he's concluded his little homily on the virtues of college.

"Good place to meet some girls your own age, too," he says, trying to soften the remark with a slight smirk.

"Jesus, Martin, give me a break." I stand up and jerk my head toward the track, and he follows me back down.

"Sorry," he says. "Can't help wondering why you're seeing a girl who's only sixteen, though."

"Martin, it's not quite so hot and heavy as you'd think," I say. "I mean, the fact that her old man burned me out makes it look like there's a lot more to it." There is something less than convincing in my voice, and he glances at me.

A gust of autumn wind hits us head on as we cross the football field, billowing Martin's windbreaker out behind him like a hunchback. "Sixteen's pretty young, though, Trick."

"Well, Horatio, I guess there are just more things in heaven and earth, et cetera, you know?"

"What the hell's that mean?"

I shake my head.

"What," he says, "you're going to tell me she's sixteen going on twenty-six, I suppose?"

"No, she's sixteen going on seventeen, that's just the point."

"You've lost me, Patrick, what are you saying—you're into minors now?"

"Yes, Martin, I'm into minors now. Jesus fucking Christ."

"Well I can't read your mind! And that wasn't His middle name. What are you telling me?"

"I don't know," I say, "it's not worth explaining, I just . . . there's something very refreshing about a girl who's still so . . . unjaded by the world. She's still got that sort of adolescent idealism about her. I like that." Which is true, though I suppose I'm equally taken by her pristine and nubile beauty—a fact I don't bother mentioning just now.

Martin watches me, waiting for more, and I shrug. "I mean, shit, Martin, half the girls my age just want to earn an M.B.A., for Christ sake. Make a killing on Wall Street."

"You just need to look harder," he says.

"Hey, you think I've been cloistered the last five years? I'll give you a typical example. I went home with a girl a few months ago, after we played Hunt's one night? Twenty-three, very articulate, *stun*ningly attractive. We get back to her place and have a few drinks, start getting a little cozy on the sofa. Somehow we start talking politics. And this girl tells me she thinks Reagan's actually been good for the country. She really likes him!"

"Lot of people do."

"Well, it was all over at that point. I mean, my flower just wilted."

"And?"

"And nothing. I got the hell out of there."

"So that's why you're seeing a sixteen-year-old?"

"Martin, it was a de*flat*ing experience, not traumatic. I told you, there's a lot I like about Vivian."

He nods. "Her adolescent idealism."

"That's one thing, yeah. There's something sort of . . . I don't know, redeeming about that. You understand redemption, Martin, right? It's this concept where—"

"All right, back off."

And at that moment I literally do stop and let him proceed ahead of me, because we've reached the narrow hole in the fence that borders the high school's playing fields. We step back onto my mother's street, where Mrs. Billaport, out raking leaves, looks up and waves at us.

"I don't know, Trick, maybe it's all harmless then. Maybe it is. I just don't like seeing you court more trouble than you need. And I've gotta tell you, if I had a sixteen-year-old daughter who was seeing a twenty-five-year-old guy—"

"Twenty-*four*, thank you."

"Okay, twenty-four. Anyway, I'd be concerned too."

"Well," I say, "it's not a spot you're likely to be in real soon, is it?"

He closes his eyes in a gesture of patient exasperation. "Try to think of Mom anyway, okay?"

"Don't I always?" I say, not meaning the remark nearly so sarcastically as Martin surely thinks I do.

That night, just as we're finishing a late dinner of whitefish and broccoli, there is a knock at the front door. When I answer it, Sheila is standing there in a blue Scandinavian sweater and black Levi's, a handsome leather purse hanging from one shoulder. "I hope you're not eating dinner," she says wincing slightly. A faint blush spreads slowly across her creamy complexion.

"No! Come on in," I say, and I call to Martin.

He wanders in from the dining room, wearing lay clothes now, and throws his head back in cheerful surprise. "Well hello!" he says, greeting her with a hearty but somehow asexual embrace.

Sheila stands on her tiptoes to hug him, her hands stiff and awkward near his shoulders. She steps back and glances at the napkin in his hand, then peers uncertainly toward the dining room. "I guess I should have called first," she says, tucking a lock of hair behind her ear. "I'm so used to eating early with the kids."

"Not at all," Martin tells her. He takes her by the elbow and leads her into the dining room, where Federal immediately begins plying Sheila with coffee and dessert. Federal, in fact, is being particularly courteous and solicitous of Sheila—too much so, which puts each of us uncomfortably in mind of the reason: last winter, about ten months ago, Sheila's husband was killed in a freak ski-lift accident. Any moment now I expect Federal to begin telling her how the first two years are the worst, but that you never completely lose a person you've known so long and so well; that strangely he is still there whenever you need to talk, that it can be like a form of prayer. Mercifully, though, we are spared that spiel.

Watching Sheila sip at her coffee there beside Martin, I remember that in one of my drawers upstairs there is a black-and-white snapshot, circa 1969, of the two of them sitting at this very dinner table. Sheila wears bangs and braces in the picture, and for some reason she is holding my father's pipe in one hand; Martin, beside her, sports a haircut that sneaks daringly over the tops of his ears, flashing his familiar lopsided smile. A cake with seventeen candles blazes before him, and I, at age seven, white shirt buttoned clear to my throat, stand at his side. His left arm is draped across my back, drawing me closer to help him extinguish the flames.

For the longest time Martin and Sheila were more or less my ideal of what a guy and his girl were supposed to be; but when Martin went away to college, already with a notion of transferring to the seminary, he encouraged Sheila to begin seeing other people. He'd always *talked* about the priesthood, but giving up the likes of Sheila struck everyone as another matter altogether. Everyone but Federal, that is, for quite aside from actively encouraging his contemplation of a religious life, she has, I believe, always perceived our girlfriends—the serious ones, anyway—as a threat to her own sovereignty. In any case, Sheila took Martin at his word, and before he was even ordained, she was engaged to a young intern she'd met at work.

At Martin's request, she has just pulled out pictures of her three children, when the phone rings and Federal gestures that it's for me. The solemn tone with which she tells the caller that yes, Patrick is here, leads me to suspect it is Vivian on the line. I excuse myself and take the call upstairs.

To my surprise, it's Detective Lebow, wanting to verify a few details from my statement. "Looks like we might have a witness to arson out at your place," he finally allows. "Jogger saw a guy with a kerosene can that night. We're going to question your girlfriend's father in the morning."

"Detective. I told you, she's not my girlfriend."

"Right, I remember now. Anyway, you keep cool, Patrick, and I'll get back to you when we know more. By the way, you're not still seeing this girl, are you?"

"No, Detective, I'm not still seeing her." Better to lie to the law, I think, than take a chance of pushing Viv's father any further. "Why do you ask?"

"Oh, I don't know," he says, "I was just thinking if you were, you might want to watch your back. Guy could mean business."

"Thanks," I tell him, "I'll remember that."

I wander into my old bedroom, suddenly exhausted, and fall down on the bed. I should go downstairs and visit, I think, I should at least remove my contacts if I'm going to fall asleep, but instead I lie there and toy with some numbers. Like six-teen. When I was sixteen, Vivian was . . . eight. Not good. Okay, when I was twenty, she was . . . twelve. Probably a very sexy little twelve, but still a definite no-no. So what about it—sixteen and twenty-four? A little out of the ordinary, but hard-ly a perversion of human nature. Twenty-one and twenty-nine? Twenty-five and thirty-three? Who'd bang war drums over twenty-five and thirty-three? Suppose J.C., at thirty-three, had told his Old Man, "Screw this crucifixion gig, I've got a great thing going with that Magdalene chick. She's twenty-five, she knows how to please a man, and she thinks I'm the cat's meow." Who'd blame him? That is, who'd blame Him? Not me. That is, not I.

But by then I must be more asleep than awake, because the whole scenario seems logical somehow.

An hour later, eyes stinging, I wake gratefully from a dream in which my mother's house is ablaze. Flames spiral out the roof and windows, and Martin stands beside me in the middle of the street. Twice he pushes me toward the house and says, "Blow it out! Jesus, *do* something, blow it out!"

I sit up and sniff for smoke, then pull my sneakers on and head downstairs for some coffee. From the kitchen I can hear Federal bidding Sheila good-bye on the front porch. I stroll into the living room and glance out the window to the drive-way, where Martin is getting into Sheila's car with her.

In a little while Federal wanders back into the kitchen car-rying several dirty cups and saucers, and dons her eternal apron.

"Tell me," I say, turning a page of the newspaper, "that wouldn't have been Father Martin I saw driving off with the lovely widow Crouse?"

She releases a breathy sound that's half sigh and half laugh. "I guess your brother's a very hip priest," she says.

"Jeans, a turtleneck, and a pretty woman—I don't know. I bet his parishioners would never stand for that."

"His parishioners," I say, "won't even take Communion from a layperson."

"Is that true?"

"So Martin says."

"Well, they wouldn't like this, then. Not that it's anyone else's business. Still, I wish he'd worn his collar." She runs a yellow sponge under warm water. "Then again, maybe that wouldn't be such a good idea either."

"Mother, he's thirty-four years old, let him be a little bit normal. Let him be a little *ab*normally normal."

"What's *that* mean?"

"I mean celibacy's odd enough—you can't expect him to banish half the human race from his social life."

"Well of course I don't. In fact, I think it's very nice that he and Sheila have stayed friends." She studies a trace of lipstick on one of the mugs, then vigorously swabs it clean. "There's no reason they can't take in a movie together," she says.

"Say it enough times," I tell her, "and you'll convince yourself."

Around eleven o'clock I'm lying on my bed listening to a local DJ who occasionally plays a single we cut last summer— a locally produced job—called "Status Quo." Frankly, it's not one of our better tunes, and this, I've discovered, is the best way of finding the song's flaws—hearing it more or less unexpectedly on the radio. The "A" side of the record, a song called "Black Sheep, White Shepherds," was our best hope for a hit, but it's a little too political for the likes of local listeners. I'm not sure I've got the right station—all these DJs have the same inane sound—so I keep toying with the dial, and every time it edges past 98.5 I hear fragments of Gary Puckett and the Union Gap singing "Young Girl" (*You're just a bay-bee i-in dis-guise . . .*). As if I needed any more advice on that score.

I'm about to get undressed and turn in for the night, when a movement outside the window catches my eye. I sit up and snap the radio off—and Jesus Christ, there's a guy in a white shirt clambering over the deck railing. Vivian's crazy father has come to finish the job!

I flick the light out, and as I do so he raises one arm as if he's about to throw something. I cover my head and dive for the closet, rooting around for a baseball bat, an umbrella, something to swing at this sick fool before he gets in here and makes a soprano of me. By the time I locate an old tennis racket, heavy and lethal in its wooden press, he's begun prying at the window.

My heart is about to pound through my chest, and I slowly edge over to the window, both hands gripping the tennis racket.

But the nose and lips mushed up against the glass are not those of a man.

"You little *fucker*," I whisper out loud, my foolish terror giving way to a heart-fluttering relief. I flick the light back on, and slide the window and storm open.

Vivian chuckles and bumps her head as she bends to climb in. "Hey, little drummer boy! Did I give you a scare?"

"Shhh! More like a cardiac," I say, leaning forward to meet her kiss. "You're lucky I didn't clobber you."

"You were really a riot," she says. "You know you're actually white? I never realized people really turn white when they get scared."

"People turn black and blue when they get beaten," I tell her. "Does your father know where you are?"

"Of course, I'm at Carol's for the night."

"This isn't smart," I say.

"Well, you said not to call you here—how else am I going to talk to you? Anyway, I brought you something, you ingrate."

And reaching behind her she draws from the back pocket of her jeans a pair of Regal Kip drumsticks, size 5A, medium-tapered tip. In red engraved letters above the manufacturer's imprint, one reads FOR P WITH and the other, L FROM V. "Don't let anyone use them for kindling," she says.

I kiss her mouth, which is cold from the night, and she takes this as an invitation to plop down on the bed, extracting from her hair her white plastic hairband and setting it on the desk.

"How'd you get up on that deck?" I ask, twirling one of the sticks.

"I dragged a garbage can over and shinned up the post. Don't worry, I cased the whole house first. Nobody's up except a guy and a woman drinking coffee in the living room. Real pretty woman—who is she?"

"Must be my brother and his friend."

"That's your brother? I thought he was a priest. I mean, he didn't have a collar on or anything."

"It's there," I say, "believe me. You just can't always see it."

She nods, smirking, fairly glowing now with the excitement of her late-night exploit. Her smirk broadens into a smile, and she lies back on the bed, nuzzling her face against my pillow. "Maybe I can just stay here tonight," she says. "I could get back into Carol's before everybody's up."

"That's a thought."

Viv kicks her sneakers off and lies there grinning on the mattress, taking in the furnishings of this old room as if they revealed something intimate about me: an uncomfortable wooden chair I built in the Boy Scouts; an autographed photo of Buddy Rich; and, stuck in an old wooden frame, a black-and-white photograph of Martin celebrating his first Mass.

I step over to the door and lock it, but can't help hearing its muffled *click* as a tongue clack of disapproval from down the hall.

Vivian hooks her finger into my belt loop, and I settle down beside her with my hand on her hip. Beneath her blouse I can make out the twin risings of her brown-nippled breasts, all taut and firm with unfinished growth. Gary Puckett is still crooning at the back of my brain: . . . *'cause I'm a-fraaid we'll go-o too faaarr . . .*

But of course that horse is long out of the barn.

Later, with the mattress on the floor because of the squeaky frame, Viv smiles sleepily and gives the sheet a modest tug that leaves only her smooth-skinned shoulders exposed.

"Better not get too comfortable," I say.

"I am comfortable," she murmurs. "Do you have an alarm clock or something?"

"Really, Vivian."

"What's to worry about?" she asks, rubbing her cheek against the inside of my arm.

"Death by fire. We've got to start being a lot more discreet. If anything."

She opens her eyes. "Wasn't this pretty discreet?"

"Yeah, I kind of wish you'd used the chimney, though."

Her expression remains earnest. "He won't know I'm still seeing you, Trick. Besides, if he only met you, I know he'd change his mind. He went back to AA this week, and once he dries out—" She stops. "What do you mean, 'If anything'?"

"I don't know." I wave a hand dismissively.

She scowls and sits up, clasping the sheet to her chest. "Your mother's been saying things, hasn't she? I could tell she hated me when I called the other night."

"Nobody hates you, Vivian—she's never even met you."

"But she's been saying things, hasn't she?"

"More my brother, actually."

"Oh, great, a whole welcoming committee."

"Viv, it's me they're annoyed with."

"But why?"

"Because. They think it's, I don't know, unfair to you."

"To *me?* But that's so . . . *sex*ist. Or ageist."

"I guess. I don't know. I've kind of wondered myself a few

times if you should really be, you know, seeing someone so much older."

She looks at me in genuine surprise. "I thought you said I was so incredibly mature for sixteen?"

"You are! You are."

"So?"

"I don't know, maybe your first serious relationship should be . . ." I shrug.

She's silent now, chewing on the inside of her lip. "But I thought . . . I don't know, I just thought . . . aren't we in love?"

Her eyes have gone glassy suddenly. To be honest, it hasn't been much discussed, love. The fact is, I've been so preoccupied with the snickering amusement and disapproval of every other person I know (and a few I don't) that I've half doubted the sincerity of my own part in these doings. After all, it's a little disconcerting to suddenly find your sense of well-being so entirely dependent upon a girl too young to remember Watergate. A girl whose womanhood only announced itself—in a friend's swimming pool of all places, shocking both young bathers into a panic—a scant three years ago. So I've kept love—both word and emotion—on a short leash with little slack, half convinced that any day I'd be supplanted by some skateboarding bopper from Driver's Ed.

But watching Viv's eyes well over into tears now, I touch the edge of the sheet to her cheek and whisper with conviction, "We are." And it occurs to me, as I fold her body into mine, that reasoning with Daddy Dementia is still not out of the question. I could take my earring off, put a clean shirt on, wear my sincerity on my sleeve. Why not? Tomorrow even. Meantime, caution.

We straddle the windowsill and step out onto the deck, where the main support post is about fifteen feet from the top of the overturned garbage can. The post is more squarish than round, which makes sliding down it more than a little awkward and uncomfortable. Vivian, however, is like a little monkey. By the time I get to the bottom I've got a splinter the size of a kitchen match sticking out of my thumb. I'm not looking forward to getting back in this way, but I don't have a key on me, and my mother locks the place up like a fort at night. "I'll walk you to Carol's," I tell Vivian, "just let me see if there's a key under the front mat."

Sheila's car is parked in the driveway, though she and Martin must be in the kitchen now, because the dimly lit living room is empty. In the darkness of the long screened-in porch, I bend to feel beneath the mat for a key. Vivian spies Tripod, my mother's three-legged cat, at the opposite end of the porch, and tiptoes quietly after him. There's no key under the mat or milk box, and I signal to Vivian to come on. In the weak light from the living room windows she's barely distinguishable, leaning against the railing with the cat in her arms.

"Com'ere," she whispers, beckoning with one hand.

I cross the creaky boards to where she sits. A few quiet strains of George Winston's piano drift out from the living room stereo. "Can you still see your brother's collar?" she says.

At first, because of the high arm of the sofa, I don't see anything. But then, beyond the sofa's arm, I see two other arms, human, clad in blue sleeves with white snowflakes and enfolding a familiar form. Martin and Sheila are lying full length along the sofa, their heads merging in a slow and lengthy kiss. They are both fully clothed, even down to their shoes.

"I'll be damned."

"I bet *he'll* be," Viv whispers, releasing a little laugh and burying her mouth in Tripod's neck.

Sheila's hand slides up Martin's back to caress his thick black hair, then traces a line down his shoulder. Viv chuckles again and I draw her away, feeling, briefly, as if I've just witnessed a kid brother's first conquest.

Tripod pads along behind us, and just as we reach the

street there is a quick metallic sliding noise from up near the deck, punctuated by a sharp *clack!* and the tinkling of glass. The storm window I left open.

Almost immediately a light goes on in my mother's bedroom, and a moment later there is another in the hall at the top of the stairs.

"Shit, I hope Martin heard that." I stand there in the middle of the street, staring helplessly back at the living-room windows as I did in my burning house dream. "Wait a minute," I tell Vivian, and I dash back to the porch.

On the sofa, Martin and Sheila are still going at it like a couple of teenagers. For a moment I consider knocking on the window or ringing the doorbell, but I hesitate. And in that moment of hesitation, Federal, in her powder-blue nightgown, appears on the bottom step of the dining-room stairs. She peeks out into the living room, squinting slightly, and then freezes. Quickly, she turns and disappears up the stairs again.

Martin and Sheila continue on making the beast with two belt buckles, both blissfully ignorant until Martin suddenly sits bolt upright and cocks his head to listen. He puts a finger to his lips and strains forward, then shakes his head and relaxes, easing back into the welcome warm arms of his old flame.

When I go downstairs for breakfast the next morning, I can hear Martin in the second-floor shower. Singing in the shower, to be precise. In the kitchen, Federal sits quiet and unmoving behind the local section of the paper, a cup of coffee cooling untouched in front of her.

"There's some bacon by the stove," she says dully.

"Thanks, I'll wait for Martin."

She half nods, curtly.

I'm none too eager to witness the greeting he's likely to receive upon making his way down here. Last night, when I returned from walking Vivian to her friend's house, Sheila's car was gone and the house was completely dark. I considered scrambling back into my bedroom like some dim-witted Romeo who's got the balcony scene backwards, but instead opted for ringing the doorbell. I figured Martin might still be awake, and after a full minute I'd just about given up when Federal came to the door in her nightgown, looking bleary and aged, and more than ever, widowed. This morning it will take her only a glance to make Martin aware that his transgression has been divined.

Setting the paper down, she now covers a yawn and says somewhat peevishly, "Patrick, I wish you'd take a key if you're going to be out so late. It's not nice getting people up in the middle of the night."

"Sorry," I tell her.

"Where did you go, anyway? I thought you were here when I went to bed."

"Just out."

She looks at me over the top of her glasses and says quietly, "Not with that young girl, I hope."

I take a sip of orange juice. "You mean Vivian?"

"Whatever her name is."

"Well I'm telling you: it's Vivian."

Her mouth tenses and she tries to stare me down, but I won't allow it, and with a twitch in her lip she silently retreats to the paper. On the surface, of course, this is a minor moment, a trivial snapshot of family friction, yet within the quirky confines of our particular dynamic it is something more. I've just drawn an updated map of her sovereign territory, and, however displeased the matriarch may be, she knows there's no disputing my cartography.

A few minutes later, Martin, his hair slicked back, dressed in a work shirt and corduroys, trots down the stairs whistling "Yuletide Garland," though Christmas is more than two months away yet. He doesn't have a clue about Federal, and I can't help feeling a certain uneasy spectator's interest.

She is standing before the open refrigerator when he enters.

"Morning," he says, and he claps me on the shoulder.

Federal turns and, apparently not opting for the quick kill, says in a vaguely ironic voice, "You're finally up?"

"It's not *that* late, is it?" he asks. He gives her a peck on the cheek, which she accepts rather stiffly.

"How was the movie?" I ask.

"Oh, it was okay. Nothing special." He sits opposite me and pours a glass of juice.

"Hmm," she says. "Sounds dirty from the review I just read."

Martin glances at me and I roll my eyes. "Well, it might be hard put to earn the imprimatur," he says, "but it wasn't so bad. A little gratuitous nudity. Nothing harmful."

"Hmmm," she says again.

Martin begins slowly tapping his fingers against the tiny juice glass; it seems he's finally begun to gauge the temperature in here. He lets out a slow breath and rubs his palms along his thighs, then draws from the wide slash pocket of his pants his limpish white collar and sets it on the table.

For all I witnessed last night, even I hadn't bargained for this.

Federal stands whipping a bowl of eggs at the sink, her hand slowing to a mere stir as she glances at the collar, at Martin, and at the collar again. Lying on its edge in a wide U-shape, it reminds me of Viv's plastic hair band.

Martin nod vaguely at the table. "Just in case you get a chance to bleach it for me," he says.

I believe I hear a literal sigh of relief pass through Federal's nostrils, though her only verbal response is a sort of grunt. She carries the bowl of eggs to the stove and drops a pat of butter into a pan. Her back turned to both of us, she says in a dullish tone, "I hope we'll at least get you all to ourselves tonight. The girls are driving over for the weekend," meaning our sisters and their families.

Martin winces slightly. "I wish you'd told me," he says, rubbing at his freshly shaved chin, "Sheila invited me over for dinner. She was sort of hoping I could meet her kids."

Facing us now, Federal blinks and turns back to the stove to lower the gas jet, then turns to Martin again. "What do you mean?" she asks finally.

"I mean eat dinner and meet her children. Eat *with* all of them, I guess."

Federal is silent.

"Those kids are probably starved for some male attention," I say. "Anyway, Em and Gloria'll be here all weekend."

Martin looks encouraged by this, but doesn't say anything. Then, turning to Federal he asks, "Okay?"

"You're a grown man," she says, "you can do whatever you want."

"Mom, give him a break, will you? So he wants to have dinner with Sheila."

"I didn't say he shouldn't. I just hope you're not . . ." and she leaves off, shaking her head in frustration.

"Oh, Jesus," Martin says. "Not what? Did I say I'm giving up my vows? Did I?! I am having dinner with my oldest friend and her three children." Standing he adds, "Now if that's going to ruin your day, Mother, I don't know what to tell you. Too damn bad, I guess," and he lurches into the living room, the front door quickly banging shut behind him.

I'm not sure whether to stay or follow after Martin at this point, but I decide he's better off with a few minutes on his own. Also, I want to be sure I don't give in to the temptation of saying something helpful, like, "Try to think of Mom, okay?" So I sit waiting for my English muffin to toast. Martin's collar is there on the table, and I touch at the silver snap, watching Tripod hobble into the room. He pauses and announces himself with an interrogative *mrrowp?* before brushing up against Federal's leg. "It's already over there," she says, jerking her head at his bowl.

Her eyes, I notice, are misty now, and she wipes her hands on her apron, looking rather glazed for a moment.

And suddenly she begins emptying dirty dishes and silverware from the main sink into the adjacent basin. Methodically, thoroughly, she sponges the sink in silence, finally plugging the drain and running warm water. She takes Martin's soiled collar from the table and squirts a few milky drops of Ivory liquid onto it. Watching her, I remember reading that the stuff was once used to simulate semen in porn films. And sitting there I wonder: How can a mother wish such a life on her son? Celibacy. Forever.

Last night Viv told me her father's problem is that he wants her to be his little girl forever, that he literally hates to see her grow up, and maybe that's also Federal's design—to make Martin always be her boy, to remain the preeminent woman in his life. No doubt she once hoped to manage me similarly, except that I learned to loosen the noose of those apron strings. Or so I tell myself.

As if in a trance now she begins soaking the soiled collar in the sink, gently scrubbing the fine linen weave, working in vain to make Martin hers again.

▼

G R A C E

▲

It's my being with Sandy at the time that gets to me. I tell Bitsy I'm going out to play some B-ball at the rec center, when I'm really heading over to Sandy's place. I don't know, I felt uneasy about carrying on with Sandy anyway, and who wouldn't feel like hell, not being home when this kind of thing happens to your wife. But it's kind of like, being off with Sandy that night, like it was almost me who did it to Bitsy. Which is something I certainly can't tell her, although I wish I could, so maybe she could free me from it. Whatever that means.

I've been trying to get it together to break off with Sandy for months, only it's always a little different once we're face to face, or lying together on her waterbed. Or it used to be. I haven't even had the urge now in about three weeks. I come home and sit down in the living room, and almost any day of the week I can see the whole thing play itself out again, as if I'd been there watching. Furniture falling, Bitsy screaming for me, the knife, the letters.

Which is the other thing. The letters. *W-I-N*—right there across her chest; eight separate cuts at least four inches long. I

didn't even notice they were letters at first, she was too much
of a mess. Even with all the blood, I could tell they weren't
much worse than surface wounds, but I figured the son of a
bitch had just carved on her at random. But when she gets
home the next night, I'm helping her put on some lotion
they gave us at the hospital, and that's when I realize. I saw
the letters, and for one weird moment I thought for sure she
must have known. Must have known where I'd been, what I'd
been doing when it happened to her. Which was ridiculous.
But then I start thinking about the guy who did it. Maybe *he*
knew. Maybe he was telling me something. And I try to think
of anyone who might know about me and Sandy. Maybe one
of her old boyfriends. So the next day I call Sandy from work,
but she says there's no one, nobody who'd care anyway. I tell
her to think hard, and she finally sighs and says this is pointless, that I'm just becoming obsessed. But I can barely hear
because somebody's putting shovels away in the tool room,
and I say, "Of course I'm upset!"

She says, "No, Wynn, *ob-sessed*, like preoccupied too much,"
as if I never heard the freakin' word before. That's the only
thing about Sandy. She graduated from the university here,
and sometimes she seems to think she's got something over
people like me and Bitsy just because of it. Anyway, she keeps
insisting the letters don't mean me at all, which might be
true, but still. She says maybe it was just some pervert saying
he'd won. WIN. But I don't buy it. I'd like to think it's just a
coincidence, but I don't know.

Anyway, the first night Bitsy's home, I'm sitting on the edge
of the bed helping her with the lotion, and that's when I realize. She's got scrapes on her back and shoulders, but right
across her chest and all those freckles, these straight little
thin-line cuts with stitches: WIN. I just stop right there, and the
stuff drips off my fingers onto her nightgown. "Bitsy," I say,
"you didn't tell me it was letters."

She looks up at me suddenly and tugs her nightgown
around her tiny shoulders. "I thought you knew."

"No," I say.

"I mean, the cop, all those people—they talked to you, didn't they?"

She buttons up the top of her nightgown.

"Yeah, but . . ."

I can remember the cop looking kind of strange when I told him my name, then he asked me to spell it. And spell it again. Then later the intern came out to talk. When I asked him about the cuts, he just said there'd be some scarring, never mentioned anything else. "Well what the hell does that mean, W-I-N?"

"I don't know! I suppose it's because I was yelling for you." She starts pulling at a loose thread in the quilt and won't look up.

"Jesus, Bitsy, why didn't *I* know about this?" I kick one of her clogs against the wall, and this palm branch Bitsy brought home from church last month drops off the mirror onto the floor. I leave it there and sit on top of the hamper.

After a while Bitsy sits up and says, "Will you pick that up, please? Anyway, what's it matter? Now you know. It's not as if it happened to you."

"What's that supposed to mean?"

"Just what I said. I mean, it's not something else we need to worry about, is it?" She reaches for the glass of 7-Up I put on the nightstand for her and takes a slow, delicate sip, barely moving her head to the glass; the son of a bitch wrenched her neck in addition to everything else.

I put the palm branch back on the mirror and go over to the bureau where the phone is, trying to remember the cop's name.

Bitsy sets her glass down and says, "Oh, baby, what are you doing with the phone book? Who are you calling?"

"That cop—or the doctor. I'm your goddamn husband, Bitsy—they should've told me about this."

"Wynn, put the phone down. They were perfectly decent men—please don't go and embarrass me."

" 'Perfectly decent men,' huh? I'd like to know what the hell was so special about them."

"Shut up, Wynn. Just shut up." That's what she tells me. "Give me the lotion, I'll do it myself."

So that's her first night home. By that point I'm almost inclined to head back over to Sandy's, but that's the last place I'm going to now. I tell Bitsy I'm sorry, kick off my sneaks, and sit up on the bed next to her, just holding her. Her hair's still damp from the bath, and her nightgown smells like the dried orange all pincushioned with cloves that she keeps in her underwear drawer. She rubs at the patch on my jeans, but then she stops and just stares off at the ceiling light.

After a while she starts pulling at her eyebrows and flicking the hairs onto the floor. I can tell from the way her mouth is set so tight that she's trying to keep herself from crying. I pull her to me and stroke her hair, and pretty soon we fall asleep like this, the lights still burning, me in my clothes, both of us lying on top of the quilt.

A few hours later Bitsy wakes up breathing hard, her eyes darting around the room, like she's done almost every night for three weeks now. It's getting to be a regular ritual, though I think she'll get over it eventually. When I first came back from Nam, I used to hit the dirt every time a car backfired or a balloon burst, but after a while they get to be cars and balloons again.

The next day Bitsy insists on going to work, so I hang around the house till about eight-thirty and take her down to the bank myself. She's a senior teller at the main downtown branch, but her friend Lydia's trying to get her into the loan department, which would be more or less of a promotion.

I'm transplanting gladiolus bulbs that morning in the beds on the main campus. Except for a couple of lazy work-study kids, it's all older men who work with me. Around noon I tell

Rupert, the only dependable one of the bunch, to make sure everyone's got something to do, because I have to go downtown for some snakes.

The little shop Sandy owns is right nearby, so when I finish up at the toy store I head over to her place. She's had this artsy card and gift shop for about two years—pretty successful apparently, and already she plans to expand. The place is empty when I go in, and I can tell she's surprised to see me. She says hello in a very concerned tone, then leans over for a kiss. I glance out the window and give her a quick one; Bitsy works about three blocks from here.

Sandy's hair looks like she's been toying with it again. She's got a sort of frizz these days, or a perm, something, I don't know. Anyway, I don't really like it, although her hair's a nice dirty-blond color and still comes down to about her shoulders. She's a lot taller than Bitsy, with a small gap in her front teeth and the sort of stunning blue-eyed look you can't ignore in a bar—at least I couldn't. She broke her nose diving off somebody's boat a couple years back, and you can sort of tell, it goes off to the left a little, though somehow it only makes her more attractive.

She asks right away how Bitsy's doing, and I tell her not too bad, that she went to work this morning.

"That's a good sign," Sandy says. Then, "What's in the bag?"

I open it and show her.

"Snakes?"

"Keeps the birds away when we put new seeds down."

She raises her eyebrows, as if to tell me it sounds pretty unlikely, but I let it go. She takes my hand in both of hers and says, "You don't look too good, you know. You're still blaming yourself for things, aren't you?"

"What do you expect me to do?"

"I expect you to let up on yourself," she says. "You're going to drive yourself nuts."

"Sandy, you don't just bury this kind of thing and forget about it."

"Look," she says, and she straightens her little credit card imprinter, "it happened, Wynn. It would've happened if you'd been playing basketball or out buying snakes. It would've happened anyway."

"That's a stupid attitude," I tell her. Because if I'd really gone to the rec center, I'd have been home by nine-thirty. At the hospital the cop had asked Bitsy whether she remembered what time it all started, and what room she'd been in before she went to the door. She told him she was ironing shirts in the bedroom, that the nine o'clock movie had only been on a little while when she heard the knock at the door, which she thought was me, that I forgot my key again. Then when Bitsy's getting X-rayed the cop asks *me* questions, including where *I'd* been. I didn't know if I should be straight with him and expect him to keep it under his hat, or what. I finally just told him I was playing basketball with some buddies, and then *I* start feeling like some kind of criminal.

"Wynn, you keep on like this, you're going to hate yourself—and resent me and Bitsy both. You've got to ease up on yourself," she tells me. But what else is she going to say? She wants me to leave Bitsy and cut out this see-you-when-I-can crap, so of course she's got to seem like some sort of merciful angel.

I don't know, I just think I liked it a lot better when things were more casual between us. I can remember back in the winter, lying in bed talking at Sandy's one Saturday afternoon. I asked if it bothered her that I was married, and she said, "No, not really, kind of makes it more exciting." But lately it's like she's trying to push Bitsy out of the picture all the time. On one level I think she's sincere about all this concern for me, but a lot of times it's as if she's just trying to seem nicer than Bitsy. Not that she even knows Bitsy—she says she went into the bank to get a look at her once—but she tries to bad-mouth her a lot, and used to say things like "Where's Bitchy tonight?" which really pissed me off, even when I was mad at Bitsy anyway.

"Listen, sweet," Sandy says, and sticks her finger in between the buttons of my work shirt. "We'd better do some talking about this soon, because you sure as hell can't talk to *her* about this one. And you're going to go bonkers if you keep it bottled up."

It seems so stupid to be talking about *me* needing help, when if she could have seen Bitsy bolting out of a sound sleep last night . . . I don't say anything, and Sandy laces her fingers with mine on the counter. "I'm glad you called me Tuesday night," she says. "I mean, that you felt like you could talk with me about it."

I wish she wouldn't say this, because it reminds me of just what a bastard I am, calling her while Bitsy was lying in the hospital. But listening to Sandy's scratchy voice saying these things, and watching the little points her nipples make against that dark purple blouse, I can feel a little life down there for the first time in days. "Yeah, maybe we can talk," I say. "Not here, though."

"Tonight?"

"Not tonight, okay? I can't leave her alone. Soon."

A lady with a kid comes into the store and nods at us. "I'll call you," I tell Sandy, and head for the door. She gives me that sad, pleading look, like won't I stay, and I feel sort of good on Bitsy's account for leaving.

That night Bitsy and I are lying across the bed watching TV, and in the middle of the local news there's this commercial for the state lottery. The TV screen shows a roulette wheel going round and round, and in each place where there'd usually be a number it says WIN. No shit. Makes me uneasy as hell, almost before I even know why, and I can imagine what it does for Bitsy. I take her hand and squeeze it, and she rolls her eyes at me.

The phone rings, and my stomach knots up a bit worrying that it's Sandy. "I'll get it," I say, but it's only Bitsy's mother checking in. I don't think her parents hold anything against me for being out the other night, though I can just imagine Joyce asking Roger what the hell I was doing out playing basketball so late. Mostly we get along pretty well, though. Bitsy and I have been together since tenth grade, and sometimes it's almost like Joyce and Roger are my own folks, though of course you never forget they're in-laws. Especially Joyce.

From what Bitsy's saying, I can tell her mother's asking her if maybe she wants to go and talk with Father Macklin at St. Joseph's, which apparently she doesn't, and I think that's just as well. Not that I have anything against priests. I knew a few decent ones when I was younger, including the guy who first showed me that gardening's a lot more than just flowers and dirt. But all this laying family problems and relationship problems at some priest's feet I can't go for. Okay, maybe the guy knows spiritual things, but there's a kind of knowledge that comes from living with a woman day after day that a lifetime wanker just can't know about.

Anyway, Bitsy's saying, "I know Father Macklin's dealt with these kinds of things, but I don't *need* to talk with him. Mom, I just won't, okay? I've got Wynn if I need to talk." She finally tells Joyce we'll be over for dinner Friday night, and eases herself back onto the bed. She's still pretty sore, and she's got some mean-looking bruises on her arms. I turn the TV off and ask, "How's your mom?"

"Okay," she says, but I don't think she's really listening. She's just lying back staring at the ceiling, pulling at her eyebrows and grinding the hairs between her fingers. She's still dressed up from work, wearing these navy-blue pumps with straps. I'm about to take them off for her to make her more comfortable—she doesn't like shoes on the quilt—but I think of how that son of a bitch must have pulled her clothes off her the other night, and I don't even want her making the association.

A car honks next door, and I remember the stuff I left out in the back seat. "Be right back," I say, and I get up from the bed and pull on my sneaks.

Bitsy sits up. "Where are you going?"

"Just out to the car."

She sits there frozen, looking at me kind of panicky.

"Really," I say. "I'm just going to get something from the car—I'll be right back."

The rear door of the Toyota, where I got sideswiped last year, gives its goddamn groan, and I grab the five roses wrapped in muddy newspaper from the back seat. They were the first ones to come up in the bed next to the president's house, and I figure Bitsy can use them a whole lot more than those folks. There's no vase in the kitchen, but there's this empty Mrs. Butterworth's maple syrup bottle up on top of the fridge, shaped like somebody's grandmother in an apron. I peel the label off, clip the stems, and fill the bottle up to the old lady's neck with cool water; with the five roses, it actually looks pretty good.

Heading back to the bedroom, I sing "Red Roses for a Blue Lady"—but when I get to the door, Bitsy's got her face in the pillows and her shoulders are heaving. I feel like a fool. "What's wrong?" I ask.

"Nothing, I'm okay," she mumbles.

"Come on, Bits. Were you thinking about it again?"

"No, I wasn't," she says, "but look at me." Her voice sounds pathetic and little-girlish. "Twenty-nine years old and I'm afraid to be in the house by myself. How am I going to live like this? You can't stay and babysit me every time you want to go out. But I *don't* want to be here alone."

I tell her she won't have to be, and massage her back till she stops crying.

After a bit, she turns over a little, facing me again, and rubs at her cheek. "Also," she says, "you sort of blame me for it, don't you, Wynn? For what happened."

"What do you mean?"

"I just think maybe you hold something against me for it. Like the thing you said about that doctor the other night. I don't know. You're just so far away all the time. Always spacing out, like you don't want to be with me or something."

"Bitsy, I don't blame you."

"I don't mean you really *blame* me. But he was going to kill me, Wynn."

She pulls a handkerchief out of my back pocket and dries her nose. She looks pathetic now, pieces of her hair all wet and matted to her cheeks. I pull her head onto my lap as gently as I can, but she starts crying again, wiping her cheek on my leg. "Bitsy, really, I know you did all you could. It's okay," I say.

"Yeah, all right," she tells me. She rubs her eyebrows, which look rashy and patchy now from where she's always pulling at them. "But I really feel bad, Wynn. I mean, bad for me, but also for you, you know? That I couldn't stop him."

"I know you do," I say. "I know it."

I don't see Sandy for a week or so, but then one Monday morning Bitsy says she's going back to her meditation class after work, and Lydia wants to take her out to dinner afterward. So Monday afternoon I call Sandy and tell her I'll meet her at her place that evening.

I get there, and I'm barely inside the door when Sandy wraps her arms around me, a real pelvic sort of hug, which I don't feel very sincere returning. She touches the tip of her tongue to the end of my nose, which she says is sunburned, and goes to get me a beer. She's wearing this gauzy white blouse and a pair of old Levi's that fit her almost like a second skin, with her red cowboy boots. I toss my fatigue jacket on the sofa and sit down next to it.

I like the way Sandy's got her place decorated—lots of plants, walls full of pictures, a big loom trailing colorful yarns in one corner. Above the sofa she's got these three black-and-white photographs of her brother carrying a bushel basket of leaves, and he's laughing a little bit more in each one.

I pick up a copy of *Rolling Stone* from the coffee table, and start reading this thing about Agent Orange, which as far as I know I never got exposed to, but who knows? Sandy's standing in the kitchen mixing a glass of red zinger. She says, "Are you reading, or talking to yourself?" That's her way of telling me she doesn't like the fact I sometimes move my lips when I read. "I'm just asking myself why you buy this crap," I say. She brings me a bottle of Tuborg and sits sideways on my lap, asking how long I can stay.

"Only for an hour or so."

She scowls and clicks her tongue against the roof of her mouth.

I don't know if Sandy really thinks I'm some kind of prize, or if she's just gotten to be thirty-one and now she's worried about being single all her life. I first started seeing her back in the winter when things were a little rocky with Bitsy, but not that bad, no worse than the problems everybody's got. I was drinking a lot, which Bitsy doesn't like, and I guess I figured her nagging was a good excuse to go spend time with someone else.

"Well, can we at least go lie down?" Sandy says.

"I guess."

"Oh, you sound real enthusiastic."

"Jesus, Sandy."

"Well, maybe I need a little more attention. I'm sick of just being somebody's monthly diversion," she says, giving me the very opening I need to take this conversation where I think it should go.

Because something's got to change. I move through every day now feeling distracted, as if something's incomplete or out of place. It got to the point where I finally called the rectory at St. Joseph's one morning, to see when this new priest was hearing confessions, but when the time came I didn't do it. It wouldn't make any difference in the end, some stranger doing the same routine he mouths for every other kneeling nitwit. What good would that do me? So I never went, and I don't mention it to Sandy, either. I don't know, it's like, sometimes you want another woman to be sort of a buddy, almost like one of the guys, but they always want to be a wife instead.

Bitsy and I watch TV that night, and there's this great relief that comes from breaking with Sandy, although something's still not back in place. Even so, I go to bed that night feeling more relaxed, and Bitsy and I fool around a little for the first time since it happened. Bitsy's cuts are healing pretty well; the scars are probably going to look like five lines—the downstroke cuts—instead of letters now. Things seem a little better all week, but not better enough, and I still can't always look Bitsy in the eye. Also, she's still full of nervous habits, and wakes up most nights for no reason.

Last night—Friday—we did some grocery shopping, and after dinner I got drunk just sitting watching this detective movie on TV with Bitsy. Later on in bed, I start feeling sick, the room's doing its circle routine, and Bitsy wakes up as I'm heading for the bathroom. But before I can get around the bed, my stomach starts somersaulting, and a corner of the quilt gets covered. Bitsy's real good about it—changes the sheets while I'm in the can, brings in a bucket, and once I'm back in bed sets a damp washcloth on my forehead. She ought to be mad, but she just holds me and whispers nice things, which means a lot at that point.

This morning—Saturday—there's no hangover, miraculously, but Bitsy didn't get much sleep on account of me, and she's still lying in bed. I haven't even got a headache, so I sweat through a set of push-ups, and I can smell last night's gin breaking through the pores on my arms. I lie back on the rug after fifty, and something's still eating at me.

I remember the one other time I was seeing another woman, years ago, feeling like I should tell Bitsy after I broke it off. Maybe that was because I thought she'd find out anyway, though, since it was a neighbor. But I never told her, and she never found out. The guilt just dried up, and I realized that was the thing to do—swallow it. But this isn't just the fling with Sandy that's eating me. It's been almost three weeks since it happened to Bitsy, and I'm certainly not operating on normal, which isn't helping Bitsy get any better, either. She knows something's wrong, and I think she still wonders if I blame her.

I think again about my idea of going to confession last week. I'm not usually that religious—Bitsy gets me to go to Mass at Christmas and Easter, and sometimes on just a regular Sunday. I used to pray a lot when I was in Nam, more out of loneliness than being afraid most times, but this was the thing: without even thinking about it, just spacing out on some stretch of road, or lying against a couple of sandbags at night, my prayers would always be spoken to Bitsy. Never to God, not dear Jesus or any of that crap, though I know it's not just crap for some. You can laugh, but it was like Bitsy, she was my God. Like everything was in her hands, or she could sort of oversee it all, anyway. Not everyone has someone like that, but like I said, Bitsy and I have been together since tenth grade, and I think maybe if you've got that kind of person, they can do for you what the nuns used to call Grace. There's just this one person who can tell you what you've done is okay, or whose forgiveness is the only thing that matters if it wasn't.

I've got to tone the story down, of course. What really matters is just her knowing where I was, what I was more or less up to when it happened. I tell myself I'm not going to run around anymore after this, but who knows what's going to happen a few years down the road, and I'm not even sure I really hope it deep down. But one thing I do know is that parts of those letters are always going to be there when Bitsy's getting dressed in the morning, or when we go swimming in the summer, changing for bed at night, you name it. And she's the one person who could make that a fact I can live with. She's lying in bed still, reading *People* magazine, which just came in the mail, and I go and kneel down by the bedside and put my face in her lap. She closes her magazine slowly and sets her hand on my head like a blessing.

DEAN ALBARELLI grew up in Burlington, Vermont, and has lived in Ireland, Virginia, Iowa, and New York City. He now lives in Provincetown, Massachusetts, at the tip of Cape Cod, and teaches in the MFA program at Emerson College in Boston. A frequent contributor to *The Hudson Review* and *Witness*, he has also published fiction in the anthologies *20 Under 30: Best Stories by America's New Young Writers* and *Voices of the Xiled*. Mr. Albarelli is the recipient of a James Michener Award, a grant from the Vermont Council on the Arts, and fellowships from the Fine Arts Work Center in Provincetown. He is married to writer Sara London.